# Mrs. Claus and the Santaland Slayings

# Mrs. Claus and the Santaland Slayings

Liz Ireland

KENSINGTON BOOKS
www.kensingtonbooks.com

KENSINGTON BOOKS are published by

Kensington Publishing Corp.
119 West 40th Street
New York, NY 10018



All Kensington titles, imprints, and distributed lines are available at special quantity discounts for bulk purchases for sales promotion, premiums, fund-raising, educational, or institutional use.

Special book excerpts or customized printings can also be created to fit specific needs. For details, write or phone the office of the Kensington Sales Manager: Kensington Publishing Corp., 119 West 40th Street, New York, NY 10018. Attn. Sales Department. Phone: 1-800-221-2647.



ISBN-13: 978-1-4967-2660-5 (ebook)
ISBN-10: 1-4967-2660-X (ebook)

ISBN-13: 978-1-4967-2658-2
ISBN-10: 1-4967-2658-8
First Kensington Trade Paperback Printing: October 2020

10 9 8 7 6 5 4 3 2 1

Printed in the United States of America

# Mrs. Claus and the Santaland Slayings

# Chapter 1

The strange occurrences that threatened to upend my marriage, my adopted city, and the potential happiness of tens of millions of children started on a December morning just nine days before Christmas with a frantic pounding on our bedchamber door. The racket sounded loud enough to wake half of Christmastown.

It was ten past six, though, so most of the town's residents were probably up already. Elves tend to be early birds.

Our steward, Jingles, shouted through four inches of ancient timber, "Nick!" In the excitement of the moment, he'd reverted to the name my husband went by before he'd assumed his title, but he quickly remembered himself. "Er—Santa! Awaken, sir! We have a very important messenger!"

Nick and I trundled out of bed, he shrugging on his red coat and buttoning it quickly and I pulling on a ridiculously heavy flannel-lined boiled wool robe. The Order of Elven Seamstresses had presented the robe as a welcoming gift upon my arrival in Santaland. Though the cynic in me had silently chortled (*ho ho ho*) at the fire-engine-red garment trimmed with fluffy white wool and a black sash, one night in frigid Castle Kringle was all it took for me to appreciate their thoughtfulness, not to mention skill and artistry. I arrived at the North Pole as prepared for the arctic cold as someone from Kansas is prepared for a volcanic eruption. I'd moved here from Oregon, which, from the perspective of Santalanders, is so far south it might as well be equatorial jungle.

Nick was halfway across the room as I was still adjusting my nightcap. A few months ago I'd never dreamed people still wore nightcaps. Then again, I'd never dreamed Santa Claus existed, at least not since I was five. Now I was married to the guy. Whoever coined the phrase *life comes at you fast* didn't know the half of it.

"Come in!" Nick called out, flipping the switch on an elaborate network of twinkling lights across the vaulted ceiling.

The eight-foot-high arched door was pushed open with effort, even though Jingles and his assistant, Waldo, kept the hinges well oiled. Jingles was puffing and out of breath when he appeared and scrambled aside just in time to avoid being trampled by the messenger.

You might wonder, as I once did, why doors in the castle should be so tall when most of Santaland's inhabitants were elves—definitely on the short side—and the Clauses, who, whatever their varying girths, were humans of average height. You'd stop wondering the first time you saw a reindeer saunter through one, its bulk and antlers making all those oversized doorframes seem modest.

At the sight of Nick, the reindeer stopped, dipped her heavy head, and pawed the stone floor with her right hoof in greeting. "Excuse the intrusion, sir. I have an important message from the village."

Though she was as stocky, furry, and snub-nosed as any reindeer, just a glance told me this was obviously a female. Most of the bucks had already shed their antlers for the winter, but females kept theirs until spring. It was one of those things that shocked me when I first came here—I'd grown up assuming most of the antlered reindeer fabled in story and song, the heroes of Christmas night, were males: all those illustrations of fantastic racks of antlers limned against the moonlit sky, pulling the sleigh. But didn't it just figure that it was the females with the stamina and patience to haul Santa around on the world's biggest errand run?

"What's wrong, Blitzen?"

Although just months ago I'd barely known zip about reindeer, the names of reindeer who drove Santa's sleigh were worn into that same brain groove that could call up the names of dwarves in *Snow White*, old soft drink jingles, and the words to pop songs I never even liked. Not just anyone had been sent galloping through the Christmas tree forest to deliver this news. All reindeer had their own reindeer names, but to people they were usually identified by their herd. Carrying the name Blitzen meant this messenger was representing one of the original chosen nine's herds. Reindeer royalty. Something significant had happened.

Blitzen's deep, rasping voice was solemn when she spoke. "Giblet Hollyberry was found dead this morning."

*Giblet.* As tense silence settled over the bedchamber, a horrible scene played through my mind. Yesterday had been the Christmastown parade and ice sculpture competition, and Nick, as the acting Santa and head of the Claus family, was the judge. Giblet Hollyberry's sculpture, *The North Pole's King*, a larger-than-life rendering of Nick's late older brother, Chris, the former Santa, had come in second. The elf, to put it mildly, had not taken defeat in stride.

The tension in the room made it clear that everyone was thinking of Giblet's curse that had echoed through Christmastown yesterday: *You're an abomination, Nick Claus—a man with no right to wear the robes of Santa, and a shame to your house. The day will come soon when Santaland will know you're also a murderer!*

With those words, Giblet had tossed his second-place ice trophy in the snow at Nick's boots and stomped down the hill toward the Christmas tree forest. Murmurs had broken out among the crowd. I'd stood stunned. *Nick, a murderer?* Had someone spiked the nog at the festival with crazy juice? Nick agonized over hurting anyone. He'd probably lost sleep over disappointing Giblet. He certainly hadn't been in bed most of the night.

And now Giblet was dead.

Despite my suffocatingly warm robe, a cold foreboding snaked through me.

"Giblet probably died in a fit of rage," Jingles piped up now, breaking the silence. "I've never seen a grown elf throw such a tantrum. Disgraceful!" He put his hands on his hips. "In olden days, an elf who spoke that way to Santa would have been exiled to the Farthest Frozen Reaches. And good riddance!"

Nick shook his head. "He was disappointed."

"Pardon me, Santa, but Giblet Hollyberry was a hot-headed nincompoop. He couldn't even live peacefully among his own people in Tinkertown."

Nick turned back to Blitzen. "How did poor Giblet die?"

"At the moment, there is only speculation, and wild talk of something in a stocking. Constable Crinkles has been alerted and is on his way to Giblet's cottage."

"I'll go there, too."

"I'll take you, sir," Blitzen said, again slightly bowing her heavily antlered head.

I moved forward, but Nick motioned for me to stop. "No need for you to go, April. I have to hurry, and you'll need to lead the castle's condolence calls to the Hollyberrys this morning. Along with Mother, of course."

That was me dismissed. Heat climbed into my cheeks, though I tried to appear calm on the outside. "Did Giblet have a wife or children?" I asked.

"No, but the Hollyberry clan is large, and tight-knit."

Jingles crossed his arms. "Not so tight that any of them wanted to live near Giblet. Who can blame them? He—"

"We won't speak ill of the dead," Nick said, cutting him off. "I need to go."

Jingles, remembering himself, scrambled to reach the door first and hold it open. "I'll prepare a lantern for your journey." He flicked a disapproving glance over my husband's figure, which, by Christmastown standards, lacked poundage. "And a snack."

Nick turned back to me with an awkward glance and a brief, apologetic smile that went a little way to soothing my irritation over being left behind. "I'll be back soon, I hope."

After they were all gone, I moved closer to the fire and let the warmth from the hearth penetrate my layers of flannel and wool. I'd never heard of Giblet Hollyberry till yesterday, yet his death disturbed me. Nick had been in an odd mood since the ice sculpture competition. I hadn't seen him brood so much since we'd first met. And when I'd woken up in the night, he hadn't been in bed. I'd gotten up and padded around the castle in search of him and had even thrown on his coat and braved the blistering cold outside to see if he was pacing around the grounds. But I never found him until I returned to bed—and there he'd been, sleeping. Or pretending to.

Now this had happened, and my husband of three months seemed to want to get away from me. Almost as if he didn't want me asking too many questions.

A few minutes later, Jingles returned, and I snapped to attention, ashamed to be caught wool-gathering when there were probably things to do. Precisely what, I wasn't sure. Castle Kringle protocol was still new to me. "I'm sorry, I've been lost in thought. Let me know how I can be of use."

"I have a castle full of elves to do my bidding."

Jingles didn't seem to know what to make of me. He wasn't used to Clauses offering to help him, and I wasn't used to being waited on. Quite the opposite.

"You might want to make your way to the morning room," he suggested. "There's a fire lit, and Mrs. Claus—excuse me, the *dowager* Mrs. Claus—is there, as is Christopher. More of the family will probably be congregating as the news spreads."

"Is it so odd for an elf to die?" I asked.

"To die at a ripe old age, no. To die suspiciously in the prime of life . . . ?" He let the question dangle.

I started toward the door. Jingles cleared his throat.

When I turned back, he said, "Mrs. Claus—the dowager Mrs. Claus—has already dressed and ordered breakfast."

Of course she had. Nick's mother, Pamela, still ran the castle. After my marriage, when I'd suggested I should help lighten some of her responsibilities, she'd pointed out to me that since she knew how to do everything, it made more sense for her to keep charge of the household. Though she didn't say so in so many words, I'd caught a few looks that conveyed her belief that I wasn't really up to managing a castle and its staff. In fact, she'd seemed astonished when I told her that I owned a successful inn on the Oregon coast, and positively flabbergasted when Nick and I announced our intention to open the inn during the lucrative tourist season from May through September.

"But Nick *can't* leave Santaland," she protested. "He's Santa."

Nick had helped me out. "Is there anything more useless than a Santa in summertime?"

Poor Pamela. I thought she'd faint at the heresy of hinting that a Santa could ever be useless. She didn't understand the economics of innkeeping, though. I could just afford to keep up the taxes and pay for an off-season caretaker. But without opening up the Coast Inn during the late spring and summer, I'd be forced to sell. And I wasn't quite prepared to give up my old life entirely.

I retreated to my dressing room and picked out a dress in a crimson so deep it was almost black, hoping it would be appropriate for the mourning calls. Then I took care getting my hair to look tidy, which wasn't easy. My reddish-blond hair had a Jan Brady tendency to be neither flat nor curly. I pulled it back and stabbed a comb with a sprig of holly into the loose bun.

As I checked my appearance in the mirror, I suddenly remembered how quickly Nick had dressed himself. Almost as if he'd never really undressed because he'd stayed out so late . . .

I tried to un-remember it.

In the spacious east-facing drawing room, a fire roared, blazing out a welcoming warmth. Facing east did the morning room little good this time of year, since the sun wouldn't show itself for hours yet. My mother-in-law, a round, petite woman with appropriately rosy cheeks, sat on the couch, knitting at her usual breakneck pace. Her hands were never idle, especially as Christmas approached. Pamela was famous for two things. First, her holiday croquembouches, amazing towers of cream puffs covered in a shell of spun sugar that by all accounts were as incredible to look at as they were to eat. This year she was insisting that I would be her helper—co-architect, she called it—in constructing her annual edible masterpiece.

The second thing she was famous for was the matching holiday sweaters she made for the family. This year she was working some bell theme into her pattern; I could hear tinkling and jingling along with the clicking of her needles. *Great, we're all going to sound like reindeer in harness.* Also, she seemed to be favoring a metallic gray yarn that, with my pale, freckly skin, was going to make me look like a shiny holiday specter.

Nick's nephew, Christopher, the son of the late Santa and next in line to the position when he became an adult, jumped up from his seat by his grandmother when he saw me. "Hey, April, did you hear about Giblet?" he asked. "What do you think happened to him?"

I was about to say I didn't know when Pamela cut me off. "Now, how would April know anything about it? She just rolled out of bed."

She was smiling at me . . . but was there something judgmental in that last sentence? It wasn't even seven o'clock yet, for pity's sake. Maybe I was being paranoid. Living with your rosy-cheeked mother-in-law could do that to you.

"Seems like a lot of fuss over a dead elf," Christopher said.

Exactly what I'd thought.

"Death is always a tragedy," Pamela scolded him. "Think of his family."

"Oh." Christopher sank back into the sofa again. He'd lived through his own tragedy recently, losing his father to a terrible accident that took place while a group was tracking a snow monster. "I'm sorry, Grandma. You won't tell Mama I said that, will you?"

She patted his knee and smiled at him. "Of course not."

I looked around for Christopher's mother. Tiffany, dressed in mourning, could usually be seen hovering about her son. Or when Christopher was occupied with lessons, she wandered about the castle, a sad lost soul. Her pain seemed as fresh as if the accident that had taken her husband's life had just happened yesterday instead of seven months ago. If anything, she grew gloomier by the day, but I supposed that was understandable. This holiday probably was a poignant reminder of all she'd lost. How different last Christmas must have seemed. By all accounts, Nick's brother Chris had been a wonderful

Santa—jolly and popular with everyone. *Born to don the suit*, as Santalanders put it.

At the thought of the man dying so young—not even forty—I started to droop, too. I was a widow myself. Or had been. Was a widow who remarried called a former widow? An un-widow?

"April, you're pale as a ghost." Pamela looked me over and chuckled lightly. "Perhaps it's that dress. Not very jolly, is it?"

Pamela was particular about appearances, although she made exceptions for Tiffany. Everyone tiptoed around Tiffany, who'd been something of a celebrity once. A former Junior World medalist in figure skating, she'd been a featured skater in an ice show when Chris had fallen in love with her. I always imagined them as a sort of golden couple reigning over Santaland, beautiful and athletic and popular. Tragedy had transformed Tiffany.

Pamela nodded toward the long, low coffee table. "I ordered nog and crumpets, April. You should have some."

The frosty pitcher and silver platter of crumpets made my stomach lurch. The amount of eggnog consumed here was appalling. I'd already gained ten pounds from tucking into the carbs that were the bulk of the Santaland diet this time of year. No wonder people here had the reputation for being jolly. The entire populace was geeked up on sugar 24-7.

"I wanted to go to Giblet's cottage, but they wouldn't let me," Christopher complained. "Why didn't you go, April?"

*Good question.* "I was told there would be condolences to pay."

"And so there shall," Pamela said. "They're seeing to the food baskets in the kitchen. We must be extremely kind to the Hollyberrys."

"Even after Giblet said that stuff to Uncle Nick?" Christopher asked.

"We won't remember that," Pamela said.

A gale of laughter came from the doorway behind me. Nick's younger brother, Martin, a portly man of medium height, was still laughing when I turned. "How could we forget? A curse on Santa Claus—a *murdering* Santa, no less! As if Nick would harm a fly!"

Delighted to see his uncle, Christopher ran over and hopped on Martin's back. Laughing, the two of them loped across the room. Martin's good spirits were infectious, and I laughed along with Christopher's whoops of glee. Martin could mimic anything, and his snorts sounded more authentic than an actual reindeer's.

Christopher was never so happy around Nick, I couldn't help thinking regretfully. But Nick and Martin were different people. Born to don the suit? That was Martin. It was just unfortunate that he'd been born the youngest of three brothers. Because of this accident of birth order, his destiny would probably be to run Santaland's candy cane factory for the rest of his life.

Although he'd be the first to assure anyone it wasn't a bad life at all.

"The important thing to remember when we visit the Hollyberrys," Pamela continued, "is to be supportive and, most of all, cheerful."

"That's just what people want when someone's died," Martin said. "A good laugh."

"I'm not suggesting we troop through their cottages like merry jokesters," Pamela insisted. "But of course they will want cheer."

Martin glanced at me with restrained mirth in his eyes. "What do you say, April? Got any good one-liners for the Hollyberrys?"

I smiled back. I needed coffee. I hoped Jingles or Waldo would remember to bring some. I was one of the few in the castle who drank it.

Martin dropped his nephew down on a chair with a plunk and then gave my dark outfit a closer examination. "Are we supposed to wear mourning for cranky elves now?" he asked. "Even the ones who slander Santa Claus?"

Christopher's forehead pillowed. "What's slander?"

"Something unpleasant," Pamela said.

"Like when Giblet called Uncle Nick a murderer?"

"Christopher!" The call from the doorway turned all our heads, and at the sight of the woman in black standing there a pall fell over the room. Tiffany, petite, slender, and pale, greeted none of us but spoke directly to her son. "Plato's waiting for you in the library. You shouldn't be late for your lessons."

Christopher dragged to his feet. "It's not fair that I have to do math while there's all this excitement going on."

"Excitement?" My other sister-in-law, Lucia, appeared behind Tiffany. "What's exciting about an elf dying?"

Next to Lucia stood Quasar, her favorite reindeer. Both were hard to ignore—Lucia because she was tall, blond, and muscular, a Viking queen of a woman, and Quasar because he had a bum foreleg that made him list to one side and a red nose that blinked like a bulb screwed into a wonky socket. The red nose suggested an ancestor from one of the noble Rudolph herd, but the rest of him . . .

Quasar's antlers were shedding velvet today, which we all tried pointedly not to notice lest we face the wrath of Lucia for criticizing him. The shedding added to his ragged look. He had to be the last male reindeer at the North Pole to lose his antlers, which just made him seem even more of a misfit.

Both of them towered over Tiffany, although Tiffany still had the presence and poise that had riveted the attention of arenas full of people in her youth. I'd never seen her skate. But just the fact that she was so accomplished an athlete impressed me. I'd never done anything sportier than take a handball course at the Y. I was pretty good at it, but not the kind of good that a person could brag about.

"Giblet might've been a jerk," Lucia said to Christopher, "but no one ever denied that he was talented and worked hard. You should do as your mom says and don't keep your tutor waiting."

If Lucia expected thanks for backing up Tiffany, she was doomed to be disappointed. Once Christopher was out the door, Tiffany swept a dismissive gaze over us all, turned on her heel, and followed her son.

Martin chuckled at Lucia. "What a hypocrite you are. I don't remember you being Little Miss Studious when we were young."

"I wasn't, but I kept myself busy with other things. I didn't waste my time listening to your nonsense."

Pamela let out a peal of clucking laughter. "No bickering, you two. There's a lot to do today."

It was, I couldn't help noting, as if Tiffany in her head-to-toe black hadn't appeared at the door at all. As if they'd all decided her sadness was something unpleasant and therefore best ignored.

My mother-in-law presented a courteous yet forced smile to the reindeer limping toward the fireplace. "Good morning, Quasar."

His head dipped, nose fizzling like a dying neon sign. "G'morning, ma'am."

Martin leaned toward me. "Don't forget rehearsal."

It took a moment to recollect that the Santaland Concert Band was meeting this morning. I'd been given the job of chairperson of the Musical Events Committee, so it wasn't good for me to miss practices, even though I had a lot on my plate this week. All the upcoming activities kept me up night, worrying. There would be Kinder Caroling here at the castle, a tea with entertainment at Kringle Lodge, the Reindeer Hop, and, most worrisome of all, the Skate-a-Palooza at Peppermint Pond. I still hadn't set the schedule for the musical acts for that last event yet; there were far more people who wanted to play than slots to fit them into, and I hated to disappoint anyone. I felt like groaning just thinking about it. And now all this business about Giblet's death, and calls to be paid to the Hollyberrys . . .

"Will we have time?" I asked Martin, who was in the concert band with me. He played a pretty good tenor sax.

"I'm sure the band will understand if you can't make it," Pamela said. "Anyway, you're not *really* musical, are you, April?"

"I play percussion."

"Exactly. They probably just felt they needed to include you in something, because of Nick." Knitting needles flew as she spoke. *Clack, jingle, clack, jingle.*

"If she's not there they might think she doesn't want to show her face," Lucia said. "Because of that scene yesterday. And now Giblet . . ."

"Well, *I'm* going to rehearsal," Martin said. "I won't waste *my* time lugging food baskets to Hollyberrys."

Lucia crossed to the sofa, flopped down next to her mother, and propped her feet on the massive low table in front of the couch. I envied her unvarying wardrobe of long wool sweaters and fleece-lined pants. She always looked warm and comfy, even if she did exude a soupçon of reindeer musk. She was the official Claus liaison with the reindeer herds and presided over all sorts of animal activities, including the neverending Reindeer Games. "There's a big race today, too. I can't miss that."

*Jingle, clack, jingle, clack.* "Surely they can do without you this once," Pamela said. "*You're* not racing."

Martin snorted. "Don't disillusion her, Mother. She thinks she's part reindeer."

Lucia chucked a pillow at him. She had a special affinity for animals, especially reindeer, although her relationship to the honored beasts of Santaland could also be contentious. She'd founded the Santaland Reindeer Rescue, which got some reindeer's antlers in a twist. No one was crueler to reindeer than other reindeer. Sorry to say, what happened to Rudolph the First wasn't an anomaly. The animals weren't forgiving of flaws in their own kind, and castoffs were often sent to the misfit herd in the Farthest Frozen Reaches to do their best among the snow monsters, polar bears, and hunters. The lucky ones, like Quasar, caught Lucia's attention before they were exiled.

Lucia let out an irritated breath. "What a mess. I suppose there'll be even more whispers about Nick now."

"Whispers?" Pamela squinted in concentration at the jangling sweater beneath her fingers. "No one's been whispering in my hearing. Giblet's death was unfortunate, of course, but it was nothing to do with Nick."

"Mom, Giblet as much as called Nick a murderer, and the next day he's dead?" Lucia's lips twisted. "Not a good look for the Claus dynasty."

"Nonsense!" Needles clacked more frantically. "It will all blow over. Little kerfuffles like this usually do. Imagine throwing a hissy fit over losing an ice sculpture competition! It's Christmas—who has time for all this nonsense?"

"Elves always have time for nonsense," Martin pointed out.

"We'll pay condolence calls this morning," Pamela insisted. "*All* of us. Smooth things over. Everything will be fine. We must be helpful, sober, and cheerful."

Martin smirked. "Solemn and jolly. Nothing weird about that."

*Clack, jingle, clack, jingle.* "Keeping up appearances is always important, especially this time of year."

"You're putting a lot of faith in food baskets." Lucia stood.

"But I'm not. I intend to go see for myself what happened to Giblet."

I was on my feet in an instant. "I'll go with you."

All gazes turned to me. I sensed they'd forgotten I was there, much the same way they didn't see Quasar nibbling the pine boughs over the mantel.

Before anyone could speak again, however, Jingles moved silently into the room, stopping next to me. "I've left your letters and your coffee in Santa's office," he said in a low voice.

"The post has arrived?" Pamela asked. She had ears like a bat.

"Yes, ma'am." Jingles acknowledged her with a bow. "There were just a few things for April. One letter in particular looked rather urgent"—he leveled a significant look on me—"so I thought she might want to tend to it *right away*."

"I'll be right there." I turned back to Lucia. "Can you wait for me? I really want to go to Giblet's cottage."

She gave my outfit a once-over. "Don't worry, it'll take me some time to get a sleigh ready. You obviously can't ride in that getup."

I followed Jingles out, but once we were in the hall I practically had to sprint to keep up with him. "I'm sorry for the subterfuge." He looked back at me and lowered his voice. "I don't know what I'll say to Mrs. Claus—the dowager Mrs. Claus—when the post really does arrive."

"There's no letter?"

"Of course not. I was just doing some straightening in your husband's office when I found the strangest note on his desk. I thought I should show you before one of the servants saw it. I would have destroyed it, but it's not my place."

Nick's study had framed world maps on one wall and floor-to-ceiling bookcases on the two walls adjacent to the door. His mahogany desk took up the space before a large picture window that overlooked the grounds around the castle, which were dotted with snow-dusted evergreens and embellished with ice sculptures that had probably stood for years. Lights on the trees provided the only illumination outside. Dawn was still hours off.

The room was scrupulously tidy except for two overstuffed sacks of mail piled in a corner. Santa letters—the tough ones. They kept Nick up at night till all hours sometimes and often preyed on his mind. Maybe that's what he had been doing last night. Even a bulletin board full of lists was arranged neatly. Looking at them made me feel a rush of love for my Type A husband. Santa was supposed to make a list and check it twice, but Nick would make a hundred lists and check dozens of times.

As I hovered over his desk, a piece of paper on the desk blotter caught my eye. I knew in an instant that this was what Jingles had brought me here to see. The note was printed in large capital letters in red ink:

*A VENOMOUS ELF. COAL IN HIS STOCKING?*

And that was all.

I frowned. "I don't understand."

"'A venomous elf'—Giblet," Jingles interpreted for me. "'Coal in his stocking.' *His stocking*—Blitzen said they'd found something in Giblet's stocking, remember?"

"But that's—"

Lucia's warnings of the gossip about Nick came back to me, and I understood why Jingles was worried. If Giblet's death was ruled suspicious, this note might strike people as a damning clue.

It looked like Nick's printing, so I didn't kid myself someone else had written it. But why had Nick put these words down? Out of irritation, anger? Neither of those emotions seemed like Nick. But how well did I know him? I'd only been married to the man three months, and had just met him three months prior to our wedding.

Besides, who could say how anyone would react after being publicly accused of being a killer? Scribbling things on a notepad wasn't a crime. It was no different than pouring your heart out in a diary.

But diaries had been used to prove people's guilt in court, hadn't they?

I hesitated, then crumpled the note in my hand.

Jingles took it from me. "I'll just put this bit of trash in the fire, then, shall I?"

"Yes. Thank you, Jingles."

He tossed the paper into the flames and we watched it burn. After a minute, he jabbed at the embers with a poker. "And now you'd better go to the carriage house. Lucia hates to be kept waiting."

I nodded, stopping only for a last glance at a few charred flakes of paper lifting toward the chimney. If only I could have burned those red-inked words out of my memory as easily.

# Chapter 2

"You picked a bad year to become a Claus."

A little impatience for my bad timing edged into Lucia's matter-of-fact voice. She sat straight as a post in the seat of the sleigh and navigated the curved icy pathway down from the castle through Kringle Heights, holding the reins as casually as if she were born driving a team of reindeer. No surprise, given her genealogy. Of course, no other Claus had a sleigh custom-built both to be pulled by and to *carry* reindeer. Quasar stood in back, his head jutted forward between us like an impatient kid's. I almost expected him to ask, *Are we there yet?*

"Christmas season is always hectic and tense," Lucia went on, "but it's definitely worse this December because of poor Chris's accident, and with Nick trying to fill his boots, and everyone trying to adjust to all the changes."

"Chris must have been a wonderful person."

I glanced at her through the maze of Quasar's scruffy antlers. She bit her lip, her eyes filling with the emotion I'd seen on the face of everyone who'd known Chris.

"He was bigger than life," she said. "So much energy. Maybe it's a cliché, but he really brought life to a room just by walking into it. He got along with almost everyone."

"Nick told me the same thing."

"I have to admit that I've had a hard time mentally adjusting over the years, being the oldest sibling and yet ineligible to inherit the prized family position just because I was born female. No female Santas, you know—especially not when there were three brothers behind me. An heir and *two* spares. I never stood a chance. It probably would have driven me mad if Chris hadn't been so perfect. Objectively, he was worthier to be Santa than I was in every way."

I nodded, understanding, though her confession made me slightly uncomfortable. Somewhere beneath what she said lay the implication that Nick *wasn't* perfect, or worthy.

"Don't get me wrong," she added, as if following my train of thought. "Nick's nice, too. In fact, he's always been my favorite brother—but it's a harder lift for him, isn't it? Chris did things effortlessly, but with Nick, you can see it's work. And he's never satisfied with the status quo. Christmastown would have trundled along as it had for centuries if Chris had lived, but Nick wants to make things better. People don't always appreciate that."

"Like the stipend rule."

"Exactly."

Members of the Claus family, both immediate and distantly related, had always been able to live in Santaland free of charge. Even if they did nothing to help with the Christmas season, they were given land and a stipend. The number of freeloading Clauses was beginning to cause disgruntlement among the hardworking elves, so over the summer Nick had decreed that every family had to contribute to the workload for their stipend, a dictate that had caused hard feelings. Some of the Clauses were having to work for the first time in their lives.

"And there's Tiffany, poor woman," Lucia continued, "moping around all the time, hovering over Christopher. And now this business with Giblet. Some holly-jolly Christmas season this is going to be for Nick—or for any of us. I can only imagine how it must seem to you."

"It's all new to me, so I don't know the difference."

"No, I guess not. That's good. And don't let Mom get you down. She'll warm up to you."

I frowned. "Pamela doesn't like me?"

"Oh." Lucia hitched her throat. "Well, you know. She worries you and Nick got married too fast, not to mention too soon after Chris's death."

These thoughts had crossed my mind, too. Having someone else voicing them wasn't helping my insecurities.

"Anyway, never mind about Mother," Lucia continued blithely. "She can't disapprove of you more than she disapproves of me. She's ferociously loyal to the Claus identity and is going to will herself to put on a cheerful front even if the castle comes down around her ears."

I hoped it wouldn't come to that.

Lucia flicked a glance over at me. "Most everybody else thinks it's a good thing Nick got married. Would've been strange to go through Christmas without a Mrs. Claus."

She made it sound as if Nick could have plucked practically any woman off the street to marry, so long as there was a Mrs. Claus in Santaland for Christmas. But it often seemed to me that there were too many Mrs. Clauses around. Three in one castle: me, Tiffany, and Pamela.

I sank down in the seat, shivering. The sun was shining, but the cold still penetrated bone-deep. "Are we almost there?"

*Who sounds like a kid now?*

Quasar's nose sizzled. "C-close."

The most populous area of Santaland was referred to as Christmastown, but Christmastown proper was the old village at the foot of Sugarplum Mountain, just below Kringle Heights, the area where most of the Claus family and their retinue lived, which of course included the castle. Kringle Lodge was farther up at the summit of the mountain. The village was small and picturesque, with a mix of Tudor-style and shingled cottages. The immaculately plowed streets were strung with white lights all year long, but during the holiday season, the town went nuts with twinkling colored lights, wreaths, bows, and other decorations.

We'd sped through the high street—everyone was used to Lucia's brisk driving and dived out of our way—and then through the more sparsely populated outskirts. Now we were in part of the Christmas tree forest.

The forest wasn't the thick expanse of woods most people think of as a forest. According to legend, the first Claus came to the barren north and planted the evergreen seedlings that became the strip of trees that snaked around the various neighborhoods of Christmastown, dividing Tinkertown and the industrial area including the Candy Cane Factory to the south from the old village. More snaking lines of the forest provided a natural barrier to separate the many rival reindeer herds. The forest varied in density, but it was at its thickest in the ring around the entire region, providing a border between Santaland and the Farthest Frozen Reaches, where the outcasts and snow monsters lived. The trees that made our hidden corner of the north so unique were pampered, pruned, and lovingly managed by the same dedicated rangers who looked after the snowmen.

Living at the North Pole gave me a new sense of the word *permanent.* Once someone created an ice sculpture, for instance, it was as permanent as Michelangelo's *David.* And a few snowmen lived longer lives than humans, elves, and elfmen. They took forever to melt, although wind eroded them, and the older ones could look fairly threadbare. The snowmen were also honored, as their slow-moving lives gave them the chance to witness things red-blooded creatures rarely saw.

For a snowman, moving took enormous effort and eroded his base. Restlessness, it was said, was almost as dangerous to snowmen as a heat wave.

Giblet Hollyberry's cottage lay outside Tinkertown, the neighborhood surrounding the Candy Cane Factory, the Wrapping Works, and the oldest toy factory, Santa's Workshop. Most of the factory elves lived in Tinkertown; I knew that much. But Lucia turned the team onto a ragged path that circled around Tinkertown. I'd never been out here before. It felt deserted.

"Isn't it odd for him to be living out by himself?" I always thought of elves as social creatures.

"Giblet said he got enough of other elves just being at the Wrapping Works all day."

*A VENOMOUS ELF.* Why had those words struck such an ominous note inside me? *Coal in his stocking* was just a general Santa term of disapproval. I doubted Nick would ever actually give a child—or anyone—a lump of coal for Christmas. He might not be the jolliest, most naturally Santa-like Kris Kringle who'd ever carried the title, but he certainly wasn't malicious.

The rest of the drive, Lucia and I didn't speak anymore, just watched the path ahead and listened to the jangling bells and hooves of the reindeer against the packed snow. Pleasant sounds. After a while, Quasar's nose blinked. "There," he said.

Giblet's unassuming abode was a rustic log cabin. Three sleighs were parked outside it—Nick's big one with a team of six, like Lucia's, and two smaller ones each pulled by a single reindeer. There were also a couple of snowmobiles bearing the Santaland logo, with the word *Constabulary* stenciled below it. In addition, sets of cross-country skis and poles leaned against the cabin next to the front door. A group of elves were gathered in the snowy yard.

"It's like a Hollyberry summit meeting," Lucia muttered.

"I'll stay outside," Quasar said.

Lucia nodded. "Good idea." As if his coming in had even been a question. I doubted a reindeer could have fit through Giblet's front door. To be honest, I wondered if Lucia would fit.

She turned to me. "I assume *you're* coming."

"Yes, of course." I hopped off the sleigh, stamping my feet to coax some circulation back into them. It was said that even when a person was used to winter weather—and I definitely was not—the cold here could sneak up on you and make you as sluggish as a snowman if you weren't careful.

My sister-in-law strode across the snow, vigor personified. I trailed after her in my fluttering skirt, feeling inadequate and unsteady, yet blazing with curiosity about what I'd find inside the cabin. A tiny voice in my head taunted me: *Are you sure you want to know?*

The Hollyberrys tracked us with silent gazes as we passed, but Lucia didn't let this bother her. "Sorry about Giblet!" she called out to them. Then she rapped perfunctorily at the door and, ducking her head, barged in.

The Hollyberrys turned their stares toward me. "I'm also very sorry," I said. "I didn't know Giblet, of course, but he seemed . . ." I struggled to find an appropriate word.

Lucia poked her head out the front door. "Come on, April."

"I'm sorry," I repeated awkwardly and hurried after her.

I entered the low-ceilinged cottage eager to see Nick, to receive reassurance by a glance or a word that the slim suspicion scratching at the back of my mind was nonsense. I'd made mistakes over the years, goodness knows, but when it came to bad life choices, marrying an elficidal Santa would put me in a league of my own.

We followed sounds of talking to the bedroom in the back—the cabin only had two rooms, and Giblet had died in the smaller one, beside a bed that looked child sized. The coverlet was still in a pile on the mattress, as if he'd just gotten up and hadn't made the bed yet. Giblet lay on the floor, curled up almost with his knees to his chest. It was clear he'd been in agony.

I looked away.

"What's the verdict?" Lucia asked by way of greeting.

"We don't know," Nick said. Seeing me behind her, he frowned. So much for reassurance. He took a breath. "Constable Crinkles, I don't believe you've met my wife yet. This is April."

The chief law enforcement officer of Christmastown, like most elves, was short of stature, but he was also more stout than average. His dark blue wool uniform bulged at the seams, and both his thick black belt and brass buttons were doing double duty. On his head perched a blue hat much like bobbies wore in old British films, right down to the chin strap. Also the Keystone Cops, although I tried to put that thought out of my mind. He peered up at me beneath the hat's shallow bill, smiling. "Well, hello there! Welcome to Christmastown!"

It was hard to know how to respond to so much chirpiness at a crime scene. I'd half expected to be shooed away, but Constable Crinkles didn't care that I had no purpose there. "How do you like it?"

Confused, I tried not to glance at the dead elf on the floor. "Like . . . ?"

"Christmastown! Santaland!"

"Oh . . . it's nice."

He beamed. "Best time to be here—Christmas! Of course, December is our busiest time. You—"

Lucia cleared her throat. "We were talking about cause of death."

Crinkles' face collapsed. "Oh. Right." He bobbed on his heels, sobering. "I'm sure it's natural causes."

Lucia, ever blunt, toed the elf's curled-up corpse. "You can't tell me that this elf died peacefully."

"Death is rarely peaceful." Crinkles jiggled in discomfort. "What else could it be, though?"

"Homicide?" I asked.

The word caused the others to gape at me.

"Santaland doesn't have murders," the constable said.

Everyone in the room except Lucia and me nodded, as if this pronouncement were just a given.

"How long will it take the coroner to reach a conclusion about the cause of death?" I asked.

The others looked incredulous.

Was the question so outrageous? It's what any character on any iteration of *CSI* would've asked under the circumstances.

"She's still new here," Lucia reminded everyone.

"We don't have a coroner," Nick told me.

"Nothing wrong with having Doc Honeytree take a look at him, though," Constable Crinkles said. "I'm sure he'll agree with me, though. Natural causes." He scratched his chin. "Or maybe accidental death."

*"Baloney!"*

At the shouted word, we all turned to the door. A short elf dressed in a dark green velvet tunic and breeches stood with his hands planted on his hips, quaking in his pointy black boots.

Nick, stooping under the low ceiling, moved toward him. "I'm sorry about your cousin, Noggin."

"Baloney!" the elf repeated, in case we'd missed it.

Crinkles was between them in two hops. "Now, there's no need for that kind of language, Noggin. We all understand that you Hollyberrys are upset."

"Not yet, we aren't. But if you're going to ask us to believe that Giblet had a very public argument with Santa one day and then *just happened* to die mysteriously the next, when we all know he was as hardy as a bear . . . well, that reindeer just won't fly. No sir."

"How can *anyone* know what happened to him?" Crinkles put his hands on his pillowy hips. "He lived out here alone, and there were no witnesses, as far as I know. Unless you've heard of one?"

"Well . . . no," Noggin was forced to admit. "Though someone said Old Charlie stayed hereabouts."

Crinkles sighed impatiently. "That old snowman's only got one eye left, and even if he is around here, chances are he isn't facing in the direction of this cottage. You can't let your imagination get the better of you. Witnesses!" He shook his head in disgust and gave Nick a sidewise glance. "Told you there'd be trouble if we didn't confiscate those pirated copies of *The Wire*," he muttered.

"We all witnessed what he said to Santa," Noggin said, avoiding Nick's eye. "Everyone heard the word Giblet said. *Murderer.* And the next morning he's dead."

Lucia stepped forward. "We also all saw that Giblet was apoplectic. He was about to have a coronary on the spot over losing that stupid ice sculpture competition."

Noggin vibrated with anger. "It wasn't stupid to him! He planned his design for months!"

"And he lost," Lucia said. "Then he freaked out and died. Nobody's fault."

"Then how do you explain the spider?"

A moment of silence followed the question. Perplexed, Lucia turned to Nick, then Crinkles. "What's he talking about?"

Nick and the constable exchanged a glance that set my stomach churning again. Something was afoot.

Noggin Hollyberry rocked back on his heels. "Don't think you can hide the truth for long. It's already out about the spider. My nephew was there when your deputy found it."

The deputy, who had a patch on his blue wool coat reading *Ollie*, stepped forward, displaying a zipper-sealed plastic bag containing what appeared to be a long red-and-white-striped elf stocking. In the bag there was also a shiny black spider. Half its body was squished, but from what remained I could make out a red dot on its once-hourglass-shaped abdomen. A black widow.

"Seems that he probably stepped on it puttin' on his stocking," the deputy said. "Squashed it to death, but not before the spider got its revenge."

"We don't need dramatics, Ollie." Crinkles frowned and then wondered aloud, "Now where would that creature have come from, I wonder."

I didn't understand. "Are spiders so rare here?"

The glances of the others told me all I needed to know, even before the sheriff spoke. "Strictly speaking, we don't have many bugs, especially not poisonous spiders like that one there. We elves aren't used to the venom, so they're deadly to us."

So Santaland had no homicides and no spiders. Except now it had both.

*A VENOMOUS ELF. COAL IN HIS STOCKING?*

The echo of those words in my mind gave me a jolt. The black widow found in the stocking was coal black—venom for the venomous elf. I clenched my hands so tight my nails pressed into my palms through my gloves.

"By itself, it proves nothing," Crinkles insisted.

"Somebody must have brought that creature"—Noggin Hollyberry pointed at the plastic bag—"to Santaland. Who? Somebody from the outside, that's who."

It was as if a celestial being with a giant straw sucked all the air out of the cabin. Who was the most notable person from the outside in Santaland at the moment? Yours truly. And I was married to the man whom Giblet Hollyberry had cursed in front of all of Christmastown yesterday afternoon.

"I hate spiders," I protested.

Nick grabbed my elbow. "Never mind, April."

But I wasn't about to stand accused without defending myself. Better to nip this malicious rumor in the bud. I took a step toward Noggin Hollyberry. "I certainly don't travel with black widows in my suitcase."

Noggin squinted. "How do you know it's a black widow spider?"

"We have them in Oregon." From the way he crossed his arms, I could tell he thought I'd incriminated myself. "It's preposterous. I haven't been south of Santaland in months. Do you honestly believe I was keeping this spider in reserve on the off chance that someone had an argument with my husband? Over an ice sculpture contest, of all things?"

The elf grumbled, "I don't know. . . . There's something fishy about the whole situation, if you ask my opinion."

"No one did." Crinkles juddered himself between Noggin and me. "Opinions are useless to us now anyhow. What we need are what-ya-call'ems."

"Facts?" I suggested.

He snapped his fingers. "Facts! That's it!"

Have I mentioned yet that Santaland law enforcement didn't inspire confidence?

"Wait till you have facts before you start throwing accusations around," the constable lectured Noggin. "Doc Honeytree will look at Giblet's body. More than likely he'll be able to tell whether or not your cousin died of a spider bite."

"I want to be there when he does his tests," Noggin said.

"A scientist now, are you?" Crinkles asked.

Noggin glared at him. "Who do you represent, Constable—the elf community or the Claus family?"

Poor Crinkles looked as if he were about to lose control. The jowls over his chin strap quivered with the effort to keep his voice calm. "I represent the law. For everybody."

Noggin threw back his head. "We'll see about that." Turning on his heel, he stomped out of the room.

The rest of us stood stunned for a moment, until Deputy Ollie broke the silence. "Perhaps we should be getting Giblet along to Doc's office," he suggested to Crinkles.

"Yes." He looked apologetically at Nick. "I'm sorry about all this. You know how Hollyberrys are."

"It's been a shock to them. My family was going to pay condolence calls, but perhaps we'll hold off on that."

"Good idea," Crinkles said. "They're in a fighting mood."

"If you need me, I'll be at the castle," Nick said.

Nick, Lucia, and I left the cottage together. The gazes of the gathered Hollyberrys followed us in silence. *Say something, Nick.* It would have been a good moment for him to rise to the occasion with soothing words about sorrow, and wanting to find the truth, and if necessary, pursuing justice for Giblet. Yet Nick, after a slight hesitation in which he looked as if he might say a few words, strode off the porch without comment. He had to duck to avoid banging his head on the porch overhang, which gave him the unfortunate appearance of skulking away.

His late brother would have made a speech. I hadn't even known Chris, but I felt it in my bones. Worse, I was sure everyone there, including Nick, was thinking the same thing.

Nick eyed Lucia's sleigh, with Quasar's flickering muzzle leaning over the bench seat.

"Why don't you come back with me, April," he said.

It was more an order than a question.

Seeing my hesitation, Lucia raised a brow at me. "Not a bad idea," she said. "Quasar and I are going to check on the Reindeer Rescue's paddock. And since now we aren't on the hook for condolence visits, I need to be there at the reindeer dash. Might be a while before we could get you back to the castle."

She was right. And if there were no calls to be paid on the Hollyberrys, then I should go to my band rehearsal in Christmastown.

I headed back toward our sleigh, where the reindeer team idled. The sleigh was not *the* sleigh—that was only used for ceremonial purposes and on Christmas Eve. This one was impressive, though. It was larger than average, and the carriage was made of wood carved into swirls around an intricate depiction of winter scenes on both sides. The back had a *C* in a calligraphy so ornate it had taken me a month to realize what it was. The whole carriage was freshly painted every year in bright colors, and cleaned and polished regularly.

One of the two lead reindeer looked up when he saw Nick. "All well?"

"Nothing to trouble the herds about," he said.

That seemed to satisfy the reindeer. They lived in their own world most of the time—an outside world of fitness, contests, and horseplay. If I'd been born a reindeer instead of a human, I'd have been chucked out to the Farthest Frozen Reaches long ago, and probably ended up on a spit over some snow monster's fire.

When we'd pulled away from Giblet's cabin, Nick shook his head. "I wish you hadn't seen that."

His words startled me. I was thinking of the note. "Seen what?"

"What happened back there. The violence."

"How did the spider get here, do you think?"

I watched him closely, but he just shrugged. "No idea. It's certainly not normal."

A laugh escaped me. "In a world of elves and talking reindeer, what's normal?"

"I don't see anything to laugh about."

Of course not. He'd grown up in this world. He didn't have to shake himself occasionally to verify he wasn't dreaming. "It's all so just different than what I'm used to."

"I did warn you."

"Sure, but being told that Santaland is real is one thing; actually experiencing it is a different matter entirely." We were crossing a section of the Christmas tree forest, but I spotted a snowman drifting down a bank, a fat gauge in the snow marking his slow progress.

"Is that Old Charlie?" I said, pointing.

Nick barely glanced in that direction. "Could be."

"Looks as if he's on the move. Is that safe for him?"

"A snowman as old as he is knows what he's doing."

He certainly looked old. He wore a stovepipe hat, like Abe Lincoln, and a red vest that had faded to a salmon pink. He wasn't just missing an eye; he'd also lost a stick arm somewhere.

"Shouldn't we stop to help him?" I asked. The snowman seemed to be going our way—headed toward town—but Nick didn't even slow down.

"You can't move snowmen in a sleigh, April. You'd just end up with a heap of snow. They have to move on their own volition."

"Okay, but maybe we should go back to see if he needs anything." *Or if he saw anything.*

"I have to get back to the castle. There are scads of Santa letters to get through in the next few days and a few problems in production. The Workshop's been texting me all morning."

"I guess I can come back later," I said.

"I don't want you driving into the Christmas tree forest by yourself. I'll send someone to take care of Charlie."

We continued in silence. Nick wasn't usually this rigid. But I'd never seen him juggling so many responsibilities at the busiest time of the year. And now there was Giblet's suspicious death. . . .

"Strange how coal in a stocking means something negative," I mused, watching Nick closely. "But a lump of coal can be vital to snowmen."

Nick's forehead wrinkled in puzzlement. "What are you talking about?"

"Coal in a stocking."

He shot me a sidewise glance, smiling a little as if he worried about my soundness of mind. "I'm not sure I get your drift."

The bells on the reindeer harnesses were loud enough that I wasn't too worried about being overheard, but I lowered my voice anyway. "Giblet's death *was* an accident, wasn't it?"

His face swung toward me, startled. "Why ask me?"

*Because of words you wrote on a sheet of paper in your office.* Had they been a prophecy, or a plan? Worried it was evidence, I'd burned the paper so no one would ever be able to use it against him. But I hesitated to explain what I'd done. It was hard to confess to your husband of just a few months that you worried he'd murdered an elf.

"How would you have described Giblet?" I asked.

He thought for a moment. "Irritating?"

"Are there other people in town who might have wanted to kill him?"

His eyes narrowed. "Other than who?"

*Oops.* "Well, his family think *you* did it."

"They're upset, naturally. Constable Crinkles doesn't suspect me."

"No." In fact, he'd almost seemed to be on Nick's side, just as Noggin Hollyberry had claimed. Of course, having Constable Crinkles as an ally probably wasn't much better than having Constable Crinkles as your lead investigator.

"You can't let all this get to you, April. We're supposed to be cheerful and jolly."

I laughed, but not exactly in a jolly way.

He glanced at me. "Well, you know what I mean. Until we hear more we should just go on as normal. It's not as if there's any lack of things to do this time of year."

"No." I looked at my watch; then I did a double take. Almost eleven already. "Just drop me off at the community center," I said.

Murder or no murder, Luther Partridge, the conductor of the Christmastown Concert Band, frowned on us showing up late for rehearsals.

# Chapter 3

My first clear memory of Nick was on a warm day in June in Cloudberry Bay. The sun was shining on the Oregon coast, giving tourists and even natives the illusion that we were a real surfing-and-suntan oil kind of place. He was standing at the edge of the beach, contemplating the expanse of gray-blue surf and flexing as if preparing to dive in.

"I wouldn't do that."

During warm summer days, lots of visitors were one plunge away from being disabused of the notion that Cloudberry Bay was Miami Beach. This man showed all the earmarks of being our next casualty. Something about the body pointed bird dog–like toward all that beautiful water. That beautiful, frigid water.

He'd registered at the Coast Inn the day before as Nick Kringle, saying as little as possible as he'd swiped his card and taken his key. He hadn't come down to breakfast. It all gave him a mysterious air, and nothing taunts me like a mystery. Youngish men on their own didn't wander into my cozy establishment often. Nick had brown hair, brown eyes, and a rather pale complexion that didn't seem to go with his muscular build, but the parts all added up to a dreamy whole. Like Laurence Olivier in *Rebecca*, only without the fake gray streaks and with a neatly trimmed beard instead of Olivier's pencil mustache.

His only response to my warning was to turn his gaze turned toward me. I'd been on an early afternoon walk and was togged out in a T-shirt, shorts, and sneakers. I usually took advantage of the post-breakfast/checkout, pre-check-in break to get a little exercise. Otherwise it was easy to become chained to the inn round the clock, a mistake I'd made when I'd first bought the Coast Inn after my husband died. Owning a small hotel can be a hamster wheel existence if you don't fence off time for yourself.

"The water's cold," I warned my guest.

"I'm used to cold."

Those were the first words I remember him saying to me. *I'm used to cold.* Understatement of the century, but how was I to know? I assumed he meant he was from Wisconsin or something. Part polar bear was more like it. I watched in amazement as he took a few steps into the fifty-something-degree water and dived in. Most tourists who did that popped right back up shrieking and streaking back to shore and the nearest towel. When Nick surfaced, he sliced through the surf in an Australian crawl without missing a beat.

There was another reason I'd been a little anxious that Mr. Kringle stay out of the water. One I couldn't exactly voice to a stranger. Until that moment on the beach, the few times our paths had crossed he'd exhibited a brooding, preoccupied air. The quiet ones worried me. I'd had a guest check in and take an overdose of sleeping pills once. I didn't want another visitor to my inn to end their stay with an ambulance ride.

That evening, the mysterious Mr. Kringle sought me out after dinner.

"Thanks for the warning today," he said.

"You didn't need it. You must be part ice cube."

"Where I'm from, most people are. But I'm here to thaw

out a little, so I appreciate your being a good hostess." He produced a small box of chocolates and presented them to me. "I brought these from home."

"Where is that?" I opened the box, picked one, and bit into the most heavenly confection of chocolate and peppermint I'd ever tasted. I may have even let out a moan, because his face cracked in a smile and he pointed to a different one in the box.

"You should try that one. It's my favorite."

As I looked at him and remembered his ripped body in that surf, it was hard to believe he was a chocolate aficionado. "I'll try it next. I want to savor this one. Where did you say you were from?"

"A little place up north—it's sort of hidden."

In the days of Google, was there any place that was still hidden? "Canada, you mean?" He had the faintest of accents, so I was fairly certain he wasn't an American.

"It's actually north of the Northwest Territories."

That cagey answer assumed I had no knowledge of the geography of the Northwest Territories (I didn't) and that I wouldn't want to own up to my ignorance of anything north of Vancouver (I wouldn't). A handsome, enigmatic stranger was leaning over me, taking me in with his dark brown eyes, and feeding me chocolates. I'd had dreams like this, and I wasn't about to bust up a living dream by volunteering the fact that arctic geography was a huge hole in my knowledge.

The next day we met again on the beach, which wasn't an accident on either of our parts. It was the start of the most romantic week of my life. We went for drives; we held hands under towering pines, listening to the music of the wind whistling through millions of needles. After two days we were having our dinners together, and every other meal, too.

*No romance with guests* had been my motto during the few

years I'd been an innkeeper. Circumstances had made it easy for me to eschew romance. I'd been newly widowed when I'd taken my money from a legal settlement and sunk most of it into the house. My husband, Keith, had died in a car accident—hit by an eighteen-wheeler belonging to a megacorporation. That was traumatic enough, but we'd been having troubles for a long time caused by infertility problems and then infidelity problems. Before the accident we'd been on the verge of separation. After the police contacted me about the crash, I realized it had occurred minutes after a phone argument we'd had.

Feeling like an utter failure in family and relationships, I'd retreated across the country, to the Oregon coast near where my grandparents had lived. It was a place that held happy memories for me. When I purchased the inn, I vowed to focus on business and to turn the Coast Inn into a place that would create happy memories for others. For three years, the friendships I formed in Cloudberry Bay and the fleeting acquaintances of paying guests fulfilled me. My no-romance policy had never been difficult to adhere to.

Yet there I was, head over heels for a guy with a week-long reservation. With Nick, I found myself spilling out more of the history of my marriage than I ever had to my best friend, Claire. More than I had to a psychologist I'd seen after Keith's accident, even. Nick listened with real understanding and sympathy that seemed deep, almost raw. On the last night, I learned why. He told me about his brother.

"Chris died two months ago. Hunting accident." The hurt rasp in his voice broke my heart—his grief was so fresh, and his face clouded with an anguished expression I hadn't seen since the day he'd arrived.

"Your older brother?" I knew Nick had other siblings. He'd mentioned Martin and Lucia several times, but I hadn't gotten the birth order down yet.

"Yes, he was older than me, younger than Lucia. Now I'm the head of the family."

It seemed an antiquated way of looking at sibling relationships, almost as if he was the heir of some principality. I couldn't help asking, "Why wouldn't Lucia, the eldest, be considered the head of the family?"

He weighed his response longer than necessary. "It's not our way."

I laughed. "Even the House of Windsor's fixed the females-last thing, you know."

"There are strong women in my family. My mother's wonderful, a force of nature. She's the glue that keeps us all together. It's been a terrible time for us."

I knew all too well what he was going through, and felt a little ashamed of my glib sparring about Lucia. Also of my thoughts about that force-of-nature mother. (But honestly, how great could a parent be if they saddled their kid with the name Chris Kringle?) I focused on helping Nick. "It's a cliché, but it's true. Time is the only thing that helps. Grief never goes away, but it recedes."

His dark gaze locked on mine. "This week with you has been the balm I needed. Spending time with you here has made me feel as if there's some hope."

I wasn't sure what that meant. Did he really like me, or was I the human equivalent of a Xanax?

"I wish you could stay longer." I'd blurted out the words before I could think about how needy they sounded.

"And I wish—"

He broke off, taking in the old sprawling house behind us, with its five gables of graying shingle, standing tall as it had for almost a hundred years against the whims of the Pacific. He shook his head. "You have a beautiful place here. You belong here, don't you?"

"I'm happy here," I said. "But I don't *belong.* I came here to get away from . . . well, I told you about all that. I've made this my home, but it's not the only place I can survive. No one should feel stuck where they are."

It was the wrong thing to say. That cloud descended over his expression again. "It doesn't always work that way, April. Maybe if it were ten years from now . . ."

*Ten years?* It seemed an odd thing to say.

"Are you going to take early retirement?" He was my age—thirty-six. "You must have started socking away money early."

He laughed a little at that. "If all goes well. We'll see. In the meantime, though, I shouldn't sit around daydreaming like a child."

Frustration filled me. If *I* was part of them, I wanted him to hold on to his daydreams. Why did he insist on talking like a slumming prince in a fairy tale, duty bound to return to his kingdom? Even as we stood face-to-face, hand in hand, the past week seemed to recede into something unreal.

He left the next day, saying good-bye quickly but brushing his lips against my cheek and then holding them there, as if to remember the moment better. Five minutes later I was helping my housekeeper, Dakota, strip beds. Back on the hamster wheel.

Where exactly was Nick off to? He'd given me an email address but never had told me the name of the town he lived in. I began to pinpoint other basic things he hadn't revealed, such as what he did for a living and what nationality he was. By the end of the day, when I was greeting new guests, I wondered if anything I thought I knew about him was true. Cinematic possibilities filled my head: He was a CIA agent. A gangster on the run. It was all a dream and he'd been a figment of my imagination. . . .

That night, I remembered Nick's chocolates, the ones he said were from where he lived. A clue! The box was right where I'd left it. *Not a figment, then.* I took the chocolate he said was his favorite and bit into it slowly. The strange flavor filling took me a moment to place, and even then I wasn't certain. *Eggnog?* The shiny red box had no writing on it, no stamp from the country of manufacture. No ingredients list, even. It must have been a pretty small outfit that had made them. And then I turned the box over and noticed one distinctive mark: a gold stamp in the silhouette of a Santa Claus waving a mittened hand in greeting.

I skidded into rehearsal just in the nick of time. In taking on the job of Christmastown Musical Events chairperson, I'd drawn the attention of a few of the music group directors, who were all interested in filling gaps in their orchestras, bands, or choirs. I'd been an easy mark. The first meeting of the Musical Events Committee, I was on the receiving end of a firing line of musical wishes:

*You aren't by any chance a coloratura soprano?*

I laughed. My warbly voice could barely carry a tune. I didn't even like to sing in the shower.

*Have you ever played oboe?*

Um, no.

*We need percussion players.* Anybody *can play percussion.*

Three months later, I was well on my way to proving that last statement wrong. Taking my place at the back of the band hall of the Christmastown Community Center, I picked up a triangle and fumbled through my music folder to find the first piece on our playlist.

Smudge, the principal percussionist of the Santaland Concert Band, noted the triangle and shot me an exasperated look. "The first song is 'Sleigh Ride,' April."

"Right!" I fumbled through my sheet music. The pages never seemed to be in order. I couldn't remember if I was supposed to be on triangle or the glockenspiel for that "Sleigh Ride." "What am I playing on that?"

His gaze turned withering. "Sleigh bells."

"Oh. Right." I scooted past where he was seated at his drum kit and picked up the sleigh bells. Harder to play than you'd think, by the way. At least for someone who was as rhythm challenged as I was. Smudge, an elf who styled himself as a hipster—or as much as anyone could who had Spock ears and tucked his faded denim pants into curly-toed booties—barely tolerated my intrusion into his world. Only the dearth of volunteers and the desperate need for sound effects in Christmas music had reconciled him to my presence on the back row.

The Santaland Concert Band was comprised mostly of elves, but there were a couple of us Claus family members mixed in. A few other members were elfmen, like Luther, the conductor.

My friend Juniper, one of the Christmastown librarians, played euphonium. She turned to me as she settled into her chair in the row in front of the percussion section. "Hi, April."

"No greeting for me?" Smudge asked, in mock hurt.

"Smudge." Juniper's eyes widened as if she were surprised to see him. Smudge and Juniper had dated once. Now they just snarked at each other. "I heard something the other day that made me think of you. What do you call a drummer in a three-piece suit?"

He frowned warily. "I don't know. What?"

"The defendant."

Luther rapped on his music stand to bring us all to attention.

Several song sheets had slipped out of my folder, and I

was scrambling to gather them all up. Juniper scooped up my second page of "Silver Bells" that had landed by her chair and handed it to me. "Everything okay?"

Was she asking me because I was late arriving, or because she'd heard rumors about Giblet?

"You seem nervous," she whispered.

The morning had unsettled me, no doubt about that. *One day you're going along, married to Santa Claus, and the next you're worried he's murdered an elf.* It wasn't something I could just blurt out to my friend, but apparently carrying around a strip of bells that jangled with every movement didn't do much to mask my anxiety.

"Is something wrong back there?" Luther asked.

I jangled back to standing. "Nope! All good!"

Juniper mouthed something at me. *We Three Beans later?*

I nodded vigorously. I could definitely use a sanity break and some caffeine before going back to the castle. Juniper was the best friend I'd made in Christmastown, and We Three Beans was our preferred hangout.

Luther raised his baton. "Let's begin."

Before he could count out the intro to "Sleigh Ride," though, Woody, our sousaphone, rose from his chair, tuba and all. "JoJo Hollyberry's not here today," he said. "On account of what happened to Giblet."

Murmurs rippled through the rehearsal room. My stomach tightened into a knot.

A flute player stood. "We're sending a card around for everyone to sign."

"Good," Luther said. "Thank you." He lifted his hands again, but Woody interrupted a second time.

"There should be more than a card. It's almost Christmas, and it's beginning to look as if an elf has been murdered. I won't say by whom."

So they *had* heard rumors. I had the unnerving feeling

that everyone's eyes were on me, although only one person turned. Martin. He gave me an encouraging half smile and a little shrug.

"As most of you know," Woody continued, "I've been working on a piece for tuba trio and orchestra for a while, and I'd like to dedicate it now to Giblet Hollyberry's memory. I'm calling it 'Requiem for Giblet.' I was hoping we could play it at our next concert."

*Requiem for Giblet?* Was he kidding? No one even liked Giblet!

"It's Christmas," Luther pointed out. "We can't be debuting requiems when everyone feels like celebrating with carols and holiday songs."

Across the rehearsal hall, the men and elfmen were all nodding, but the elves directed stony stares at Luther. "Not that I don't think it isn't a wonderful idea for a tribute, Woody," Luther added, reading the room.

Giblet's death, I worried, was going to tear Christmastown apart.

Smudge flicked an angry glance at me. "Stop jangling," he hissed.

I hadn't realized that annoying sound was coming from me. I tried to keep it together for the rest of the rehearsal. After it was over, when we were all packing up our instruments and gear, someone passing by me murmured, "Everyone heard what Giblet said to him, but no one guessed it was actually true."

"Hear that?" Martin, coming up behind me, asked in a low voice.

I nodded.

"I was getting strange looks all through rehearsal," he said. "I'm guessing Nick didn't do very good PR this morning at Giblet's cottage."

"PR's not his forte. But I do think Constable Crinkles

will help. He seems to be on our side. Not that he's covering up," I added quickly, "but he is keeping an open mind. As long as nothing else goes wrong, we should be fine. Nick should, I mean." God, I was babbling. "Have you ever heard of a snowman called Old Charlie?"

Juniper jumped in. "He's very old." As soon as the words were out, a red flush rose in her cheeks. "You probably guessed that, though."

"Nick said he usually stayed near Giblet's, but we saw him heading into town."

Smudge frowned. "No one's seen Old Charlie in Christmastown in a long time. He likes the country."

"Maybe he was just restless because of all the activity going on around Giblet's," Juniper said.

I nodded. For a snowman used to stillness, it was probably annoying to see sleighs, skiers, and sleds whizzing by.

"Need a ride back to the castle, April?" Martin asked.

"Thanks, but Juniper and I are going for coffee."

He looked down at Juniper and her cheeks brightened even more. She'd mentioned Martin a couple of times to me before, but it finally dawned on me why. The way she was blushing, it probably dawned on Martin, too.

"I should drop by that place more often," he said. "Though I'm not much of a coffee drinker."

"They have other things besides coffee," Juniper said quickly. "Tea, hot chocolate, eggnog, soft drinks, and spritzers . . ."

Martin laughed. "Do you own We Three Beans stock?"

Her face continued on to a deep crimson hue, and I jumped in to help her out. "It's our hangout," I said. "We've got the menu memorized."

"Well, good luck getting there today," he said. "The sidewalks were already crowding up for the race before rehearsal started." He edged past us and left the hall.

Juniper looked as if she might pass out. Luckily, the band hall was emptying, so few were around when she swooned into a chair. "Did I just sound like an idiot, or what?"

"Not at all," I assured her.

"I did, though, didn't I?" she said.

"Not that anyone would notice," I said.

"I noticed," Smudge said, putting away his cymbals.

"Smudge noticed," I said, "but Smudge doesn't count. Martin might have noticed, but probably only in the way that you wanted him to."

"Right," she said. "There's noticing and there's *noticing*."

"I'm positive he good-noticed you," I assured her.

The Christmastown Reindeer Dash drew even more interest than the rest of the never-ending Reindeer Games did. In the last contests of December, the culmination of tournaments all year long, the stakes were the nine slots of the sleigh team. To Santalanders, the final Reindeer Games were the Super Bowl and World Cup rolled into one. Last year there had been a last-minute surge by the representative of the upstart Fireball herd. Several elves had lost their cottages making bad bets.

Juniper and I squeezed our way through the crowd to We Three Beans, placed our orders, and then claimed a corner table in the cozy timbered-ceilinged room—me, Juniper, and Juniper's euphonium case. Juniper tried to calm my worries about the investigation. "No one thinks Santa killed Giblet."

"You didn't see Noggin."

She rolled her eyes. "No one with any sense, I meant. Noggin Hollyberry's been a rabble-rouser his whole life. A couple of years ago he tried to get the elves at the Candy Cane Factory to walk out two weeks before Christmas."

"What happened?"

"Someone showed him Christmastown's SSR."

I shook my head, clueless.

"The Strategic Sweets Reserve. There's enough candy stored in Sugarplum Mountain to send all seven continents into a diabetic coma. And that stuff doesn't go bad—candy canes, especially. Those have longer storage life than uranium waste."

"The Hollyberrys must be quite a clan."

"No one will listen to them, especially if what you say is true and Giblet just got bit by a bug. Who could possibly blame your husband for that?"

*Someone who'd seen the note written on his desk.*

"The elves were awfully solemn at the rehearsal when the requiem was brought up," I reminded her.

"Well, most elves live to a ripe old age, you know? For that matter, it's rare that anyone dies around here in an odd way. You should have seen the mourning commemorations after the last Santa died, this past summer. A hunting accident. That was a shock to everyone."

"Did they ever catch the abominable?"

Juniper's blue eyes widened, surprised that I had to ask.

"It's not a subject my in-laws ever talk about," I explained, embarrassed by my ignorance.

"No. A lot of men were out on that hunt. The snow monster probably saw the hunting party coming from miles off. You have to be sneaky when hunting abominables."

A shadow passed over us and Juniper and I looked up. My stomach roiled. As if the day weren't turbulent enough, Therese Jollyfriend glared down at me, her eyes shooting daggers. "Maybe you should take up snow monster hunting. You seem very good at sneaking, *Mrs. Claus*."

Every eye in We Three Beans was now directed toward our table. Ever since my arrival three months before, Therese had made no secret of her belief that I'd stolen Nick from her. Apparently they'd been an item at one time, although not at the time I met Nick. Nevertheless, his marriage had caused something inside the young elfwoman to snap.

"Give it a rest, Therese," Juniper said in disgust, projecting her voice so that all who were listening could hear. "One date to an elf clogging show doesn't equal a lifetime commitment."

The titters from the tables around us further incensed Therese. "What do *you* know about it? What does *anyone*?" She was practically trembling now, and her long black spiral curls shook, too, as her eyes narrowed on me. "Everything was fine until Nick went away and you preyed on his grief to get your claws into him. Others might not know about the destruction you leave in your wake, but *I* do. And now look what's happening! You're going to bring Nick down."

Pottery clattered on the tables of We Three Beans, and then the floor started shaking. Attention pivoted from Therese's tirade as people leapt up to press against the windows or run out to the sidewalk. The first time I'd experienced anything like this, I'd thought I was about to die in an earthquake and had created a scene by doing a duck-and-cover under the nearest table. Now, though my hand was trembling, it wasn't because of fear of natural disaster. Therese's words had rattled me.

When I glanced up again, though, she was gone.

Hoofbeats thundered past, and cries and whoops went up all around us. Juniper stood on her chair, craning to see out the plate glass windows. "Cupid colors in front!" She hopped in excitement.

I nodded, feigning as much interest as I could in a reindeer race when worries and suspicions clouded my thoughts.

*Others might not know about the destruction you leave in your wake, but* I *do. . . .*

Had Therese found out about what had happened to my first marriage? That had to be the destruction she'd been referring to. But how could she have known? No one in all of Santaland knew about Keith . . . no one except Nick.

I couldn't believe he would have told her.

"There's never been a Cupid at the head of Santa's team before," Juniper said, sinking back down into her chair. "This will be a first, if he manages to hold on to the lead in the hurdles."

Hurdles for the elite class of flying reindeer meant stands of trees and small ponds. The Reindeer Hop would be the last big event of the Christmas festivities. December in Christmastown was a never-ending parade of lunches, soirees, outdoor events, and parades.

December in Christmastown also meant more work than the inhabitants did during the rest of the eleven months of the year combined. It was North Pole life on steroids. I was already looking forward to January and hoped the questions surrounding Giblet's death would be cleared up by then.

Juniper's brow pinched in worry, which caused the tips of her oversized ears to tilt slightly, as if they were concerned, too. "Are you okay? You're not going to let crazy Therese bother you, are you?"

"Oh no," I lied.

Hoofbeats thundered down the street again, but this time they weren't as heavy. The race was over, so people turned curiously to see the few reindeer galloping through town. One stopped in front of We Three Beans, while others continued running up the hill toward Kringle Castle. The reindeer that had stopped was lathered and breathing hard. Elves and people got up and headed for the door to find out what the hubbub was about. Juniper and I followed.

The animal, which had a comet blazed on his flank, puffed his nostrils and then took a deep breath.

"Old Charlie's gone," he announced to the crowd gathered around.

"Where to?" someone yelled.

I wondered the same thing. Nick and I had just passed Old Charlie on the forest trail. Snowmen couldn't move fast enough for him to disappear that quickly.

"Not just gone," the reindeer elaborated. "*Killed.* Poor old guy's nothing but a puddle. Somebody melted him."

# Chapter 4

By the time I arrived on the scene, Charlie's melted remains had frozen solid. His vest, his stick arm, and his one eye and button nose were all preserved in an icy puddle.

Constable Crinkles stared at the sad sight in disbelief. The befuddled lawman was in shock. Everybody had liked Charlie, and it was difficult to keep away the scores of elves and people who had trekked out to witness the scene after hearing the news. In a rare show of model police work, Deputy Ollie had roped off the area, hoping to preserve what evidence there was.

Only Claus privilege had allowed me through.

Two deaths in one day couldn't be a coincidence, and that thought gave me a little relief—mixed with guilt at my relief. Whatever suspicions I had concerning Nick were completely unfounded if Christmastown had a psycho killer on the loose. Entertaining the notion that Nick had a grudge against an angry elf had been a stretch for me; imagining my husband on a killing spree, however, was impossible. He'd never harm a helpless old snowman. And I even knew where Nick had been when Charlie was killed. He'd just dropped me off at rehearsal and then gone . . .

*Where?* I frowned. Where *had* Nick gone?

Crinkles tugged at his chin strap. "It must have been a powerful blast of heat to melt him like that, so fast. Some kind of blowtorch, maybe."

Everyone within hearing range shuddered in horror.

"Were there any footprints?" I asked.

The constable's eyes blinked at the question, and then, belatedly, he glanced around.

Nick pointed to a swath of sweeping marks in the snow. "Looks like someone cleared them away, probably with a branch."

"Whaddaya know," Crinkles said. "That's what it looks like, all right."

I despaired. "Maybe you should start canvassing people to see if anyone owns a blowtorch."

A light dawned in Deputy Ollie's eyes, as if he'd never thought of this angle before. "And then we could ask those folks where they were when all this happened."

"But we can't say for sure when Charlie was melted," Crinkles argued.

"Of course we can," I said. "Nick and I saw him moving along the road just a few hours ago. It had to have happened sometime soon after, especially given that he's frozen solid now."

Nick draped his arm over my shoulder. "We should get going and let the constable and deputy do their job."

Had I been getting in their way? I thought I was helping.

Ollie went to his sleigh and returned with a pickax. He hefted it with the handle over his shoulder, like a soldier with a musket.

"What do you intend to do with *that*?" Crinkles asked.

"You said we needed to remove the body."

"I didn't say we were going to hack poor Charlie into ice cubes. Have you gone crackers? Folks are watching."

Ollie's face scrunched in confusion. "So what do we do?"

"We're going to lift him off the snow—gently and respectfully—and carry him back to the office."

Ollie sighed, and I could see why. That was quite a chunk of ice to haul away. Nevertheless, he returned to the constabulary's motorized sleigh and backed it closer. Ollie, Crinkles, and Nick wedged the block of ice off the ground and hefted it into the back of the sleigh. No easy feat.

When they were done, Ollie leaned over, puffing out an exhausted breath. Staring at the indentation the snowman's remains had left in the snow, he squinted. Then he leaned in and picked something off the ground.

"That's funny," he said. "Charlie just had the one eye, right?"

"Of course. It was coal. He lost the other one in the blizzard of 2012."

"Huh." The deputy turned over the item in his hand, which on closer inspection turned out to be a button. "We found his button nose frozen in the ice . . . so where'd this one come from?"

We all stepped in closer to examine the brass button.

"That's not the type of button a snowman would have for an eyeball," Crinkles said. "Even if he needed a spare."

"Maybe it came off his vest," Nick said.

Ollie wiped it off and inspected it more closely. He glanced up at Nick, more nervously now. "More likely it fell off yours."

Dread roiled in the pit of my stomach. Minutes before I'd been appalled at how bad the constables were at their jobs. Now that they seemed to be picking up on clues, I wished they'd stop.

Still, I wanted to know. I had to know. I leaned in to inspect the button. It was large and perfectly round, with the same waving Santa emblem I'd seen on the box of chocolates Nick had given me last summer. The same kind of button was on many of Nick's clothes, including the coat he was wearing now.

Strained silence ensued. "Did you just lose it, maybe, when we were picking up Charlie?" Crinkles asked hopefully.

Nick stared numbly at the button. It was obvious he hadn't just lost it. We had only to look at his coat to see all its buttons were accounted for. Was that the same coat he'd been wearing this morning, though? I honestly couldn't remember.

"Could be you lost it a while ago and it just happened to be here," the constable said.

"What are the chances of that?" Ollie asked.

The constable shot him a look.

"It would be quite a coincidence," Nick said in the deputy's defense. "And I haven't lost a button—at least, not that I recall."

I didn't, either. Not that I was a button-sewing kind of wife. Nick's mother probably was. In fact, I doubted there was a missing button in Christmastown that could escape Pamela's eagle eye.

"I'll have to keep the button," Constable Crinkles told Nick apologetically. He lowered his voice. "It wouldn't be good if word of this got out. The Hollyberrys are already clamoring for me to call in an outside investigator."

"Maybe you should," Nick said.

Crinkles looked from Nick's face to mine, then shook his head. "We'll see."

Nick bade him a good day and steered me toward his sleigh. The head of the reindeer team watched us approach. I was still terrible at guessing which herd the animals came from.

"It's true, then?" the reindeer asked. "About Charlie?"

"Yes," Nick said. "He's gone. Killed, most likely."

The animal hung his head low. "Strange times."

"Yes."

"And a Cupid won the race today," the reindeer added. The others nodded as if that were as strange a portent as two homicides in one day.

I stepped onto the sleigh and covered myself in a lap robe. This was probably another side of my outsiderness to locals. *She's always cold!* I could hear them saying.

We rode half a mile with only the muffled clop of hooves against packed snow to break the silence. Finally, Nick spoke. "Go ahead, April. Say what's on your mind."

"Who says I have anything on my mind?"

He shot me an amused look. "You usually do."

I wondered if this was a time to bring up Therese's sneak attack in We Three Beans and her strange reference to my last marriage. On second thought, *never* seemed the best time to bring that up, so I focused on more recent events. "If you must know, I don't appreciate being shut down like you did back there."

"When?"

" 'Let's let the constable and his deputy do their work,' " I said, doing a fair impression of Nick. "As if I were butting in."

"Weren't you?"

"I was trying to help."

"They don't need help. They're the law."

"Are you kidding me? It's like Barney Fife times two."

He stared at me, uncomprehending. "Who times two?"

My husband hadn't grown up watching *The Andy Griffith Show* reruns, or any other TV shows, except the few who made it on to North Pole television, which from what I could tell was mostly weather, Lawrence Welk reruns, and weather. Satellite dishes had changed things a little, but entertainment to Nick's generation had been elf clogging recitals, the Elf-men's Chorus, and umpteen Christmastown Little Theater productions of *A Christmas Carol.* Most pop culture—aside from a few toy tie-ins needed to do his work—was as much a mystery to him as things like proms and pep rallies. We came from two different worlds, and I had blithely eloped to Santaland thinking I could fit in, when even my name marked me as an outsider.

But my name and fitting in were the least of my problems today. "Where did you go after dropping me off at rehearsal?" I asked.

He glanced over at me. "Why are you asking?"

More interestingly, why wasn't he answering? "In case Constable Crinkles ever asks me, I should know."

"In case I become a suspect, you mean." His mouth turned down.

"You're already a suspect. That button . . ."

"That button could have come from anywhere. It might have been stolen from one of the Santaland seamstresses who make our clothes, or it could have been a hand-me-down donated to the charity store in Tinkertown. Or it might simply have fallen off one of my coats somewhere else."

"And was planted at the scene of the murder." The idea that someone had planted a clue to implicate him made me uneasy.

It didn't sit well with Nick, either. "Who would have done that?" he asked. "A Santa hater, in Santaland?"

"The Hollyberrys didn't seem very friendly toward Clauses."

"They're grieving, April."

It was so frustrating. "Would you stop being understanding? I'm trying to think of things that could clear you."

He laughed. "You should wait till I've been accused to worry about that."

"By the time someone is accused, the minds of a lot of people are already made up." Also, I couldn't help noticing Nick was still avoiding telling me where he'd been. "So after you dropped me off . . ."

"My brother's grave," he said, almost resentfully. "I went to be near Chris. I do that sometimes. And after this morning . . ."

The reminder of his grief chastened me. What was wrong with me? Ever since Jingles woke us this morning, the craziest thoughts had been flitting through my mind. "I'm sorry," I said. "It's been such a strange day."

"For everyone." He looked straight ahead as he drove. "That's why we need to keep our spirits up and present a calm, united front."

That was what Pamela had said.

"United against what?" I asked.

"Against suspicions, gossip, and hysteria. Those things can sweep through Christmastown quicker than a blue norther. You don't know this place like I do."

"I wasn't trying to fuel hysteria. I was just trying to find out what happened."

"That's not your job."

Right again. "Maybe that's the problem. I don't have a job."

Shocked, he turned toward me. "You're Mrs. Claus."

The words almost made me laugh—the way he said it made it sound as if being the wife of Santa Claus was as responsible a position as that of the CEO of a Fortune 500 company. "I'm *a* Mrs. Claus. Your mother runs Castle Kringle. And Tiffany . . . well, she's also Mrs. Claus, and everyone respects her as Chris's widow." Or at least they stayed out of her way. "Meanwhile, I wander around in an overcarbohydrated funk and play the triangle."

"You do more than that."

Sure. I had an Excel file of musical acts I kept up with. I was like a one-person talent agency. Although there was a lot of busywork involved, being Musical Events chairwoman didn't feel as fulfilling to me as running the Coast Inn. "I know, but it's not . . ."

I couldn't bring myself to finish. I was used to running a business, handling staff, juggling accounts, barely getting everything done by the end of the day. I sometimes forgot how wearying that had been. How I'd wake up at three in the morning worrying about what would happen if I stopped getting enough guests, or if I got too many at once and had turn them away. I worried about repairs, and guest complaints, and taxes. There were always taxes. And repairs. And whiny guests.

My phone pinged inside my purse. Grateful for the distraction, I checked my messages. As if the universe had known I needed a reminder, a long email popped up from Damaris Sproat, owner of the Pacific Breeze bed-and-breakfast down the road from my inn. I laughed. In fact, it might have come out as a demented cackle.

Nick glanced over nervously. "What's up?"

"Damaris Sproat's latest email. You have to hear this.

**"TO: APRIL**
**FROM: DAMARIS**
**SUBJECT: CLOUDBERRY BAY CHRISTMAS REGULATIONS**

**"April, I'm afraid you might have forgotten the ordinance (506.C) passed by the town council last year pertaining to holiday decorations within the Cloudberry Bay business district corridor. To wit, all businesses within said corridor must display appropriate holiday decor to attract and appeal to seasonal tourists. Naturally, I understand that you are**

**still with your new in-laws; however, when I checked at City Hall yesterday I discovered you had not applied for a variance.**

**"This puts you in violation of 506.C, which of course carries a fine. Unless, of course, you intend to remedy the situation. Right now there is a black hole in our Cloudberry Christmas Lights Walk where your inn is.**

**"I have never stuck my nose into your personal business, April. Perhaps you're one of those Christmas-hating heathens. I will hate to see you fined, but I'm sure you'll agree that no one—newlywed, heathen, or otherwise—is above the law.**

**"Sincerely,**
**Damaris"**

After finishing reading it aloud, I laughed. "A Christmas-hating heathen!"

Nick frowned. "They can penalize you even if you're not there?"

"Evidently."

I'd forgotten all about the ordinance. The last thing a person thinks about when they're eloping in the summer is stringing up holiday lights and setting them on a timer.

Nick's jaw worked, his desire to take my side warring with his natural revulsion at an undecorated house at holiday time. "What will you do?"

I snapped my phone cover closed and dropped it back into my bag. "Pay the fine. What else?"

He sagged in relief. "I was worried you were going to say you wanted to go back to Oregon."

"To string a few colored lights across my porch? Irksome

as it is to hand Damaris a victory, I'm not insane. Not yet, at least."

He laughed, and I joined in.

It was easy to laugh then. Neither of us knew what was coming.

# Chapter 5

"Goodness me, you were out a long time," Pamela said. "I can't keep up with any of you children anymore. Always on the go!"

I bumped into my mother-in-law after I'd returned and changed into something more comfortable—an oversized red sweater, black jeans, and a pair of boots I'd had since forever. She gave my casual, minimally seasonal sartorial choice a disapproving once-over.

"It's been a strange day," I said.

The comment—it seemed so innocuous—made her draw up to her full height. Pamela Claus was the only person I knew who could make five foot two look formidable. She was in a red-and-green wool suit with a skirt featuring felt mistletoe appliqués, and her gray hair was piled into a bun that added another three inches to her. "During times of crisis, it's more important than ever to stick to routines . . . and the formalities." She gave my outfit another jaundiced up-and-down sweep. "And perhaps stick closer to home."

"I went to the scene of Old Charlie's murder."

"Murder?" Her voice looped up. "Who said it was murder?"

"It was twenty below out and the poor creature melted. He didn't spontaneously combust."

Her manicured hands fluttered as she mentally reached for a response she couldn't find. There was no reason Charlie would have melted the way he did without being the victim of malicious action. "I don't know why you should have gone out there, though. If you must play Sherlock Holmes, you can try to find Tiffany for me. No one knows where she is."

"Couldn't you just look for Christopher?" Tiffany usually stuck to her son like white on rice.

"He's having his lessons."

"Wouldn't she be in the west wing, then?"

"Naturally, that's the first place we looked. I haven't been able to find her, and neither has Jingles. You might try the Old Keep. Maybe she's wandering around there." She shooed me off with a wave. "Tell her that we'll have a special tea in the salon at four."

The prospect of tea, at least, cheered me. I hadn't eaten much at breakfast, and had only drunk a cup of coffee since.

And yet . . . the Old Keep. The name was an understatement. The Old Keep was ancient, abandoned completely several generations earlier because it was so difficult to maintain. The stone was crumbling, all the mortar needed repointing, and bits of roof occasionally caved in. There was no way to heat it efficiently. Not to mention, the Old Keep, situated on the edge of Calling Bird Cliff, was expected to eventually tumble into oblivion as weather eroded the promontory.

"I'm not sure I—"

Pamela's hand clamped down on my arm. "Just do your best. We need to look after each other now."

She clicked away on her sturdy two-inch pumps. *Look after each other?* What did that mean? It almost sounded as if she suspected Tiffany of something.

In all my months in Santaland, Tiffany and I had spoken only rarely and we'd never had what I'd call a tête-à-tête. We sometimes bumped into each other in the morning in the empty breakfast room and shared a silent meal for a quarter hour. Usually Christopher was with her, and in that case I chatted with him while Tiffany lurked guardedly close.

I doubted she would appreciate my spying on her.

But to placate Pamela, I'd give the Old Keep a look-see and then come back and have my tea with a clean conscience.

The castle consisted of four parts. The aforementioned west wing was the modern section built on the west side of the Old Keep. "Modern" in this case dated back to the 1800s. Tiffany and Christopher occupied the first floor, while Lucia, Martin, and Pamela lived on the floor above. Nick and I had our quarters on the second floor of the main part of the castle, which was several hundred years older. Below us was the main hall, and behind that was the kitchen, and Jingles' quarters. Attached to this section was the east wing, where there were salons, and the big meeting hall. Behind all of these structures was the Old Keep, mostly hidden from the vantage of the drive up the hill and from Christmastown, except for the high, crenellated tower that rose above the main wing's roof.

I breezed through the modern west wing's first floor, just to double-check Tiffany hadn't returned to her room. Down the corridor where Tiffany and Christopher lived came the droning of one of Christopher's teachers, but a quick look inside the doorways of that hall produced no Tiffany sighting.

I sighed. On to the Old Keep, then.

My footsteps slowed as I walked down the echoing corridor that led to the Old Keep's entrance from the main castle. Evidently, the family had kept using the grand hall of the Old Keep for festive occasions up until the 1970s, when the roof had collapsed under the weight of too much ice. It was a miracle no one was killed.

The vaulted ceiling still made me nervous, although Nick had sworn to me that it had been stabilized. I crossed the empty hall nearly at a run just so I'd be at risk of being crushed by roof tiles and ice for a slightly shorter duration. The only reason I risked it at all was because I saw a heavy door ajar across the abandoned great hall and could feel a draft coming in from it.

The door opened on to a large stone spiral staircase. It led down to a cellar—no way was I going down there—and up to the old tower. I looked up, debated with myself, and decided to go. It was exercise; I'd earn myself a piece of cake with my tea. At this point, though, I moved slowly. The only time I'd come here before, with Nick, we'd encountered a strange wooly ice rat on these steps. My heart was still recovering.

When she'd heard about the rat, Lucia had said she would put poison around—not to spare my worries, but because the wooly rats carried fleas that could transfer to her reindeer. Priorities.

I moved carefully, squinting at first in the darkness, cursing myself for forgetting to bring a flashlight until I remembered my phone had one. I turned it on and almost immediately heard a squeak, followed by the scritching of tiny feet against stone. So much for Lucia's efforts.

As I wound up the staircase, the way became lighter and the temperature dropped. Someone had left the heavy door to the walkway along the castle tower wide open.

I peered through it and swallowed a gasp. Her straight, narrow back to me, Tiffany was sitting on one of the crenellation's depressions, dressed in nothing more than a dress and a wool cape, her feet dangling over the side—where there was a hundred-foot drop to the cliff. Cold wind howled around the tower walls. One strong gust could blow her petite body right off into the void.

I stepped out, moving cautiously. I'd never felt secure on this aerie walkway, and now I also feared startling Tiffany.

When I got close, though, she turned her head calmly as if some sixth sense had warned her of my presence. "Oh, it's just you," she said.

As opposed to whom?

I edged closer, leaning into an icy breeze. "Do you think it's safe to be sitting there?"

"Perfectly safe." She patted the space next to her, inviting me to join her on her lunatic perch.

I gulped. I didn't want to be taken for a complete coward, even if I was . . . at least when it came to being blown off a tower and smashing to the rocks below like a watermelon dropped from the Empire State Building.

I gingerly wedged myself next to her but kept my body facing the castle and my feet on terra firma. Tiffany was staring out at the distant mountains of the Farthest Frozen Reaches. From far away, the peaks looked like a picture postcard—pale winter light reflected off the snow, making the treacherous passes and glaciers resemble peaks of fondant icing. Yet those mountains held danger and tragedy. Chris, Tiffany's late husband, had fallen into a crevasse on Mount Myrrh, whose summit loomed highest on the distant horizon. I was sure it was that mountain Tiffany had been contemplating.

"Frightened?" she asked me.

"N-no."

She tossed me a knowing smile. "It made me nervous at first, too. Chris used to bring me up here to talk, sometimes for hours. He loved the view. But Chris wasn't afraid of anything."

*And that's how people die in snow monster hunts.* I shook my head at the uncharitable, un-Clausian thought. Her husband had died protecting Santaland and all its elves and people.

"What did you and Chris talk about?" I asked.

"About our lives before we knew each other, and the future, and our families. Our likes and dislikes . . . including people."

"From what I've heard, Chris liked everyone. Or at least everyone liked him."

She shook her head. "People say nice things now. I know better."

I squinted out at Mount Myrrh. "How often do you come up here?"

"Why?"

"Well, maybe it's not the healthiest thing to dwell so much on"—I gestured with my head to the far mountains—"the accident."

She eyed me with scorn. "Do you really think a sportsman like my husband fell through a crevasse?"

I blinked. The thought of Chris's death having not been an accident had never occurred to me. The word *murder* had never crossed anyone's lips—at least not until yesterday, when Giblet Hollyberry had spat the word at Nick.

"Now today there have been more deaths," she said. "Who else will die before it ends?"

"Giblet's and Charlie's deaths had nothing to do with Chris."

The look she gave me was tinged with pity. "You've become one of them quickly, haven't you?"

"One of what?"

One side of her mouth screwed into a sneer. "A Claus."

The malice in her voice and the way she was looking at me made me even more uncomfortable on that ledge.

"Maybe we should go in," I suggested. "Pamela's prepared a special tea."

"A special tea for a super special day." She laughed, which dissolved into a wrenching sound of despair. She twisted and took my arm, clamping her hand around it like a vise. Despite her Tara Lipinski build, she was surprisingly strong, and my heart thumped in my chest. If she jumped now, I'd go down with her. "Don't you get it?" she said, her eyes crazed. "This isn't a safe place."

No kidding.

I certainly didn't feel safe at the moment. I tried to avoid any quick movements, the way one would around a dog foaming at the mouth. A gust of air chose that moment to whip around the tower. I leaned into it, and away from her. Away from the terrifying drop she was so close to bringing us both to.

"Don't look at me like that." Her tone dripped contempt. "I'm not crazy, or suicidal."

It was the possibility of *homicidal* tendencies that made me nervous. One good tug and that would be the end of me.

"I've got my son to think of," she continued. "You can't usurp *him*."

As if I'd usurped anyone. "I have no intention to," I assured her in a steady tone. "Christopher's wonderful. He's the nephew I never got to have—I don't have brothers or sisters."

She eyed me skeptically, and then slowly the blood pressure cuff of her grip let up. She dropped her hand.

Liberated, I slid off the wall and gave my butt a quick swipe to get the dusting of ice off. "Pamela asked me to tell you that tea was ready if you want it."

She stared at me for a moment, the crazy draining from her gaze. She turned her attention back to those mountains, seeming as placid as if the whole previous conversation had never happened. "Thanks. I might come down later with Christopher."

"Great!" I chirped. "I'll let Pamela know."

I walked away as calmly as I could, though once I hit the stairs, my feet moved considerably faster, wooly ice rats be damned. I couldn't decide if I'd just escaped an untimely death or if I was just jittery from the strangest day I'd experienced since the afternoon the man I loved had revealed his true identity.

What was all that nonsense about Chris being murdered?

Of course, after her husband died in a horrifying way, Tiffany's mind was bound to play all sorts of tricks on her. I'd had the experience of being the widow left behind trying to put all the pieces together. Sometimes it wasn't possible. Sometimes you had to accept that there were things you would never know.

*You've become one of them quickly, haven't you?*

If she was imagining Nick and me—or, even more laughably, Pamela and me—being part of a cabal plotting to undermine her, she was truly delusional.

"Did you locate the elusive Tiffany?" Martin asked when I entered the evening salon. He popped a sandwich triangle in his mouth.

"She was outside," I explained. "She said . . . well, she might be down in a little while." I didn't want to go into the real subject of our conversation, at least not in front of Pamela. I was leery of talking about Chris's death around his still-grieving mother.

Lucia, lounging with Quasar in front of the fireplace with a plate of currant scones, had no such qualms. "That woman needs psychiatric help. Chris's death sent her over the edge."

"Piffle." Pamela, in an armchair, stared intently through her bifocals at her knitting. Next to her sat a half-finished cup of special Christmastown spiced tea. "Please don't let Christopher hear you say such things."

"You think he hasn't noticed? She smothers him."

"She's just being a good mother."

Lucia rolled her eyes. "Oh, come on. Christopher hardly ever leaves the castle anymore. Tiffany doesn't let him have any friends over, either. He wants a dogsled, but she won't let him have one—she's afraid of accidents, she says. But I think it has more to do with her not wanting him to be able to move around independently."

"He's only eleven," Pamela pointed out.

"The perfect age for a kid to have a sled and a few dogs," Lucia said. "I did at his age."

Martin laughed. "And look how you turned out."

Lucia stuck her tongue out at him.

"I confess I'm just as happy not to have any more animals wandering around the castle," Pamela said, never stopping her knitting. We all pointedly avoided glancing Quasar's way. "And dogs shed so."

"What about a cat?" Lucia asked.

Martin and I exchanged confused looks. "Do cats pull sleds?" he asked.

"I'm talking about as a pet," Lucia said.

"*Especially* not cats." Pamela shuddered. "Unsanitary things."

Again, there was a reindeer in the room drooling on the stone floor, but sure. Cats were unsanitary.

"Tiffany's no-dogs rule isn't about shedding," Lucia said. "Or cleanliness. It's about control. She's a control freak and a little nuts, if you ask me."

I didn't feel as if I had anything to add to Lucia's frank but spot-on assessment, so I started loading a plate with finger food. Tea was becoming my favorite meal. I'd already decided that when I opened the Coast Inn again in late spring tea would be a new tradition there. Although maybe not the overly sugared spiced tea popular in Christmastown.

"You're very quiet, April," Martin said. "Did Tiffany say something to disturb you?"

"No," I lied. "I was just thinking how wonderful Pamela's teas are."

"Guess who wins the gold star in sucking up today," Lucia muttered through a mouthful of scone.

"I mean it," I said. "I'm going to start having tea at the inn."

"We'll all have to visit this place," Martin said. "The Coast Inn. Sounds like a place you'd cruise up to in an old convertible."

"You should plan a trip to Cloudberry Bay," I told him. "I'll give you a family discount."

"I don't see why any of us should go," Pamela interrupted in that impatient tone she used when people weren't behaving the way she wanted them to. Which was often. "For that matter, why should you and Nick go down there at all? You don't need the money."

Before we got married, Nick and I had struck a bargain that we would spend part of the year in Oregon, which would allow me to keep my hand in the innkeeping business and hold on to the property I'd come to love. If we didn't continue operating the place at least part of the year, it would be nothing but a money drain—the most inconvenient beach house ever.

"It's not just about the money." Maintaining a toehold in my former life was as much for my sanity as anything else. "It's a wonderful place. Nick liked it."

"So much he went back twice." Martin, who was lounging across the sofa, winked at me. "But I don't think it was just the accommodations he returned for."

I sat down in the chair next to Pamela. "The inn is my baby."

"Hopefully it won't be the only one!" she exclaimed.

It was natural that Pamela would want grandchildren, but she was barking up the wrong tree, not to mention reopening an old wound. Nick and I couldn't have children. *I* couldn't have children, which was what had made my first marriage hit the rocks. Infertility treatments didn't work, and Keith, my late husband, had said he was against adoption as a solution to our troubles. But he was very much pro-cheating, I discovered after he was gone. I got to meet his pregnant girlfriend at his funeral.

Eyes trained on the floor, I gulped down a sip from my cup, waiting for the urge to pour hot sweet tea over my mother-in-law's head to pass. Getting over Keith, and getting past the disappointment of not being a mom, had taken years. But talk like Pamela's still needled me. What bothered me most was that I let it.

Happily, Martin saved the situation.

"Speaking of sperm," he said, "where's Nick?"

"Don't be crude," Pamela barked at him. "We don't use words like that in Christmastown."

Next to the fireplace, Lucia sniggered.

"What word?" Tentatively, Martin asked, "Sperm?"

Pamela jolted as if she'd been jabbed with a pointy stick. "Stop that!"

Lucia grinned at me. "No sexy talk in Castle Kringle."

She and Martin guffawed. They were both punchy, and showing about as much maturity as Christopher.

"There's no reason to talk about *s-e-x* at all," Pamela said.

"But you were the one who brought it up, Mother," Lucia pointed out, "telling April to get busy with the grandchildren."

"I didn't mean it *that* way."

"There just can't be too many immaculate conceptions from Mom's perspective," Martin told me.

"Where *is* Nick?" Pamela asked impatiently. "If he's in his study, we should let him know there's tea—or, better yet, have Jingles or Waldo take some to him."

"I'll go," I said.

But Pamela, exasperated with the present company, was out of her chair and halfway to the door before I could half rise. "You stay right there," she said. "You have that over-loaded plate of food to eat."

When she was gone, Martin and Lucia collapsed into whoops of laughter.

Taking advantage of Pamela being out of the room, I decided to bring up what Tiffany had mentioned. "Was there ever an investigation into Chris's death?"

I might just as well have fired a shotgun into the air. Their eyes went wide. Martin sat up straighter. "What makes you ask?"

"Tiffany raised the possibility that her husband's death wasn't an accident."

For a moment they blinked at me as if I'd been speaking in tongues. Then Lucia stood, spilling scones on the rug. Quasar stretched his neck to reach the nearest one.

"You see?" she said to Martin and me. "She *is* crazy. Something needs to be done about that woman."

"Like what?" Martin asked. "There aren't any psychiatric hospitals here."

"Then someone needs to go south and have her committed."

"Lock the widow in the loony bin?" Martin mused.

"It's not a joke. She needs help."

I thought of Tiffany dangling her legs off the top of that tower as casually as if she'd just been sitting on a bench. Then I remembered her taking my arm, and the fear I'd felt in the face of all that wild vehemence. All I'd thought about was getting myself away from her. Now the words she'd hissed played back to me: *This isn't a safe place.*

And here were two Clauses arguing over whether to lock her up.

Come to think of it, neither Martin nor Lucia had answered my question.

"What if she's right about what happened to Chris? It sounds as if there wasn't much of an investigation. Did Constable Crinkles even ask you where you were that day?"

Lucia frowned. "Why would he? Everybody knew I wasn't on the mountain. I was tending to a sick reindeer that day."

"And I was slaving away at the Candy Cane Factory, as usual," Martin said. "I remember being in my office when word came back about what happened."

"Nick told me it was an accident," I said.

"Of course it was," Martin said. "Everybody loved Chris."

Lucia seconded his statement. "Nobody would've wanted to kill him."

It was a rare moment of agreement between them. Even stranger was the fact that they both sounded so definite. The cult of Chris was strong in Santaland, and his mythic status seemed especially inviolate here in the castle . . . but what man alive was beloved by everyone?

"Anyway," Martin said, "who would benefit from killing Chris?"

"Nick."

I thought it, but Lucia had said it.

Martin laughed. "Oh, right. We all know how much he relishes being Santa." He shook his head. "He wouldn't consider it benefiting. Donning the suit was never his dream. He would've much rather kept beavering away in the Claus business office and the Christmastown Planning Commission."

"You're right about that," I said.

"The point is," Lucia said impatiently, "Chris's death was declared an accident months ago and Tiffany can't accept the truth. We can't have a crazy woman running around the castle pointing fingers at Nick."

"She didn't point at Nick, exactly," I said. "She implied

that Chris's death and the deaths of Giblet and Old Charlie were linked somehow."

This stunned them into silence, at least for a moment.

"Aren't the Hollyberrys adversarial enough?" Lucia asked. "The last thing this family needs now is to have one of our own pointing fingers at us."

"It's especially bad for Nick after Charlie's melting." I told them about the button.

Lucia looked distressed. "What a mess!"

"It's all nonsense," Martin said.

"What's nonsense?" Pamela asked, sweeping back into the room.

The three of us clammed up.

Luckily, Pamela was distracted by the sight of Quasar devouring the last of the scones on the floor. She clucked. "You shouldn't let Quasar eat those currant scones, Lucia. You know what dried fruit does to his digestion."

I looked to Lucia for an explanation. She mouthed the word *gas* at me.

Martin laughed.

"It won't seem a laughing matter when the whole castle starts to smell like a methane factory," Pamela declared primly.

I tried to look serious, as did Martin and Lucia, but Quasar chose that moment to let loose an impressive cloud of wind, accompanied by a sound that reverberated around the room like a moose call. The three of us dissolved into hysterics. But Pamela was right. That smell cleared the room.

Out in the hallway, Pamela stopped me. "You didn't ask me about Nick."

He hadn't come back with her, so I assumed he was too busy for a tea break. "Is something the matter?"

"I never found him," she said. "Jingles said he left right after dropping you off."

As she spoke, she tilted her head, studying me as if she

expected the words to have some specific effect on me. It was true that Nick normally spent afternoons in his study, but today had not been a normal day.

"I'm sure he'll turn up," I said. "He told me he had a hundred things to do."

She stepped close to me and took both my arms as if she were going to give me a bone-rattling shake. Instead, she said ferociously, "Watch him, April. There should be nothing more important to you right now."

When she released me, I stood reeling long after she'd bustled away. *Watch him.* I couldn't tell if that was a simple directive, or a warning.

# Chapter 6

Disturbing dreams kept me tossing and turning all night. One example: I was sitting on a ledge with Tiffany, who was insisting that someone murdered Chris. I fell backward, face to the sky, arms and legs flailing. Above me, peering over the stone wall to watch my plunge, was Nick.

A little later, another dream: I was getting married at the justice of the peace office where Nick and I were married, but after the ring was slipped on my finger I looked up and realized I hadn't married Nick at all, but a horrible green-faced creature with a red nose and hair of orange and red flames. It was Heat Miser from *The Year Without a Santa Claus.*

I bolted up in bed. If it hadn't been morning already, I would have been afraid to close my eyes again.

I turned to say good morning to Nick—and yes, to reassure myself that I wasn't Mrs. Heat Miser—but his side of the bed was empty, the covers smoothed back, unslept in. I'd left him working in his study the night before. He'd returned for dinner, during which everyone had behaved as if nothing at all odd had happened that day. Which just made the horrors of the past twenty-four hours seem even more surreal to me. Despite his attempts to appear normal, Nick had clearly been preoccupied.

Or felt guilty?

*Preoccupied*, I repeated to myself. With a deadly crime wave underway, why wouldn't he be? For all intents and purposes, he was Santaland's head of state. Acting head of state. The Santa regent to Christopher's claim.

*Who benefited from Chris's death?*

I got up and dressed in my favorite Mrs. Claus dress—a green fitted velvet number with a skirt trimmed with white wool. I pulled on black boots with four-inch heels, did my hair, and put on makeup as if arming myself for battle. Mostly it was my own suspicions I was fighting. Fighting and winning. I was going to follow Pamela's example. The events of yesterday had nothing to do with my family, and especially not with the generous, kind man I'd married.

Before I went downstairs, I unplugged my phone from its charger and looked at my email. One glance elicited a groan. A new message from Cloudberry Bay had landed in my inbox overnight:

**FROM: DAMARIS SPROAT**
**SUBJECT: CHRISTMASTIME FINES**

I didn't want to open it, knowing I would be annoyed. And yet it was sitting there on my screen like a mosquito bite, an itch to be scratched.

Reader, I tapped:

**Since you haven't bothered to reply to my previous email, I can only assume that you are perfectly happy to let the issue of your lack of both town and holiday spirit be taken to the city council. It pains me to do this to you, April. I would be grieved if you think this complaint stems from any personal animus**

**on my part. Far from it! Even though my great-uncle, Homer Sproat, was one of the town forefathers and practically built every inch of your beautiful home with his own two hands, and even though you basically snatched it out from under my nose right after Uncle Thornton died, I have never once uttered a peep against you, or your acquisitiveness, or your butting into city affairs that you know little of, being a relative newcomer. You'll recall that I even stood up for you when you painted the house a non-town-approved color. You wouldn't believe the number of people who came up to me and asked, "Damaris, how can you stomach looking at what a monstrosity that girl's making of your uncle's place?" But I mind my own business, and that house that was in my family for generations is no longer my affair.**

**Which is just my way of saying that I bear you no grudge, and would certainly never do anything so petty as fining someone out of spite. I hope we're still good enough friends—Thursday Night Book Club notwithstanding—for you to believe me when I say that this is nothing personal.**

**Attached you will find the estimate of the fine to be levied against you, which amounts to $532.**

**Cheers,**
**Damaris**

I'd completely forgotten demented Damaris. She'd even mentioned the Thursday book club we belonged to, which she quit in a huff when a majority of us had voted to read *A Man Called Ove* when she was dead set on *Atlas Shrugged.* In protest, she'd written a letter to the book club president as thoroughly argued and opinionated as a Supreme Court decision.

I scanned the message again and laughed at the absurdity of it. A perfect study in passive aggression. At times like this I missed my friend Claire, who enjoyed Damaris's ridiculous shenanigans as much as I did. Claire owned Cloudberry Creamery, the local ice-cream shop, and we'd dubbed a popular bitter lemon slushee she sold "The Damaris Freeze" after the lip puckering its first jolt of bitterness caused. An added splash of vodka made a Drunken Damaris, which we enjoyed during those winter months when there weren't too many tourists around. In other words, right about now.

I forwarded Damaris's emails to Claire with a brief note telling her I thought she might like to know that I might have escaped the winter off-season, but I was still getting an icy blast of Damaris. I hadn't confessed the truth about Nick to Claire yet—I'd just told her his family were big landowners in the far north. Her curiosity about my whirlwind marriage was intense, but she wasn't naturally nosy. Perversely, this made me more inclined to confide in her. I just didn't know how to start.

*By the way, I married Santa Claus. . . .* She'd suspect I was actually living in a rubber room somewhere.

After sending off the email, I decided to tell Nick about Damaris's note. He could probably use a laugh today.

I met Jingles in the corridor. "Is Nick in the breakfast room?"

The question seemed to surprise him. "No, he's in his study. It's already been quite a morning. Constable Crinkles was here."

I gulped. "Why didn't anybody tell me?"

He gave me a dubious look. "They probably didn't want to bother you."

"They?"

"Santa and Mrs. Claus—I mean, the dowager Mrs. Claus. They were shut up in the study for half an hour after the constable left." He lowered his voice. "Not that I was listening at the door, but as I was standing in the hallway I *might* have heard them mention something about the investigation, and *bringing in someone.*"

Bringing in someone . . . like a lawyer? Did they even have those in Santaland?

My jaw tightened. "Thank you, Jingles."

I stood in the hallway, reminding myself of pertinent facts, trying to tether myself to sanity: *Hiring legal counsel is no indication of guilt.*

*A morning meeting with one's mother is not a personal cabal against me.*

*I did not marry an elficidal Santa.*

This whole double-murder situation was making me paranoid. Especially with crazy Tiffany's ravings about Chris being murdered thrown into the mix. Or *was* she crazy? If she wasn't . . . well, she'd come as close as possible to implicating Nick as she could have without physically pointing a finger at him.

That's what was making me second-guess everything. The only person anyone was pointing to as a suspect was Nick. As far as I knew, there were no other suspects. So far, the evidence was scant but it all pointed to Nick.

Someone needed to do some digging to find out who really was behind this crime spree. And given the head-scratching ineffectiveness of Constable Crinkles, I was pretty sure that someone was going to have to be me.

Filled with newfound investigative fervor, I grabbed a quick bite in the breakfast room—miraculously empty—

tapped into my inner Poirot, and revved up my little gray cells. Who would have killed both Giblet and Charlie? The trouble was I'd barely known Giblet. And as for Charlie . . . did snowmen have enemies?

I needed to start at square one. The clues. First up: the spider. If what they said was true and poisonous spiders weren't native to the North Pole, then how did one get to Giblet's cottage and into his stocking? It had to have come from somewhere.

That decided my course of action. I put on my coat and gloves, and before anyone—especially Pamela—could waylay me I slipped out the side door of the castle and took the funicular down the hill into Santaland. Several cars went up and down the long incline toward the castle all the time, so I wasn't completely dependent on the castle's chauffeured fleet of sleighs and snowmobiles. Stealth was the goal. Unfortunately, as I settled into a corner seat for the ride I felt as if I was being examined. I was used to standing out; I was taller than an elf, had reddish-blond hair, and I was Mrs. Claus. But this was something different. A hair-standing-on-edge sensation.

I looked around the car and found my gaze locked with Therese's.

*Great.* All I needed now was another public confrontation. I braced myself for a demented harangue like I'd been treated to in We Three Beans. To my surprise, however, she didn't come forward to make a scene, and when I rose to leave the car at the first Santaland stop she merely smirked at me. I would've at least expected her to stick out her leg at the last minute and send me sprawling to the ground. Subtlety wasn't her style, so her holding back left me almost as unsteady as a blizzard of angry words would have. I stepped off the funicular and very pointedly did not look back. Mistake number one.

My destination was the main branch of the North Pole post

office. Think your post office is crowded during the holidays? You should see mine. The strange thing about the Christmastown P.O. is that the pileup isn't caused by people sending packages, it's caused by the sacks of mail—all addressed to Santa—and tables and tables of elves sit sifting through the letters and directing them to the correct department at Tinkertown, or, for those really tough letters, to the castle itself, where Nick and his assistants deal with the children who want things like a new brother, or a house, or an end to war. I'd already seen those stacks of letters and how they affected Nick. Santa Claus wasn't just about tossing toys down chimneys. It was about giving hope.

Employees everywhere, and no one to talk to. On speakers from above, 101 Strings sawed happily away at "Sleigh Ride." I waited through it and Bing's "White Christmas" before a harassed elf clerk came to the window. "Can I help you?" When he looked up at me, he gulped and straightened his cap.

"I want to inquire about a package," I said.

"Do you have the tracking number?"

"No . . . in fact, I'm not even sure it was sent at all. I was just wondering if there were any deliveries made recently to Giblet Hollyberry's cottage?"

At the name, the elf frowned. "Giblet. Oh. Well, I wouldn't know. Unless it was a tracked package. Any other deliveries would just go out with the normal mail and we wouldn't have a record."

I didn't have a number, of course. I'd made the mistake of thinking that everything in Christmastown would be magically simpler, even the postal service.

So much for my little gray cells.

"We'll be sending a sack of mail up to the castle later today," the clerk said.

"Thank you."

I was about to leave when the elf lowered his voice. "I'm not supposed to plug the competition, but what the heck—it's the holidays, right?"

I leaned in.

"SPEX," he said.

I frowned, uncomprehending.

"Santaland Parcel Express," he said. "They might be able to help you. Lots of folks around here use them, especially this time of year. They don't have to handle letters to Santa."

"Thank you."

The elf's eyes widened again. "Not that there's anything wrong with Santa letters. It's our bread and butter."

"You do an amazing job sorting them all out," I assured him.

He stood a little taller. "We try."

He gave me the address for SPEX and I left, heading for the parcel office. As I walked, I felt a frisson of awareness, as if I was being watched. Or followed. Remembering my encounter with Therese earlier, I slowed down at a corner and looked around surreptitiously. She was nowhere in sight. The sidewalks teemed with the usual December traffic, elves and people bundled up and going about their business. A dogsledder mushed past, the dogs wearing jingle bells on their harnesses like reindeer. The wonderful aroma of hot chocolate from the Hoppie's Hot Drinks cart lured me over for a quick drink. As I downed a cup, I took in the twinkle lights winking against the snow-covered streets and rooftops. It was hard to believe that anything sinister could have happened in this cheery, festive world.

Maybe it hadn't, I told myself. Maybe the spider bite was just happenstance and the melting of Charlie was . . .

Well, it was hard to say what that could have been besides deliberate malice.

The difference between this SPEX office and the post

office was stark. A lone employee, middle-aged and tall for an elf, slouched behind the counter, bored out of his mind. Seeing me—recognizing who I was—he straightened and lit up like a Broadway marquee. "Mrs. Claus! How may I help you?"

"I came for some information. I need to know if any packages were delivered to Giblet Hollyberry's recently."

The enthusiastic smile on his face froze into a pained rictus. "I can't give out information like that. Confidentiality, you know."

I glanced at the name tag on the elf's tunic. *Filbert.* "The clerk at the post office said you might be able to help."

"I'd like to. . . ." Filbert practically writhed.

Guilt shot through me at the position I was putting him in. I wasn't an arm-twisting kind of person. I took a step back. "It's all right. I understand."

His head tilted. "Are you working with the police? I didn't tell them anything, either."

*That* caught my attention. "They've been here?"

"Yes—asking me all sorts of questions, probably about the same things you want to know. Suspicious packages at the castle, that sort of thing."

"What did you tell them?"

His mouth tightened, as if he was physically barring any information from passing to me.

I'd underestimated Constable Crinkles. He hadn't seemed inclined to do much in the way of real investigating, yet he'd worn out a little shoe leather coming down here to try to figure out who had sent that package to Giblet.

Maybe he wasn't as hopeless a detective as I'd thought.

"Was the constable satisfied with what he found out?" I asked.

"The constable?" the clerk repeated.

Did he think I was so ignorant of Christmastown that I didn't even know who the law was? "You don't have to tell me what you said to him. I understand."

"Wait!"

I stopped, and Filbert came around the counter. "I didn't like the way the questions were being asked by that detective. Everything was about the new Santa, and did he ever come here to pick anything up, or was there a suspicious package delivered to the castle."

My mouth felt dry. So it was as I thought. They suspected Nick. "What did you say?"

Anxiety crossed his face, and then he stepped back around the corner. "I'd love to tell you, but first, I'd like to show you a video I made of my youngest daughter, Willa. She's a tap-dancing, singing dynamo!"

Before I could protest, he'd flipped his monitor around and had hit *Play* on a video of a little elf girl tapping and singing "All I Want for Christmas Is My Two Front Teeth." She was cute as a bug's ear, although her mastery of pitch left something to be desired. I tried to keep smiling as she warbled and tapped her way through the song.

When it was over, he grinned at me. "Wouldn't she be great for opening the Skate-a-Palooza?"

My mouth dropped. First, the Skate-a-Palooza was a huge outdoor event featuring big acts, like our local rock band Figgie and the Nutcrackers. Open with this kid and I might have a riot on my hands. "I'm not sure . . ."

He hit the button and the monitor went black. "Of course, if you don't want to know what suspicious package was delivered to the castle . . ."

So this was it. A shakedown. And now I had to weigh which was stronger: my integrity, or my curiosity.

"Willa will be a dynamite opener," I said.

He beamed. "I hoped you'd think so. That wasn't even

her best outfit. Her mama just made her a new one, with sequins."

I cleared my throat. "What about this package? What did you tell the police?"

"That *I* never took anything like a suspicious package to the castle, which is the truth."

I frowned. Was this a joke?

He smiled slyly. "What I didn't say is that my coworker, Frank, said he'd taken a special delivery over just last week. He said the package was marked *Live Animals* and had directions to be delivered immediately."

*Live animals.* My heart rate sped. "What was in it?"

"Frank said he didn't know. It was a big box, though. Came from Alaska, I think—at least, that's where it went through before it got here. He said it was kind of heavy."

I wasn't sure if I was relieved or disappointed. "Too big to be spiders, then."

He frowned. "Well . . . they could have put the spiders in one of those glass things."

A terrarium. I hadn't thought of that. "Who was it addressed to?"

"Lucia Claus. But she wasn't the one who took the package. A man did."

"Nick—I mean, Santa?"

His brow furrowed. "Frank didn't think so. Neither of us had ever really seen Nick Claus up close. He's not like Chris was, or even Martin. Those two were always the friendly ones." My expression must have changed, because he suddenly looked stricken. "Meaning no disrespect."

"None taken."

"I hope you won't hold what I said against little Willa. She's got a mighty talent."

I bit my lip. "No, I wouldn't do that."

"The Hollyberrys were always hotheads, Giblet most of

all. None of us sane elves think the Claus family would kill anybody. Especially not Nick Claus. Gosh, everyone knows he's a private sort of person. Keeps to himself."

He sounded like a guy on the news replying to a reporter's questions about the serial killer next door. "Thank you for the information," I said.

Filbert leaned forward, lowering his voice. "You know you're being followed, don't you?"

The uneasiness I'd felt on the street came roaring back. "I thought so. Thanks for telling me."

I left the store, feeling frustrated and paranoid again. If someone was following me . . .

As I reached the corner of the building, a hand darted out and caught my arm, whirling me back. A man in a black trench coat and hat looked at me with eyes as gray as flint. "Are you April Claus?"

I tried to shrug his hand off my arm, but his grip remained firm. Firm and cold. Iciness seeped through the wool of my coat. "I am."

"You'd better come with me, then. I have questions."

"I have one, too," I protested. "Who are you?"

"Name's Frost, ma'am. Jake Frost. I'm a detective."

"Jack Frost? Are you serious?"

"*Jake*," he said with the studied patience of a man who'd made the same correction a hundred times. "Jack was a distant relation."

"Have you been following me?"

"As it happens, yes."

"Why?"

"Someone tipped us off that you were acting suspiciously."

"Who—?"

All at once, I remembered that smirk I'd seen on the funicular on the face of my would-be rival, Therese.

# Chapter 7

"Why were you asking the postal and delivery clerks about Giblet Hollyberry?" the detective asked me.

"Why do you think? He was murdered."

We were sitting in the main room of the Christmastown Constabulary, which was a cottage repurposed as a police station. My glimpse of the "jail" revealed it to be a bedroom with a button lock on the hallway side, although I was assured that the windows had been painted shut. Clearly, Christmastown didn't expect any criminal masterminds to be passing through in the near future. Understandable, I supposed, for a city that had never seen a murder until yesterday.

Detective Jake Frost perched on a chair all the way across the room from me, while I was as close to the hearth as I could manage without going up in flames. The mantel was festooned with evergreen, holly, and mistletoe. No one would confuse this place with Alcatraz.

The gaze Frost leveled at me brought the temperature down a few degrees, though.

I jumped in before he could ask his next question. "I'm glad they've brought you in, Detective Frost. Maybe now we'll find out who killed Giblet and Charlie."

"That's the intention."

My attempt to ingratiate myself didn't impress him. "Well . . . anything you want to know," I said, continuing my effort to seem biddable. "I'm only too happy to help."

Except I had no intention of helping to convict my husband or anyone else at the castle if Frost was going to rush to judgment. I especially wasn't going to tell him about that package delivered to the castle until I discovered more about it.

Frost's lips quirked. It was hard not to stare at him. I'd become so used to the doughy folk of Christmastown, Jake Frost had seemed to swoop in a like a bird of prey among a warren of plump bunnies. Everything about him was angular and dark, except his eyes, which were a disarming slate gray.

"Where were you the night Giblet Hollyberry was killed?" he asked.

Of course I'd known I was a suspect—the Hollyberrys thought so, and Jake Frost was here at their insistence. But I hadn't yet heard *that question*. Suddenly I felt like a bug pinned on a board. I began to sweat like a suspect. I scooted my chair a little farther from the fire and cleared my throat. "I was in bed asleep, of course."

"All night?"

I shifted, remembering how strange that night had been. How restless I was—almost as restless as Nick, who'd disappeared.

"Mrs. Claus?"

He may have said it twice. To be honest, I still had difficulty associating that name with me. "April, please," I said. "I might have gotten up for a drink of water . . . or something like that."

"Uh-huh."

His eyes narrowed as if they could laser right through to my soul. For all I knew, they could. An air of unreality hung about him; his possessing supernatural powers wouldn't surprise me. Once you find yourself in Santaland, the bar for something to seem fantastical is set high.

"I didn't speak to anyone, if that's what you mean," I said, hating the way my voice looped up. *Don't sound guilty.* "There's no one who could give me an alibi."

"Not even your husband? Surely he was with you."

I flushed. "Well, yes, but he was asleep." *Part of the time.*

He watched me carefully, taking his time. If I had been interrogating me, I would have thought I was guilty. Because I *felt* guilty. I was lying, but I wasn't sure why. I didn't think Nick killed Giblet, and I was sure *I* didn't, so why didn't I just tell the whole truth?

Because the truth looked so bad: A restless Santa wandering around during the night an elf who'd insulted him was murdered. What detective wouldn't leap to the obvious conclusion?

"I didn't kill Giblet," I said. "That's why I came into town to ask about the packages that had been delivered to Giblet's cottage. Would I have done that if I were guilty? Of course not. In that case, I would've known where the spider came from, and when and where it was delivered."

"*If* it was delivered."

"How else could it have gotten here?"

"Someone might have brought it by hand."

"If you're thinking I brought it to Santaland, that's ridiculous. I would have needed future sight to know there would be an elf in Santaland I wanted to rub out. When I came here I was newly married, fresh from a honeymoon. I wasn't thinking about elves or murder or anything like that. Transporting spiders to kill Giblet Hollyberry was certainly not at the top of my agenda. I'd never even heard of him."

"You'd heard of him before he was found dead, though."

"Only because of the ice sculpture competition. And even

after the ice sculpture kerfuffle, I didn't bear him any ill will. I just felt sorry for him—he'd lost and pitched a childish fit."

"He called your husband a murderer."

"That was just ridiculous. I had no idea what he meant. . . ." Even as I left the sentence dangling, I could have kicked myself.

"But now you understand," Frost guessed.

"I've gotten wind of a wild conspiracy theory about the previous Santa's—Nick's brother's—death. It's completely unfounded."

"People are saying your husband pushed his brother into that crevasse."

I drew up, doing my best imitation of Pamela. "Anyone acquainted with Nick knows he would never do such a thing."

*Except, apparently, Tiffany*, a little voice in my head contradicted.

"How well do you know him?" Jake Frost asked.

"He's my husband."

"Of three months. According to my sources, you two hadn't known each other very long before the wedding."

There were people—sources?—talking to the police about Nick and me? The thought made me queasy.

"There have been women married to men for decades who never understand their dark secrets until the police start unearthing bodies in the backyard," he finished.

*For Pete's sake.* "Nick's a good person, conscientious and kind. When I met him he was grieving for his brother."

"I've seen a widow grieve for a husband after she put arsenic in his coffee."

"You don't lack for gruesome examples, do you?"

"All I'm saying, ma'am, is that sometimes guilt looks an awful lot like grief. The two things can get all mixed up in a person's head."

*If that person is a murderer.* "What you're saying is that you've swallowed a lot of absurd rumors about Nick and you aren't interested in looking further."

"As far as I'm concerned, the investigation is still wide open."

Sure it was. "Is that why you'd take the word of a flake like Therese Jollyfriend and follow me around?"

He shifted. "As to that, I didn't actually believe her. If I had, I would be asking you questions about trying to set up your husband for murder and bring down the House of Claus and maybe the entire tradition of Christmas itself."

"She said that about me?"

"Let's say it was the direction she was heading. Mostly I wanted to see what kind of woman could manage to make that strong an enemy in just a few months. What *did* you do to her?"

"It's one of those hell-hath-no-fury scenarios. Except as far as I can piece together, Nick never scorned her. They only went out once or twice."

"Could be she's just gone a little snow crazy. Not everybody is cut out for living here."

As I burrowed deeper into my coat—I hadn't taken it off at the station—I wondered if I was one of those people. Only time would tell. Of course, if Therese was as unhinged as she seemed, there was a chance I wouldn't live long enough to find out.

"Do you think Therese is dangerous?" I asked.

He shrugged. "She seems more nutty than violent."

"Could she have planned all these terrible things to set *me* up? I mean, to make it look like I was somehow masterminding a plot to make Nick look guilty?"

"Instinct tells me she couldn't set up a tiddlywinks board, even with instructions. But as I said, I'm not ruling anything out at this point."

That should have been a relief—I wanted someone keeping an eye on Therese—except that it also meant he wasn't going to rule out Nick. Or me.

The second I crossed the castle threshold, pinpricks of panic hit me. The foyer was deserted, but singing echoed down from the great hall—youthful voices trilling out "Ding Dong Merrily on High."

*Oh God.* Realization hit me and my body went clammy.

*The Kinder Caroling.*

*Shoot, shoot, shoot.*

This was a big deal. All the schools of Santaland sent children to the castle to sing. In return, the lady of the castle—aka me—treated the carolers to punch and pastries and handed out simple favors and a "gold" coin good for a treat at the Santaland Sweet Shoppe. A Mrs. Claus had been handing out favors in this tradition forever.

In Santaland, forever meant centuries.

Jingles swooped down on me like doom, taking my handbag and divesting me of my coat, gloves, and scarf. "Where have you been?" he whisper-growled at me.

"In town."

"I had half the elves in the castle hunting for you." His sweeping gaze gave me a head-to-toe assessment. "Well, you've looked worse."

"Thanks for the confidence booster."

"Children aren't the most persnickety about appearances." He turned me toward the hall. "You'd better scoot in there before you miss the whole thing. Mrs. Claus has been doing the honors in your absence."

I arched a brow at him.

"The dowager Mrs. Claus, I mean."

I swallowed, wondering if being late would almost be

worse than not showing up at all. My mother-in-law wouldn't view my absence favorably, but most people might just assume I was sick. Perhaps Pamela had even told them that. If I walked in now, it would be obvious to all that I was merely scatterbrained.

*It's for the kids*, I told myself. This was one event I'd really been looking forward to.

I hurried off to the great hall, a long gallery of marble and stone and leaded glass windows, with tapestries made by the Santaland weavers centuries ago covering the stone walls. The Tinkertown Tots choir started singing "Marshmallow World." I slunk in a side door and tried to make my way inconspicuously to where Pamela was standing next to the massive decorated tree. She appeared especially queen motherish today in a suit of cranberry red with a matching hat and satin gloves. As I sidled up next to her, the quick, sharp smile she aimed at me was as withering as any glare.

"Where have you been?" she said under her breath.

*Out trying to clear your son.* I mouthed, *Sorry, I forgot.*

"Goodness me, April. It's not as if you have onerous duties. You could at least show up for the few events you're scheduled for."

"I'm here now," I whispered.

Even though I'd Mrs. Claused myself up this morning, I was looking the worse for wear after my dash around downtown. Pamela's glance strayed more than once to my boots, which were streaked with marks from the salt that was spread everywhere to keep the sidewalks from being like a hockey rink.

"Marshmallow World" ended and everyone clapped. "Are there any more toys to hand out?"

She gestured to a brass box next to me shaped like a treasure chest, which held the fake gold Santa coins. They were mostly gone. I scanned the room to see if Lucia was nearby, although I couldn't imagine her patience lasting through more than one kiddie choir. "Was Martin here helping you?"

Her eyes widened. "Don't be silly—he's at work. Luckily for me, Therese happened to drop by and leant a hand."

*Happened to drop by?* Sure she did. Because she'd known I wasn't going to be around—she'd seen me leave and then sicced the detective on me. I was about to protest when Pamela shushed me. "Time to talk afterwards, April. Duty first."

I took the box.

"And for pity's sake, smile."

I smiled, although it would have been impossible not to when a whole line of adorable tiny elves were filing past in their velvet suits, hats, and pointy boots. I only wished I could shower them in real gold.

The only bad moment came when I caught sight of Therese darting out a side door. She must have loved seeing me arrive late and witnessing Pamela's irritation with me. It struck me as very disloyal of Pamela to let Therese stand in my place, but then again, I was the idiot who'd forgotten and Therese was her goddaughter. Maybe Pamela had harbored hopes about a marriage between Therese and Nick, too.

"You simply must try harder," Pamela lectured me when the hall had emptied out. "Heaven knows I do what I can to include you in things. Just this morning I tried to find you. I wanted to show you my design for the croquembouche."

A pastry needed a plan? "I went out to help your son, and thanks to Therese, I got nabbed by a detective looking into the Giblet Hollyberry case."

"You talked to the detective?"

All at once I understood. This was what Jingles had overheard Pamela and Nick talking about. It was the detective who'd been sent for, not a lawyer.

Pamela's brow furrowed. "What did he ask you?"

"He wanted to know if I had an alibi for the time of Giblet's death."

"Did he ask you anything about Nick?"

I hesitated. Bringing up the subject of Chris's death was difficult—especially in front of Pamela. "There's a lot of gossip in town."

"Of course there is. Everyone loves to chitter-chatter about the castle. But surely the police aren't listening to such nonsense."

"From what I could glean, they don't have any real leads."

"Then they're not looking hard enough." Pamela was pacing, a sure sign that there was at least some disturbance happening underneath that cool exterior. "Although I'm still not convinced Giblet Hollyberry *was* murdered. It might all be a lot of hysteria over nothing. Who knows how that spider got here? It might have hitched a ride on someone's suitcase, unbeknownst to that person."

But then how had it made its way to Giblet's cottage? I felt much more inclined to believe the spider had something to do with the package delivered to Lucia at the castle. I needed to find out more about that.

And what of Charlie? How to explain his malicious melting, unless he'd been a witness to what had happened at Giblet's cottage that morning?

"I'm sure it will all blow over," Pamela continued, "especially if we stay out of it, remain cheerful, and put on a united front. You shouldn't be running around talking to detectives. Why were you in town to begin with?"

"I had something to check on." My interrogating postal employees wouldn't go with her directive to stay out of it. "Is Nick here?"

Pamela gaped at me as if I'd lost my wits. "Santa appears at the beginning but doesn't ever sit through the entire Kinder Caroling. That's why *you* were supposed to be here."

Every castle event seemed planned out as precisely as Kabuki theater. I vowed to try harder the next time.

The more I thought about the police investigation, the more worried I became. Presenting a united front in the hopes that the matter of Giblet's death would blow over didn't seem much of a strategy to me. I wanted to talk all this over with Nick, so I headed for his study.

I knocked at the door and waited for his "Come in" before entering.

"April." He smiled but barely looked up from whatever it was he was studying on the desk blotter before him. "Is everything okay?"

"Fine." I decided against telling him about the concert's slipping my mind. "The kids were adorable, but that's not what I want to talk to you about."

One of his brows crooked, but he was jotting down something and within seconds seemed to forget I'd spoken.

"I talked to Detective Jake Frost this morning," I announced.

"Mm?"

"They certainly got him here fast." When he didn't respond, I repeated, "I said, they certainly got him here fast."

He looked up, frowning. "Who?"

"The detective. Jake Frost."

"Is he in Christmastown already?"

My mouth crunched into a wry smile. "You know, I'm getting the oddest feeling that you're not listening."

"I'm sorry—my mind is consumed by Pudgy Puppers this morning."

"What?"

"Pudgy Puppers. Every other kid in North America wants one, and the supply is woefully low. The shortfall wasn't really something we could have predicted six months ago."

Six months ago this place had been plunged into the crisis of Chris's death. Of course they hadn't been thinking of Pudgy Puppers. Still, it was hard for me to believe that Nick was concerned with stuffed animals when his future was at stake. "The detective was asking about you."

"Not surprising. That's his job."

"It's his job to find someone to pin this murder on, and he's looking straight at you, Nick. Aren't you worried?"

"I'm worried about Christmas."

"But—"

"I'd be more worried about the investigation if I weren't innocent."

It was all I could do not to roll my eyes. "Innocent people have been accused, tried, and convicted."

He studied me. "Sometimes it seems you don't have faith in me."

"Of course I do. I told him you're innocent, but . . ." *Where were you the night Giblet died?*

"But what?" he asked.

Questioning my own husband the way Jake Frost had questioned me wouldn't be a very good way to show my belief in his innocence. "But sometimes it seems like I'm the only one in the family taking the murder inquiry seriously."

"It's the constable's business, and the detective's, not the castle's."

"But we in the castle are the prime suspects. No, actually, that's not true. *You* are the prime suspect."

That caught his attention. "The detective said that?"

"Not in so many words, but from what I gathered, you probably are. And there's so much gossip flying around—"

He let out a sigh. "Gossip, that's all it is. Everyone around here loves to gossip, but there's no time for that now. It's December."

"I just think you should pay attention. There was a package delivered to the castle not long ago. According to the clerk at SPEX, it was addressed to Lucia and contained live animals."

"So?"

"A spider is a live animal," I pointed out.

He tapped his pencil. "So is a hamster, or a cat, or a reindeer. Lucia has always been an animal freak. There's no telling what was in that box."

"Shouldn't you at least ask her?" I said.

"If the constable or detective thinks it's important, he'll ask."

*Not if they never find out about it.* I ducked my head. "I can't believe you're so incurious."

He took off his reading glasses. "This is my first December at the helm, and I really don't need distractions right now. Especially seeing you frantic over a bunch of rumors."

"It's not just—"

He didn't wait for me to finish. "In January I'll gossip with you all you want. We'll talk about Giblet twenty-four/seven after the new year. But for now, tens of millions of children are counting on me to stay focused on the task at hand: Christmas."

He put his glasses back on and turned back to his notes.

I stood up. "Fine. But by January, you might be in the hoosegow. Granted, it's not exactly Sing Sing. More like a B and B. But I'll still be sorry to see my husband living there as a jailbird."

He shook his head. "You're panicking over nothing."

Choking in frustration, I left the room, almost smacking into Jingles on my way out. The keyhole was practically embossed in his cheek.

"Something wrong?" he asked.

I'd just been warned against gossiping, but it was such a relief to run into someone who seemed as concerned about the goings-on as I. True, up until now Jingles tended to view me more as an interloper than a real Mrs. Claus. But I needed to confide in *someone.*

"They've brought in an outside detective, and I think they're focusing the investigation on Nick. No one here seems to think this is an emergency."

"They suspect Santa of murder?" His eyes bugged. "We have to do something!"

Dear Jingles. It didn't take *him* long to ramp up to a Battle Stations level of panic. I wanted to hug him in gratitude. "I've launched my own investigation. I could probably use some help."

Jingles straightened to military attention. "Where do we begin?"

I wondered for a moment how much Jingles *could* help. Then again, Mr. Ear-to-the-Keyhole might prove himself invaluable.

"A package containing live animals was delivered to the castle recently. It was addressed to Lucia, but a male took the delivery. Was that you?"

He drew back. "Not that I recall." Beneath his cap brim, his forehead scrunched in thought. "I wonder what she's brought into the castle now. Let's pray it's not another ferret. The last weaselly creature she adopted shredded two sofas."

"I'm more worried about spiders than weasels."

"You think . . . ?" He sucked in a breath. "Not Lucia, surely."

"Then the person who intercepted the package, maybe."

"That could have been anyone." He frowned again. "Oh, dear. I never imagined I couldn't trust my own castle staff."

"We shouldn't jump to conclusions," I said, channeling Nick.

"All the same, I'll ask. Anything else?"

"We need to find out if Giblet had any particular enemies, so if you know anybody in Tinkertown . . ." I doubted he would. Jingles didn't seem to hobnob much with the hoi polloi outside the castle. A fine pair of detectives we would make: a stranger in town and a persnickety snob.

But Jingles surprised me. "Oh, yes I do. A very important someone. I'm a not-too-distant cousin of Punch, the elf who beat Giblet in the ice-sculpting contest."

# Chapter 8

Jingles arranged for me to meet Punch at the Tinkertown Tavern, but he wasn't able to accompany me there. When she heard where I was headed, Juniper had insisted on tagging along. "You don't want to go to the tavern by yourself," she warned.

"Rough?" I asked.

"People vape there," she'd said with an anxious quaver in her voice.

The Tinkertown Tavern was a dive bar in the same way Applebee's could be considered a greasy spoon. The low-ceilinged room had bare board walls and lighting partially supplied by candles in mason jars on all the tables. The only holiday decorations were old bulb lights strung around the doorframe, and corner speakers were playing a Glenn Campbell Christmas album. The patrons were mostly factory elves in their off-hours, but they weren't exactly intimidating. In fact, the barkeep was a jolly bald elf with a substantial paunch beneath his snowy apron. His relentlessly cheery manner made me suspect that he took regular nips of his special house grog.

As I sipped at the grog I'd felt obliged to order, I could understand the temptation. The syrupy concoction was made with rum and warmed to just the right temperature to defrost your bones after coming in from the cold. I could have slurped down the entire mug in a few swallows, but I was mindful that this was my second outing as an investigator. I needed to stay on my toes.

At Juniper's suggestion, I was wearing one of her elf caps, slightly tight on me, and a traditional embroidered elf tunic. The outfit made me feel slightly ridiculous, but even though I had to scrunch up to fit in the booth that was just slightly too small for me, I did seem to blend in better with the clientele.

A few elves across the bar playing darts looked over at me, gazes assessing. I looked away. "Don't stare," I told Juniper under my breath, "but there are a bunch of guys over there looking at us."

She angled a glance at them and then looked back at me. "You don't know them?"

I shook my head.

They were coming over. As a group. Their dead serious, purposeful demeanors as they approached made me wonder if they were Hollyberrys coming over to tell me I was married to a killer Santa . . . and not in an admiring way.

The four of them stopped right by the table. They didn't seem thuggish, exactly, but why were they staring at me so intently?

"Hey, guys," Juniper chirped.

One, the shortest, cleared his throat. And then he began to sing "Good King Wenceslas." The others joined him in a tight four-part harmony. Their singing battled with Glenn Campbell singing "Pretty Paper" until the barkeep turned the sound down. The rest of the bar went silent, watching as I sat trapped with a smile frozen on my face.

So much for feeling as if I blended in.

The impromptu barbershop quartet serenade continued for another three verses—who knew the song had so many?—

before Juniper nudged me and nodded to someone coming in the door.

Even for an elf, Punch the sculptor was short, but he walked with a swagger of someone certain of his worth. At Juniper's wave he nodded and headed over to us, frowning at the quartet. He didn't wait for them to finish.

"What is this? Amateur night?"

The singers broke off, and I awkwardly tried to thank them, and they even more awkwardly tried to hint that their group would be perfect to perform at the Peppermint Pond Skate-a-Palooza. I jotted down their names on a coaster advertising Winkie's Hard Sauce Ale.

"Go peddle it somewhere else," Punch growled at them. He slammed into the bench seat opposite Juniper and me. He had a bulbous nose, small eyes, and rough hands. Ice-chiseling hands.

The quartet retreated to their corner.

"You the lady that wanted to talk to me?"

I nodded. "I know your cousin, Jingles."

His lips turned down. "Jingles. He always thought he was better than everybody else because his ma married a man from up by the castle."

I didn't know what to say to that. Jingles hadn't mentioned animosity between them—maybe he didn't realize there was any. Or perhaps he did know and that's why he hadn't come with me.

"Would you like something to drink?" I asked.

"You buying?"

Juniper hopped up. "I'll get it. What would you like?"

"Grog."

What else?

"Make it a double," he said.

Juniper hurried away. I faced my interviewee. Now that

I had him here, I didn't know quite how to start. Obviously bringing up the cousin connection hadn't helped. I fell back on etiquette.

"Thank you for coming to talk."

He snorted. "You're not the first who's wanted to speak to me, but this time I figured I'd at least get a tankard out of it."

"You've spoken to the detective?" I guessed.

"Sure." He sat up straighter, proud of being a person of interest. "I won the prize over Giblet, and everybody saw how upset he was."

"Did you and Giblet have words after the prizes were awarded?"

"Sure. He came up to say congratulations."

"And?"

Punch looked at me with a combination of amusement and pity. "See, it's like what I told that spooky detective. Giblet and I were . . . well, I wouldn't say friends, exactly. We were two artists, and we admired each other's work."

Juniper hurried back and set down the oversized metal tankard in front of him. He nodded at us both and took a healthy swallow. *He* didn't seem too worried about keeping his wits about him, which was fine with me.

"Sure, Giblet was angry about the contest result," the elf continued, "but he wasn't mad at *me*. All of his rage was for your husband, the new Santa."

"Why?"

Punch lifted his rounded shoulders. "He seemed to have a real fixation on Nick Claus—seemed to want to needle him for some reason. Back when he told me what he was planning for the contest, I thought it was a bad idea. *The North Pole's King.* A depiction of the late Santa? Right off, I told him that idea couldn't win."

"Why not?" I asked.

"Think about it. Even if he liked what Giblet did, your husband's a quiet, modest guy, and he wouldn't want to appear biased by the subject matter. On the other hand, if what some people are saying is true—"

"Of course it isn't."

"I said *if.* In that case, he wouldn't want to be reminded of how much more everybody loved his brother than him."

I tried to put my own bias aside and consider the matter logically. "Not necessarily. If Nick really had a guilty conscience, he would want to cover his resentment—and what better way than by awarding Giblet first prize?"

Punch shrugged. "Well, I'm a sculptor, not a psychologist."

Maybe so, but I wasn't ready to stop picking his brain. "If you told Giblet his sculpture would lose, why did he persist?"

He took a deep drink. "Cussedness. That was Giblet all over. He never did believe in doing things the easy way. And when he lost, he planned to go down spitting in the eye of the powers that be."

"That's a terrible attitude," Juniper said. Cussedness and spitting in someone's eye were foreign concepts to her.

But I'd noticed something else in what Punch had said. "You said *'when he lost,'* as if it were a foregone conclusion."

"Of course it was," he said. "He was never going to win, no matter what he made."

"Why not? Because of the reasons you gave before?" I asked.

"No, because I'm the better sculptor." He drained his tankard, smacked his lips, and smiled with egotistical gusto. "You see, Mrs. C., you're skidding down the wrong sled path. At least if you're looking for people who had problems with Giblet. He and I were friendly rivals. If you want to find someone who *really* didn't like him, you should talk to Starla Winters at the Wrapping Works."

I glanced at Juniper, who indicated with a subtle nod that the name was familiar.

"Starla pitched a fit when Giblet was promoted over her as the Wrapping Works Director of Operations—said it was the worst miscarriage of justice in the whole history of Santaland. There were times when it was so bad between those two that Giblet told me he thought he might quit the works entirely and move out to the Farthest Frozen Reaches and become a full-time freelance sculptor."

I frowned, wondering whether Jake Frost had already gone down this investigative trail.

"You go ask Starla Winters what *she* was doing the night Giblet died," Punch said. "I'll bet you get closer to the truth of the matter than you have talking to me."

He left us to go visit with a friend at another table.

"Did you believe what he told us?" I asked Juniper.

"About Starla?"

"About everything."

Juniper considered the question for a moment before a strange transformation came over her. Disbelief and barely concealed pleasure flushed across her face, making me pivot to follow her gaze. Hunched at the bar, Martin smiled and waved. In the next moment, he muttered something to his elf companions and came over to our table with his drink.

"I thought I was the only Claus who ever hung out in Tinkertown," he said, sliding easily onto the bench seat Punch had just vacated. He nodded at my cap with puzzled amusement. "You *are* a Claus, aren't you? Looks like you've gone native."

"Juniper loaned me some things for our night on the town."

He smiled at Juniper, who'd been struck dumb. "That was a good idea," he said. "Get April out of the Claus comfort zone."

She didn't respond except to turn the color of a boiled lobster.

Martin leaned in and peered into her mug. "Your drink's almost gone. Can I get you another?"

She blinked. "For me?"

As an afterthought, Martin looked at mine, too. "I'll get you both refreshers."

He dislodged himself from the too-small booth and hurried to the bar. For a large man, he moved very easily.

The moment he was out of earshot, Juniper sank against the bench. "I'm acting like an idiot, aren't I? Do you think he thinks I'm an idiot?"

"Why would he? You've barely said anything."

"I know! I'm tongue-tied. All sorts of things are going through my head, but then I look into those eyes of his and I just go numb. And then I want to kick myself because it's all so stupid—he's Martin Claus and what am I?"

I laughed. "You're Christmastown's favorite librarian, and a damn fine euphonium player. And you're pretty foxy, too, in your going-out finery." Her tunic was purple and green, with sequins making her look sparklier than usual.

"Foxy? Me?" She snorted. "Right."

"Smudge thinks so," I said.

She drew back, startled, and not in a good way. "That's all over. He hates me."

"That's right. I keep forgetting, because he watches the back of your head during rehearsal more than he watches the conductor."

"Staring daggers."

"No, daggers is the way he looks at *me*," I said. "The way he looks at you is more smoldery."

Juniper absorbed this, then shook her head, tossing a glance at Martin, who was taking both our drinks from the barkeep. "Smudge isn't my type. He's not at all dapper, you know what I mean?"

Only in Santaland, where potbellies and double chins were in, would Martin be considered anyone's dream lover.

He came back, smiling as he sat down as if he knew he'd been the topic of conversation. "Get your stories straight?"

In unison, Juniper and I piped up guiltily, "What?"

"You were deep in conversation about something, and I can only imagine it was how to explain your meeting the illustrious ice sculpture artist."

How much could I tell Martin about what I was doing? I trusted him—somewhat. He was my ally, I knew that, but he loved to gab with people, and I didn't want everyone at the castle to know I was running a shadow investigation. Also, I didn't trust him not to tease me about my sleuthing at inconvenient moments, when others would overhear.

"Are you thinking of getting a statue of your own winter hero done?" he asked. "Maybe Nick would like that for a Christmas present."

"He wouldn't like anything less, and you know it."

"So you were talking to Punch about . . . ?"

"Giblet," I admitted.

Understanding dawned. "I see. You're trying to figure out who Giblet's enemies were and outwit the detectives. Not that it would be difficult to outwit Constable Crinkles, but that other fellow . . ."

"You heard about Jake Frost?" I asked.

Martin laughed. "You think that guy can blow into town without everybody noticing? He's been famous since solving the toy heist ten years ago." I frowned and he explained, "There was a greedy elf stealing toys from Santa's Workshop and selling them on eBay from his cottage basement. Took calling in Jake Frost to find the toy embezzler."

"I hadn't heard of that," I said.

Martin smiled at Juniper. "We're not supposed to talk about crime in Christmastown. It's like the old Soviet Union—crime is anti-Christmas, so we pretend it doesn't exist. Until an elf is killed."

"And poor Charlie," Juniper said.

Martin nodded at her reminder. "Now that a killing spree is underway, we all have to own up that maybe Santaland isn't the idyllic place we try to tell ourselves it is."

"It's still pretty darn nice," Juniper said loyally.

"And probably one of the safest places on earth," Martin agreed. "Except for during the past two days. We can't kid ourselves that none of this happened. Who's to say we might not all still be in danger?"

"Why?" I asked.

"Because the killer wasn't caught. Maybe there's a pattern to the violence that we haven't made out yet. Any one of us might be next."

Juniper shivered. "That's a terrible thought."

"Just be careful," Martin said. "Don't go out alone if you can help it. And if you don't mind my saying, maybe you shouldn't be visiting odd places like the Tinkertown Tavern."

"You're here," I said.

"I work in Tinkertown—the Candy Cane Factory isn't far from here. I come here occasionally and rub elbows. I like getting away from the castle sometimes."

"So taverns are fine for you, but not for me?"

"It's not the tavern that's dangerous; it's the traveling back and forth. In fact, I should escort you two back."

Juniper looked as if she might expire. "There's no reason for you to go to any trouble for me," she said, ignoring my pointed glare. "I don't live far—and no one would want to kill me."

"Sure about that?" he asked. "No broken hearts in your wake, or angry second-chair euphoniumists?"

She laughed. "Not that I know of."

"We'll drive you home, just in case. You're on our way back."

"How do you know where I live?" she asked.

He leaned in and confessed, "You're in the directory and I'm the nosiest person in Christmastown—at least about people I like."

And with that, my friend's soul left her body. R.I.P., Juniper.

On the way home, Juniper sat between me and Martin on his sleigh's bench seat. His was a more modest model than the one Nick traveled around in—it was less ornate and less comfortable—but he clearly enjoyed driving it. He kept the reindeer at a brisk gait, and he and Juniper gossiped about band members. I knew most of the people they were talking about, but my mind was already wandering to my next interviewee. I wondered how best to approach Starla Winters—at home or at work? I liked the fact that she hadn't spoken to the constable or the detective yet. Maybe I could catch her off guard. Not that I knew she had anything to be *on* guard about.

The sleigh slowed and then stopped in front of a modest Tudor-style house. I was going to hop off to let Juniper out, but Martin beat me to it, handing her down and bidding her a good night in a way I had no doubt made her go weak in the knees. I'd be hearing about this tomorrow, and probably for weeks to come.

"I'll call you in the morning," I said. "About that other thing."

For a moment her expression fogged; she'd forgotten all about the investigation and Starla Winters. Finally, it dawned on her. "Oh, right. Good night!"

When we got underway again, Martin said, "She's talkative once you get her going."

"She's wonderful—the best friend I've made here."

He glanced at me, his eyes merry in the moonlight. "Is that a warning to me to stay away from her?"

"Not at all," I said, hunching into my coat. "Though she *is* probably too good for you."

His laughter echoed along with the jingling reindeer harness as we crossed through the quiet evening streets of Christmastown. "You're probably right. Well . . . we'll see what develops."

"You're not going to lead her on, I hope."

"Of course not. And don't worry—I won't take her away from your investigation."

"I'm not investigating anything."

He leveled a doubtful stare on me.

"Okay, I'm investigating, but it's not what you would call official. And Nick doesn't approve, so not a word of this to him."

"Newlyweds already keeping secrets?"

"Cut the arch tone or I won't tell you anything." I crossed my arms. My teeth chattered. Would I ever get used to bone-deep cold?

"Okay, okay," he said. "Any suspects yet?"

"Not really. I just wanted to see what Punch had to say about Giblet."

"Let me guess. . . . He told you he didn't kill Giblet."

I nodded. "They were friendly."

"And you believe him?"

"I'm not sure. He talked a good game."

"Most elves do after a few tankards." He shook his head. "It's freezing out here. Reach back and get the blanket behind the seat."

I did, and spread it across both our laps.

"Do you know I'm probably the only Claus who hates winter?" he asked. "I can't wait to retire to Florida."

I laughed. "Heretic."

His smile disappeared. "Given the crime wave up here, maybe I should retire sooner rather than later."

I wished I could whisk Nick away. Maybe not to Florida, but at least to Oregon. We could decorate the Coast Inn and avoid Damaris's fine. And not worry about who was committing all these murders up here . . . and who might be the next victim.

# Chapter 9

The next morning, after checking with Jingles that my presence wasn't necessary until late afternoon, I considered the best way to get myself over to the Wrapping Works. It was a long trip. I'd have to take the funicular down through Kringle Heights, then catch the Christmastown trolley out to Tinkertown, and I wasn't sure of the way once I got off there. Asking the stables for sleigh transport might alert Nick or Pamela about what I was up to, and for now I wanted to keep my sleuthing stealthy.

I broached this dilemma with my castle confederate. "Is there a way to get there on the sly?"

Jingles opened his mouth to answer, then slammed it shut again.

"What?" I asked.

His head shook. "No—never mind."

Quasar's uneven gait clopped down the hallway behind us.

Jingles' gaze caught sight of the reindeer over my shoulder, and he seized upon a new idea. "Why not take Quasar?"

I stared at him dumbly. I'd rarely seen Quasar leave the castle without Lucia.

"Lucia is judging the yearling Reindeer Hop this morning and Quasar doesn't care much for competitions, so he's at loose ends." He called out, "Aren't you, Quasar?"

Quasar, who was grazing on a garland, was startled to hear his name. "W-what?"

"Can he do that?" I whispered to Jingles. I'd seen Quasar riding *in* sleighs but never pulling one.

Jingles put his hands on his hips. "He's a reindeer. Their whole raison d'être is eating and dragging things around."

It was worth a shot. "But what will Lucia say?"

"If you leave now, you'll be back long before she is—those games go on and on. And you don't have to worry about Quasar spilling the beans. He's not much of a talker."

No argument there.

I turned and approached Quasar, whose nose blinked unevenly as I drew nearer. "I need to go to the Wrapping Works," I said. "Could you take me? On a sled, I mean?"

His nose sustained a glow for a few seconds and then went out like a cigar ash. "M-me?"

"Why not?"

He seemed paralyzed.

"I'm in a bit of a bind. Jingles thought you could help me."

He lifted his head. "You m-mean it's an emergency?"

Not life-and-death, but . . . "I need to get there this morning."

Something in my words brought out his inner Rudolph. His eyes brightened and momentarily his nose blazed to a blinding red. "I will t-take you! Meet me at the front in ten minutes."

"Can we make it the side? I need to get there without too many others knowing."

He nodded, sending a little flurry of antler velvet sloughing to the floor. "Of course." He clopped away noisily, moving faster than I'd ever seen him go, until a corner of an antler hit the doorframe, sending him stumbling back. He twisted back to check if I'd seen.

"Are you all right?" I asked.

"I will get you to the Wrapping Works! N-never fear!" He charged successfully through the door and out of sight.

A quarter hour later, he came loping crookedly at the head of a small uncovered sled that looked like something a dog musher might drive with the help of a few huskies. But Quasar was in harness and hooked up to the contraption, raring to go.

"It's s-steadier than it looks," he said.

I climbed on, worried more about his steadiness than the sled's.

"Hang on!" he called out.

I'd never driven a sled, but apparently that didn't matter, because Quasar knew where he was going and he was ready to get there with all due speed. All I did was perch myself at the barrier at the front of the sled, like standing in front of a podium with reins in my hands. Though this sled was not technically flying, as the gangling Quasar loped unevenly over bumps and icy potholes it occasionally felt as if we were leaving the earth. The sled had no shocks, so every yard of packed snow we traveled over was tooth rattling.

Once, after an Arctic hare dashed in front of our path, a startled Quasar nearly dived into a ditch, but he righted himself, and the sled managed not to pitch over, and we were soon on our way again.

By the time we pulled up to the Wrapping Works, a warehouse-sized half-timbered building, my legs were noodles from the strain of holding my body rigid and steady. I dropped the reins and wobbled off, looking up at the lit Santaland logo at the top of the peaked roof. It reminded me of the little chocolate box Nick had once given me, which had so intrigued me.

"Thanks for getting me here," I told Quasar. "I won't be long. I just need to speak to someone."

Was it my imagination, or was Quasar standing a little straighter? "I'll be waiting right here, ma'am."

Inside, the Wrapping Works was a noisy hive of activity. Though almost all the workers were elves, the rooms were bigger than the ones in the castle, especially the main room in which a series of conveyor belts carried toys to various stations along the building's three floors. The motor driving the belts, though unseen, whirred heavily as background sound that echoed throughout the cavernous room.

A foreman elf carrying a clipboard and sporting a pencil behind one ear found me talking to a security guard by the front door. "Lady says she needs to talk to Winters," the guard said.

"Winters can't talk now—she's busy." The security guard gave him a nudge, and the foreman's eyes widened as he noted who I was. "Oh! Mrs. Claus. How can we help you?"

"I need to speak to Starla Winters."

"Of course! Right this way." He waved me forward, tapping his clipboard. "We're very busy here. And Starla was just promoted to leader of her section, so you can imagine . . ."

"I'll only need to speak to her for a few minutes."

We walked past an open workroom. A group of elves stopped what they were doing to stare at me. Far from smiling, they looked almost belligerent.

"Well?" the foreman asked them. "What are you gaping at?"

They said nothing, but the hostility in their eyes spoke for them. *The wife of an elf killer.* It was a reminder that all was not well in Santaland.

"Get back to work," the foreman ordered.

"It's okay," I said under my breath, not wanting to fan the flames of resentment.

Happily, we started walking again.

I had to practically skip to keep up with him. "You said Starla was recently promoted." Didn't take her long to get Giblet's job, apparently. "Isn't that an odd step to promote someone in December, when things are so busy?"

"It's not as if we had much choice, shorthanded as we are. And you might say, 'Well, Giblet Hollyberry was just middle management,' but those are the employees who really keep the belts moving around here."

"You must have felt his loss keenly."

"Oh sure. We don't have an elf to spare. Not in December. And Giblet, for all his faults, was a real artist. He knew what looked good and what didn't."

"Did everybody like Giblet?" I asked.

He nearly stopped in his tracks. "Everybody? Try almost *nobody.* But that doesn't matter here. At the Wrapping Works, we don't expect elves to be jolly all the time. No ma'am. Wrapping is serious business and an art, and we like to foster an atmosphere of what we call industrious expressiveness. If emotions and egos come into play, it's bad for morale. Wrapping is the highest calling in Christmastown, and we need strong workers in all places."

"I take it you didn't like Giblet, either."

"He was okay as long as you didn't cross him. And as long as there were anise-flavored icebox cookies available to him. He loved his breaks."

At the top of the stairs he led me into a long room with perhaps a seven-foot ceiling, where elves worked at long metal worktables lined with roll after roll of wrapping paper of all designs. A conveyor belt brought a series of boxes with various stuffed animals inside, some with heads poking up as they watched themselves being carried toward the elves who would tape up their boxes and wrap them.

The foreman noted my interest. "Boxing's done on the

first floor, wrapping second, and then ribbons and labels are added on third. Then the packages are moved back down by freight elevator and taken over to be labeled and sorted according to which part of the world the recipient lives in. Don't want to waste your husband's time making him backtrack on the big night."

The wrapping elves worked at lightning speed.

"They must get a lot of paper cuts."

From behind me, a deep voice rasped, "Just a hazard of the trade."

The foreman peered around me. "Oh, Ms. Winters. Just who we were looking for. Mrs. Claus needs to speak to you."

Stocky, with her black hair in a buzz cut as if she were a US Marine, Starla Winters was dressed in bizarre green overalls—drab olive green, not the perky kelly green that you saw most often in Christmastown—tucked into her ankle booties. Her eyes were assessing me, and not in a friendly manner. I'd never known a person a full foot shorter than I was could appear so intimidating.

"What do you want?" she asked.

"Is there somewhere we could speak in private?"

The foreman nodded. "Take the break room. No one else is using it this time of day."

Starla led me to the room he'd indicated and shut the door behind us. To be honest, I felt a little hesitant now that I was shut up in a room with her. If there was ever a match for Giblet Hollyberry, it had to be this drill sergeant of an elf in front of me. Her mouth flattened into an impatient line.

"What is it you want?" she asked. "Not to be disrespectful, but it *is* the week before Christmas. Maybe that doesn't mean much to you Southerners."

*Southerners* in arctic parlance meant anyone south of the Yukon. "We have our own Christmas rush down there, too."

She sniffed derisively. "We hear all the stories of stampedes of people at big-box stores. And then we also hear stories of people who don't even start thinking about Christmas until Christmas Eve. Procrastination's a luxury elves don't have."

I'd always been a bit of a holiday shopping procrastinator myself, a trait I'd never felt shame about until I fell under Starla's withering gaze. "I was hoping you could tell me a little bit about Giblet Hollyberry," I said.

Her jaw worked, and she crossed her arms. "I can tell you he's dead."

"Yes." I shifted, looking around. The break room had a long table, and across the back wall there was a counter that extended the whole length of the room, which was broken up by a two-burner stove. There was some kind of drink dispenser on the counter, alongside a long platter of iced Christmas cookies.

The kind Giblet was so fond of, I imagined.

We sat at the table, in what I realized at the last minute were elf-sized chairs. My knees poked up past the tabletop. Starla noted my position with a smirk.

"Okay, what do you want to know about Giblet?" she asked.

"I heard there was some controversy about his getting hired over you."

She shrugged. "No controversy. He got the job and I didn't. It was pure sexism, of course."

"Sexism?" I repeated.

"Sure—don't you have that where you come from? These male elves all stick together, especially the ones with artistic pretensions."

"Giblet *was* very talented."

Evidently, that was the wrong thing to say. She practically vibrated with irritation. "As a sculptor, maybe. As a wrapper, he didn't know squat. Could he cut a straight edge? Did he know how to fold a curved end? Did he know the difference between grosgrain and curling ribbon? Heck no. Let me tell you, a package gift-wrapped by Giblet Hollyberry was a package you wouldn't wish on your worst enemy. The tape would show from a mile away."

I hadn't realized wrapping was something a person could get so het up about, but every skill had its obsessives.

"Did you work your way up at the Wrapping Works?"

"I sure did—my first job was gathering scraps off the ribbon-cutting floor when I was knee high to a gumdrop. I've been in practically every job here, and I'm one of the better wrappers in Santaland, if I do say so myself."

"And Giblet?"

She sniffed. "He came on a few years ago, after losing his job at the Candy Cane Factory."

"That must have been irritating, having him jump ahead of you."

"Try *infuriating*—but that's the way things go around here. It's not how hard you work; it's who you know. I shouldn't say that to a Claus, of course. . . ."

"Are Clauses all-powerful?"

"Boy, you really did just poke your head through the spring ice, didn't you?"

"I'm new here, if that's what you mean."

"Well, you'll learn. In this country, Clauses can get away with murder."

"The murder of Giblet Hollyberry, for instance?"

She seemed taken aback that I would extrapolate something so concrete from her metaphor. "I didn't accuse anybody of murdering Giblet."

"No, but having a Claus under suspicion doesn't hurt you any, does it?" I leaned forward. "It took me exactly one day of asking around about Giblet's enemies before your name came up. Everyone knows you hated that Giblet was promoted over you. You don't even try to hide your animosity toward him and he's only been dead a few days."

"Why should I try to hide anything? *I* didn't kill him. Giblet was an egotistical, cranky jerk, and he shouldn't have come anywhere near a management job in this place, but the abomination of his promotion took place almost two years ago. If I'd wanted to murder him, I'd have done it long before now."

"Not if you were smart."

"Excuse me?" she asked.

"If you were smart, you would have bided your time, waiting for a moment when everyone had forgotten that you were stung over the promotion kerfuffle. Just hang back until a busy moment in the year, or after Giblet had just made a public show of temper toward someone else. Or after all three of those conditions had been met. Then even the police wouldn't think to talk to you."

Her eyes narrowed.

"The police *haven't* talked to you, have they?"

"Why would they? I didn't do anything."

"And you have an alibi for the night Giblet died."

"Of course." She frowned. "That is, not exactly. I was home all that night, with Cletus."

"And Cletus can vouch for your whereabouts?"

The question brought a chuckle. "Cletus is my dog. A wolf pup, actually. He's five years old now, but he'll always be a pup to me."

"He lives in the house with you?"

"Where else?"

"Don't you worry he'll hurt someone?"

"He'd only do that to protect me." She tilted her head. "Tell me—did that dimwit constable find any wolf tracks around Giblet's cottage?"

"Not that I heard of."

"There you go, then. I never walk anywhere at night without Cletus. He'd take on a snow monster to protect me."

So the wolf was her alibi, in a way.

I stood. "Thank you for talking to me."

She got to her feet, too. "Sorry I couldn't have broken down and confessed for you. I suppose that's what you were looking for, wasn't it?"

"I just wanted to find out more about Giblet," I lied.

"I'd give a lot to know who sent you here," she said in a low rasp. "But I don't suppose you'd tell anyway."

I remained silent.

"That's what I figured. I'm guessing it was someone like Tinkles."

"Who's that?" I asked, bird-dog alert.

Starla came close to laughing. "If you're going to play at the detective game, you really ought to practice your poker face." She shook her head. "I guess Tinkles is off the hook. He's the manager that works under me now. I thought maybe he was thinking he could score a bloodless Wrapping Works coup by having me pegged for Giblet's murder. But maybe I've got more enemies than I thought I did."

"It wasn't an enemy," I assured her. "Though I had no idea the Wrapping Works was such a hotbed of competitiveness."

"It's an elf-eat-elf world, Mrs. Claus."

I said good-bye and made my way down to the main doors, wondering what my next step would be. As I was walking out of the factory, my calculations evaporated when I saw a small herd of reindeer surrounding the place where I'd left the sled. Not just surrounding it—menacing it. Hooves were kicking up snow, and I couldn't see either Quasar or the sled.

Without thinking, I let out a banshee yell and charged down the steps two at a time.

# Chapter 10

"Hey! Get away from him!"

Reindeer heads swung toward me. I flapped my arms, although I'm not sure what good that would have done if these delinquent reindeer had decided to stand their ground or stampede toward me. Instead, like the cowards they were, they caught one look at who was running at them and, with a few unintelligible grunts and snuffles took off, sprinting and fly-hopping away before I could identify any of them.

Not that I *could* have identified them, even if I'd had a longer look. But they didn't know that. All of them had to be older juveniles, since they were skipping the yearling Reindeer Hop.

I still couldn't see the sled, but Quasar's head protruded out of the newly formed snowbank they'd kicked over him. I hurried over. "Are you okay?"

"Y-yes, ma'am." His nose fizzled. One of his antlers lay in the snow while the other was still in place, giving him a strange, lopsided look.

"Who were those guys?"

"Reindeer," he said.

"I *know* that, but what was wrong with them? Why would they do this to one of their own?"

I could have bitten my tongue. *Because they don't consider Quasar one of them.* Because he was a misfit.

Reindeer were jerks. #notallreindeer.

"I'm rather c-cold, ma'am," Quasar said, obviously hoping I would stop ranting and extract him from his predicament. I began digging with my gloved hands, but half a minute later I was back in the Wrapping Works asking the guard for a snow shovel. The foreman not only obliged me with a shovel but also sent several elves out to help me dig my reindeer and the sled out. At least these elves were a little friendlier than the group that had given me the evil eye. They even sang as they worked, and I heard my first "White Christmas" of the day. And it wasn't an impromptu audition.

Once freed, Quasar thanked everyone, although he seemed rather subdued and depressed. Who could blame him? It was like a fraternity hazing, from a fraternity that had been rejecting him all of his life.

I couldn't make him drag me all the way back after what he'd been through, so I tugged the sleigh and walked alongside him as he limped back to the castle. Keeping up a conversation was harder than keeping up with his crooked gait.

My thoughts returned to the marauding gang that had attacked him. "We should go to the constable and report those reindeer. What herd were they from?"

"A lot of different ones. There's n-no point filing a complaint. That's just the way they are."

"Animals," I muttered. "This is Santaland, not the Wild Kingdom. Not the jungle." Quasar tripped in a dip in the snow and stumbled toward me. I just managed to avoid getting my foot stomped by a large hoof. "Of course I know the Rudolph story, but you'd think *that* would at least have taught them not to bully one of their own."

"They don't really see it that way. To them I'm just a . . ."

He didn't say it, but I knew we were both thinking the dreaded *m* word.

I felt a little like a misfit myself. An April in a land of perpetual winter. More a budding Miss Marple than a Mrs. Claus.

"I'm at least going to tell Nick what happened to you. Lucia will be upset if we do nothing."

His big eyes widened, showing the whites. "Lucia can't hear about this. P-please don't tell her!"

"If she's your best friend, she'll want to see those reindeer punished."

"I-I'm not so sure she is my best friend now." His head hung lower. "She's not the same. She's secretive, and spends time without me, and sometimes when she comes back she smells."

Could she smell worse than a reindeer? "Smells how?"

His withers twitched. "Like danger."

"Maybe you're just imagining that."

He tossed his one-antlered head and continued in his Eeyorish voice, "Anyway, she's already brought enough trouble on herself for befriending me. I know the Claus family doesn't always like me around."

"That's not true," I lied.

He hung his head. "Pamela's never liked me since I ate most of the Christmas tree one year. But I woke up in the night and I was so hungry. Times like that I can't help nibbling."

One of the downsides of being a ruminant.

"Well, never mind that. I know you don't want to cause trouble, but something ought to be done. Otherwise those hooligans will start taunting more reindeer."

It took longer than I expected to get back. Quasar wanted to stop to dig for fungi, which apparently is a delicacy reindeer with sensitive noses can smell through feet of snowpack. Far be it from me to stand between a reindeer and his nutritional mold, especially when he's had a traumatic morning. I didn't rush him. It was afternoon by the time we made our way up the long, winding drive to the castle.

As we neared, a figure at the portico loomed larger. It was Lucia, hands on hips, not pleased. Hadn't Jingles said she'd be gone a long time? Of course he hadn't known how long the trip to the Wrapping Works would end up taking me.

She lunged off the front steps to meet us. "Where have you been? I've been worried sick!"

"I had to go to the Wrapping Works."

She rounded on me. "I wasn't worried about *you*. I meant Quasar."

"He went with me." I sniffed, but I couldn't smell anything on her but her usual leathery, reindeer-musky scent.

Her gaze took in Quasar's lopsided antler situation and then the sled. "You made Quasar drag you out all that way?"

"He wanted to go."

"Of course he *said* he wanted to—Quasar's the sweetest reindeer in Santaland. That doesn't mean you should exploit his kindness."

Exploit? That's not how it was, but on the way home Quasar had muttered a few times that he didn't want to let Lucia know what had gone down outside the Wrapping Works, and I didn't want to break that confidence. It was hard, though, with her flaring at me like an angry mama bear.

"Are you okay, Quasar?" She took in his sheepish expression. And that antler.

"Fine," he blurted. "Th-there was no trouble with other reindeer."

He was the world's worst liar. Lucia groaned. "Did they kick rocks at you again?"

"Just snow," he said. "It's not like they b-buried me alive. My head was free."

She rounded on me, apoplectic. "I'm going to give my friend here a thorough going-over, and if I find one thing wrong with him you will never be allowed within ten feet of another animal in this land again."

I was too exhausted to tangle with her. And, to be honest, in retrospect my actions had not been well thought out. Why hadn't I just taken the trolley, or at least asked if there was a stronger reindeer available?

I remembered Jingles suggesting Quasar, and a frisson of doubt traveled through me. I thought I could trust him. Had he done this on purpose?

No sooner did I enter the castle, tired and ragged, than Pamela swooped down on me as if she'd been lying in wait just behind the massive oak front door. Her jaw dropped. "Oh dear!"

I'd just hiked three miles in the snow with a lame reindeer. "Nothing that a long soak in a hot tub won't fix," I said.

"There's no time for a long soak now. The big sleigh's been ordered and will be here any minute. We'll be leaving for the tea in a quarter hour."

"The what?"

Her smile froze as if she were being forced to communicate with a half-wit. "The tea, the tea at Kringle Lodge. Don't you remember? You booked the elf cloggers yourself."

Cousin Amory's tea. This morning it had seemed a far-off event.

"Nick looked for you, but he had to leave early. You'll come with me in my sleigh."

I was disappointed—both at having missed Nick and at the prospect of a frigid drive up the mountain with Pamela—but I tried not to show it. "Great! I'll change and be right back down."

She wrapped a hand around my arm. "My dear, I realize this is all new to you, but you really must try harder to stay focused. It's December. In January you can space out all you like, but December needs your attention."

Her words reminded me of Nick's the day before. In January I could swap gossip with my husband, zone out, or hibernate till spring. The trouble was, the Clauses didn't know that their whole world could tumble down around them by then if Nick was fingered as the Santaland serial killer.

But try explaining that to a mother-in-law in full social panic.

I made my voice sound sober and soothing. "I will try," I vowed. "I'll be back down in a jiffy." I turned and took the stairs two at a time. My legs were exhausted from the march through the snow, but escaping Pamela's nattering put new life in my step.

The ride up the mountain to Kringle Lodge was blessedly short but just as frosty as expected. In front and behind us sleighs made their way up the mountain, which echoed with the cheery sounds of jangling harnesses and voices raised in wassailing songs. The temperature dropped as the sleigh climbed to the summit, and my mother-in-law's demeanor didn't warm things up any. I'd managed to do a fairly decent job freshening up and changing. My green crushed velvet with red piping wasn't my favorite—the materials might have made a wonderful sofa sometime in 1972, but as formal wear it left something to be desired. Still, it was newly made by the order of seamstresses, and it was pressed and clean. Pamela looked satisfied with the dress; with me, not so much, especially as I pinned up my hair in some semblance of an updo. Sleigh primping wasn't a done thing, I presumed. Together as ever in white gloves and an ice-blue wool suit with matching pillbox hat, she eyed my every movement as if I were flossing my teeth at a banquet table.

"I've finalized the plans for the croquembouche," she said. " 'A Tribute to Castle Kringle.' "

I blinked. "We're talking about a pastry, right?"

"Yes—a pastry in the shape of the castle. I've drawn up a blueprint. And on the morning we make it, we'll use an overhead projector to outline the plans on a giant Plexiglas board that's been dusted with powdered sugar. Then we'll mark the outlines of the blueprint in food coloring."

For a moment I thought she was pulling my leg, but her voice was dead serious. "Are you sure you want me to help you with this? It sounds . . . involved."

"It will be a nice bonding experience for us. One year I made it with Tiffany, and last year Therese and I created a croquembouche swan—and I have to say, it was my most successful ever."

The name Therese set my molars to grinding. Pamela had guessed the surest-fire way to keep me involved in her daffy project.

By the time the sleigh slowed in front of the lodge, we'd joined a procession of other arrivals. I looked around for Nick, but I didn't see him among the other parties. Liveried elves stepped out to help us down.

"I'm going to hurry ahead and make sure the cloggers have arrived and have everything they need," I told Pamela.

I hurried up the lodge's wide steps, which had been newly cleared of snow. The lodge was a long, two-story building fashioned from old-growth cedars a century ago. Lights had been strung all along the front, and a wreath half as big as the door itself hung at the entrance. Candles and torches were lit everywhere to add warmth and light to the path leading to the door. From the lodge's porch, I looked down the valley past the castle's roof and turrets, and farther to the lights of Christmastown, and then even farther, across the forest line to the Frozen Reaches. I paused a moment to take it all in—

though the sun was still fighting the good fight overhead, winter's early twilight was falling fast, casting a reddish glow over the whole snowy landscape.

A dark presence, like the twilight itself, appeared next to me. Jake Frost's gaze surveyed the scene I'd just been admiring. "Looks harmless from up here, doesn't it?" he asked. "Very serene."

"Christmastown, you mean?"

"I was thinking of the Reaches. You'd never guess there were snow monsters out there."

"I wouldn't guess from looking at Christmastown that there was a monster there, either. A murderer ranks worse than a snow monster in my book. One's a monster by nature, the other a monster by choice."

"Sometimes murderers are the way they are by nature, too."

"I never understood the impulse to sympathize with a killer," I said.

"Understanding and sympathizing are different animals."

I raked my gaze over Jake's dark hat, coat, and boots, which was what he'd been wearing the last time I'd seen him. He wasn't dressed for a party. "What are you doing here? Did Amory invite you?"

"I invited myself." He came close to smiling. "The law has its privileges."

One possible explanation for his presence here made my heart race. "You aren't here to make an arrest, are you?"

He shook his head. "Just observing."

I looked around at the gathering guests. To Jake Frost, we were probably all like bugs in a terrarium. Interesting beings to observe. Who would exhibit incriminating behavior?

"Are you here all alone?" he asked.

"No, I came with my mother-in-law."

"Where's your husband?"

Good question. Nick obviously hadn't been watching out for my arrival. "He had business to attend to. He left the castle before I did."

"Interesting."

Never had that one word seemed to carry so many ominous undertones.

"No, it's not," I piped up, lest he extrapolate something incriminating from our separate arrivals. "It's perfectly normal. Goodness, does everything strike you as suspicious?"

"I just think it's strange that a newly married man wouldn't want to escort his bride to a party."

His dark gaze held mine, and heat mounted in my cheeks.

"I need to check on the entertainers," I said. "These events always have an element of stress to them for the Clauses, you know."

"What's the entertainment?"

"Elf cloggers."

He winced.

He wasn't alone in his reaction. Elf cloggers were the morris dancers of the North Pole, it seemed. They got no respect. "They're very talented," I insisted.

"So are some kazoo players, but I don't go out of my way to hear them."

"I've never heard a talented kazoo virtuoso, and neither have you."

"All right, April. You caught me in a lie."

"Very suspicious."

He laughed. The sound of it, though dry, made me smile.

"There you are!" Lucia appeared at my side.

Come to tell me I could no longer even look at a reindeer, no doubt. I would have liked to ask her a few questions—like what was in the package addressed to her and delivered to the castle. But I couldn't forget Jake was there and would overhear everything.

I gestured to the detective. "Lucia, you know Detective Frost, don't you?"

She glanced at him and darted out her hand. "Jack Frost? I've heard of you."

"Jake, actually," he corrected with strained patience. "Jack was a distant relation."

Lucia didn't seem to care what his name was. She was focused on something else. "Maybe you can help, Detective. Santaland's juvenile delinquent reindeer problem is getting worse. You should catch them and take them with you back to the Reaches. Teach them a lesson."

"Reindeer are a little out of my line," Jake said.

"Even ones that attempt murder, like the pack of them did this morning?"

She had Frost's attention now. "Murder? When?"

Lucia pointed to me. "Didn't April tell you? They surrounded my friend Quasar and nearly buried him alive."

He glanced sharply at me. "You were okay, though, I hope?"

"Of course April was okay. Those fiends targeted Quasar. He shouldn't have even been at the Wrapping Works."

"What were *you* doing there?" Jake asked me.

I stammered, "I-I just had to talk to someone."

Lucia frowned at me. "You're even starting to sound like Quasar."

"I had to speak to an elf who works there. Starla Winters."

"The wolf lady?" Lucia asked. "What'd you want with her?"

Amused that Lucia was doing his job for him, Jake awaited my answer.

"Private matter," I said, groping for a response to throw both of them off my scent. "I had a specific wrapping job I needed done."

Lucia shook her head in disgust. "I'd heard you Southerners were useless, but I assumed you at least could wield your own wrapping paper and ribbon."

I glanced around. "I really should go check on the elf cloggers."

Before I could flee, a hand clamped on my arm. I expected the hand to belong to Jake, but it was Lucia gripping me. "I owe you an apology, April, for blowing my stack today."

An apology from Lucia was so novel that under most circumstances I would have been agog with gratification, not to mention vindication. But Jake Frost was observing us closely.

"Quasar admitted that when you asked to take him to the Wrapping Works he really wanted to go. Whatever you were doing there, I know it wasn't your fault that he was attacked. He said you rescued him, too, and I'm grateful to you for that."

"It was nothing," I said, and excused myself.

Should I have told Jake Frost that I'd been at the Wrapping Works to interview Starla Winters because she'd had a contentious history with Giblet? Maybe. But Punch had given me that information. If it became known that everyone I spoke to would be under official investigation soon after, who would want to talk to me? Besides, I hadn't unearthed anything particularly incriminating against Starla.

It was a good thing I decided to check on the elves, because there was drama enough in the small room where they were getting ready and warming up to distract me from my worries. The cloggers wore bright red and green jumpsuits under boiled wool vests decorated with sequins, rhinestones, and bells. Their wooden-soled boots created a clop with every step, so everyone seemed to be in a frenetic state of sparkling, tinkling, and clomping. The vests differed in the size and number of tinkle bells according to each elf's part in the production.

The elves had worked up a routine to a medley of songs

loosely gathered under the thematic umbrella "Christmas on the Silver Screen." They'd lacked a wow finish until someone had dreamed up the idea of turning "There's No Business like Show Business" into a holiday number. Until you've seen and heard thirty elves sparkling, stomping, and ringing with a gusto to rival even Ethel Merman's, you don't know show biz.

Due to the elves' verve and enthusiasm, their vests often needed repairs, and today was no exception. A quick run-through had jostled dozens of bells loose. I set to work with a needle and thread. This was a big show for the group—entertaining at the lodge was considered an honor—and nerves were on edge. One elf had misplaced his cowbell and had a meltdown until the thing was found behind a poinsettia. I gave the group a final pep talk, assuring them they would be a hit, something that I hoped more than knew.

After leaving them, I headed to the lodge's cavernous main hall, which was situated in the back half of the first floor where the tea was being held. I hadn't even greeted our host yet. Amory Claus was a Claus through and through, large and round, with florid cheeks and bright blue eyes. With his thick, dark, and neatly trimmed beard, he reminded me of Sebastian Cabot, the actor who'd played the butler on *Family Affair.* A cousin of Nick, Lucia, and Martin, Amory was next down in the pecking order of Clauses.

He smiled at me in a way that was more wry than merry. "Hello, April. Sneaking in the back way again?"

His wife, Midge, must have told him what had happened at the Kinder Caroling. Scuttlebutt traveled fast on this mountain.

"I was checking on the cloggers. I hope everyone enjoys them."

Amory stroked his beard like an old sage. "Well, everyone will pretend they do. Of course, they would have genuinely enjoyed the Swingin' Santas."

This had been a sore spot with Amory and Midge ever since I'd chosen the elf cloggers over the Swingin' Santas, who'd performed at this lodge event the past three years in a row. It seemed only right to give some other group a chance.

Amory's attention had already moved on. "Nick's not here yet. I suppose he wants to make a big entrance." He framed his face with crazed jazz hands and said, "Santa!"

"He doesn't like to draw attention to himself; you know that."

He darted a hand out to reach for a mixed drink off a passing tray. "I know he *acts* modest, but we'll see. That red suit does something to men's heads. Nick wasn't on the job two weeks before he started issuing ridiculous dictates. It's always been enough that my family managed Kringle Lodge. This year I'm supposed to do make-work jobs in addition to everything else." He sniffed. "Overseer of Santaland Plumbing! *That* shows what your husband thinks of me."

"Plumbing's important," I said.

"It's a no-glory job. You think he wasn't sending a message to me? People only think of plumbing when it's not working. The rest of the time it's a joke."

I didn't want to argue. Amory was the loudest Claus and his dislike of Nick's Claus Employment Policy was well known.

"It was all totally unnecessary," he said. "There's hardly enough jobs even for all the elves to do around here, without us Clauses being shoehorned into the workforce. Mark my words—pretty soon you'll see a rise in elf unemployment and dissatisfaction. It wouldn't surprise me if this little crime wave we're having proved to be the first sign of that."

"Two murders is hardly a 'little' crime wave."

Amory wasn't listening. He polished off his drink in one slug. "Dear old Nick even makes his wife work," he grumbled, "although of course *you* were given a plum job."

"As opposed to a *plumbing* job," Martin said, sidling up to us.

I could barely conceal my relief at having someone rescue me from this increasingly awkward conversation. "I don't mind working," I said. "I miss running my inn."

"I assume you were better at that than at arranging entertainment," Amory said. "Elf cloggers! This is going to be an endurance test."

Before I could defend my elves, our host stomped off to greet another guest.

"Dear Cousin Amory," Martin said, leaning in. "How long was he giving you an earful about his grievances?"

"I suppose Nick's work policy did seem like a burden."

"It's not as if Amory's crawling in the sewers himself." Martin laughed. "Better chance of getting a camel through the eye of a needle than squeezing Amory Claus through a manhole entrance."

Amory had a point, though. "It *is* an added responsibility. And he has the lodge to take care of."

I expected Martin to respond, but he wasn't even listening to me. His attention, like everyone else's, was on the doors where Christopher and his mother had just entered. In the corner, a pianist had been playing "The Christmas Song," but now even the piano fell silent. Christopher was in a black velvet suit to match Tiffany's full-length jet-black dress and veil, which was attached to her head with a tiara of sapphires.

"Good grief," Martin whispered. "If you'll pardon the expression. It's like Death has crashed the party."

Poor Christopher. He was clearly uncomfortable with everyone gawping at him, but he was sticking to his mother's side while the stares were on them.

Midge, Amory's wife, bustled forward in a large pink satin dress with a tulle shawl collar that made her look a little like a cotton candy cone. She gestured impatiently for the pianist to resume playing. A bouncy version of the "Dance of the Sugar Plum Fairy" covered whatever she said to greet the newcomers.

"Maybe Lucia's right and Tiffany should be sent to a psychiatric clinic," Martin said. "Showing up at a Christmas party dressed like Doom isn't something a well-adjusted person does, even if they are grieving."

I wondered if grief was the whole story. What if Tiffany had some crazy plan to stop the tea and accuse Nick of pushing his brother into a crevasse? To torture myself more, I imagined Jake Frost arresting my husband right here on the suspicion of three murders—his brother, the elf, and the snowman.

After all, maybe I should be relieved Nick had decided to absent himself from this event. It looked bad, but not as bad as having his sister-in-law publicly denounce him would have.

"Should we go say hello to Christopher?" I asked.

As I spoke, however, several cousins of Christopher's age arrived and lured him away with them, probably a more welcome intervention than Martin and mine would have been.

"That just leaves the child's mother hovering like the angel of death."

I tried to make excuses for her. "Lots of people wear mourning."

"Sure, in Victorian novels."

Tiffany turned then and spotted me across the room. The hubbub of party chatter had resumed, yet I felt her hundred-watt stare almost as if she were standing in front of everyone saying, *There stands the woman who married my husband's murderer.*

"You okay?" Martin asked.

I gave myself a shake. "Just worried about my cloggers. The show should be starting soon."

Martin shook his head. "I can see why you'd want to put your own stamp on things, but you don't have to go overboard. Everybody liked the Swingin' Santas."

I groaned. "Not you, too."

"I always enjoyed dancing to them, but then this year . . ." He sighed. "Tiffany's obviously in no mood to dance, Lucia prefers reindeer, and you look as if you're waiting for a meteor to strike the Earth." He glanced around. "I was hoping your friend Juniper would show up, but—"

My brother-in-law's face paled, and he looked with something akin to horror at the doorway. My immediate fear—that Tiffany really was going to make a spectacle of herself and cause trouble for Nick—died when I saw my husband himself standing there.

Not alone, though. He was with Therese. *Very much* with her.

They'd just arrived, and they'd obviously arrived together. Nick was dressed in his best red Santa Suit, while Therese wore a low-cut, tight-fitting, full-length dress in bright red satin, with spiked heels that brought her close to Nick's height. It looked as if they'd coordinated outfits—Santa and his sexy helper. They appeared to be arm in arm, although on closer inspection she had merely placed her hand in the crook of his arm, perhaps just before they walked in. Or maybe they'd been like that for some time.

Either way, Nick wasn't shrugging that well-manicured hand away now.

Immediately, curious gazes turned toward me, people no doubt wondering if I would melt in humiliation or explode into tears. But before I could react, music blared over the loudspeakers set up in the corners of the room and the spectacle of thirty jingling, clogging, singing elves danced into the room.

# Chapter 11

I should have booked the Swingin' Santas.

I had to hand it to the elf cloggers, though; they gave it their all. So much so that the hall reverberated with jangling and stomping and my head began to pound in time with those pointy-toed wooden shoes. It was hard to take my eyes off the spectacle of that many small beings hopping, stomping, sparkling. And yet . . .

Was I being paranoid, or did it seem as if *no one* was really paying attention to the elves? I felt as stiff and uncomfortable as I'd been the moment I'd spotted Nick and Therese together. This wasn't just Therese stepping into my shoes for a kiddie event to show me up to my mother-in-law. This was her announcing herself to the world as my rival, and demonstrating to all of Santaland—and specifically the gathered Clauses and friends—why Nick had made the wrong choice of bride.

Martin leaned close to me. "Don't forget to breathe."

If he hadn't said that, I might have expired then and there, a victim of suspended respiration. I sucked in air, feeling a rush of oxygen to my head. Then I laughed.

*Stop acting like a twit.* It was just a stodgy family event, not the junior prom. Of course Therese looked stunning. She was beautiful and had no qualms about showing off her assets. She'd been the Siren of Santaland long before I'd arrived here, yet Nick hadn't chosen her. He told me he'd never even thought of marrying until he'd gone to Oregon and met me.

I was no Therese, nor did I want to be. I just wanted her to let go of my husband's arm. She was still standing too close to him in that low-cut dress of hers and clinging to him like a deer tick.

Guess I'd picked the wrong day to wear an outfit that made me look like Grandma's sofa.

The last strains of "There's No Business Like Snow Business" rose to a crescendo, and I forced myself to pay attention. When the elves took their bows to healthy if not quite heartfelt applause, though, I couldn't help glancing at Nick and Therese.

Her hand was still stuck to his arm.

"You think they had some mishap with Krazy Glue?" Martin asked.

I smiled and clapped more enthusiastically for the cloggers. "We might have to get them surgically detached."

"I'm guessing there was some Galahad impulse behind all this," Martin said. "That's the thing few people realize about my brother. Most of the time he's a quiet, steady fellow. But then he'll do something big and impulsive and sometimes stupid."

*Like asking a woman to marry him after staying at her hotel for a week.*

Would he also have followed an impulse to shove his brother at the very worst moment?

*I did not marry a homicidal Santa.*

I dragged my gaze away from Nick again and ended up staring into the inscrutable face of Jake Frost.

In the next instant, he was gone.

How had he done that? Was he like a genie who could appear and disappear whenever Constable Crinkles or someone else summoned him? The thought unnerved me.

After the clogging, I sought out the elves and congratulated them on a job well done. Then I returned to the hall and made a beeline for the drinks table, hoping to find something stronger than tea there. Unfortunately, Therese got there before me.

"Oh, hello, April." She acted surprised to see me. "What a sweet little entertainment you put on for us."

Her condescension put my back up. "The elves did all the work. Of course they didn't know they'd have competition."

"From whom?"

"Some late-arriving attention seekers."

"I don't remember seeing anyone else come in." Mascara-laden lashes blinked innocently. "I thought Nick and I were the late arrivals."

I swerved away from her, wanting to cut this encounter short before I tackled her in irritation. No need to turn Amory's party into a scene worthy of a women-in-prison movie. I attempted to maneuver closer to Nick, who of course was in a crowd of people. One thing about being Santa—with that suit on, it's hard not to be the center of attention. I veered back toward the beverage table instead, after first checking that Therese had vacated the vicinity.

I'd drunk two tumblers of nog when Midge found me. "Wonderful elves, April."

"Thank you." I waited for the "but."

She smiled. "They weren't as good as the entertainment we've had in the past, of course, but I'm sure we'll appreciate the Swingin' Santas more next year."

Would there be a next year, here, for me? I tried to envision surviving a year in Santaland, going through all the motions again . . . and again and again. The prospect would have turned my stomach had I not known I'd have my stretch in Oregon to recharge my battery. At the Coast Inn, I knew what I was doing. I could handle Damaris Sproat, the town council, and anything else life threw at me down there. I enjoyed dealing with all the day-to-day challenges, handling all the routine matters. I even enjoyed changing sheets—getting a room ready and imagining the impression the clean, cozy appearance would have on a weary traveler was one of the most satisfying chores.

I'd dreamed of returning to that world with Nick. Of having a helpmate and confidant. But what if that didn't happen? Nick could wind up in whatever lockup this strange land would devise for a serial-killing Santa. Perhaps there was a VIP jail here, like Club Fed. Or would he be banished to the Farthest Frozen Reaches, with the monsters, polar bears, and misfits?

"April? Are you all right?"

Midge's voice snapped me out of my funk.

"Don't let Therese get to you," she said.

"I wasn't thinking of her."

"Good. My advice? Don't let anyone even suspect you are. The moment gossip starts, you lose. That's what Amory always says, anyway. Amory's very wise—you should remind Nick of that."

The advice struck me, although not necessarily for the reason Midge intended. "*The moment gossip starts, the person being gossiped about loses*," I paraphrased, weighing each word as I spoke.

Midge glanced anxiously at the empty tumbler in my hand. "How many of those have you had?"

"Just two."

She clucked. "I told Mistletoe to go easy on the hooch, but you know how help is. *They* don't have to worry about the bill from Santaland Spirits."

"Amory doesn't like his job as the head of plumbing operations, does he?" I asked.

Her breath caught, and she put a hand on my arm. "Honestly, April, I don't like to pull strings, but if you could just have a word with Nick? It's inhumane to make Amory spend so much time on storm drains and sewer pipes. He's been *such* a loyal member of the family."

Had he been loyal? I wondered if some of the malicious gossip against Nick could have been instigated by Amory. Revenge against Nick for coming up with the compulsory work policy.

"Was Amory on the snow monster hunt when Chris died?" I asked.

Midge's face wrinkled in confusion at my change in topic. She dropped her hand. "He was, but he told me he was nowhere close when the accident occurred. Chris had separated from the rest of the group, Amory said. And of course Amory has been so upset about that horrible day. If you could see how he's suffered with post-traumatic stress. I know he wishes he could have done more to save Chris, who was so brave."

She added quickly, "Not that Amory's a coward. He went on the hunt, after all, and nothing compelled him to. He volunteered. But he's not the hero type to go charging headlong into danger." Her smile faded almost as fast as it appeared. "It was a terrible accident, and Amory's always been sure to tell everyone it *was* an accident. From the very first day he's been insistent that Nick had nothing to do with Chris's death. Nothing whatsoever."

Had he professed Nick's innocence in Chris's murder so vociferously that people began to suspect the opposite? That snow monster hunt, I decided, needed looking into.

The ride back down the mountain with Nick started out peacefully. In the sleigh gliding down the trail, with only the sound of hooves on packed snow and bell collars jangling as accompaniment, I leaned my head back and drank in the sky overhead. Gossamer swaths of green and blue streamed across the heavens, a display of northern lights that seemed tailor-made to distract me from my problems. *Look*, that sky was telling me. *You wouldn't see this in Oregon. . . .*

"I thought your dancing elves did a great job," Nick said. "Very original . . . for elf clogging."

The poor elves. Even Santa was lukewarm about their talents.

I sighed and pushed myself up. "You put on quite a show yourself."

He was holding the reins with two hands—he was always a careful driver—but he looked over at me, eyes off the road for many seconds. "What are you talking about?"

His expression was screwed into such obvious puzzlement that I laughed. "Your arrival with Therese? It created quite a stir."

"That was her," he said. "And that dress."

The red dress would have commanded attention no matter what, given that it fit her like cling wrap. But showing up on the arm of someone else's husband—Santa Claus's arm, no less—had to have been calculated. "A little of the hubbub had to do with you standing there with her arm in arm."

He turned in surprise, almost offended. "We were never arm in arm."

"Okay, when you arrived with your arm crooked and her hanging on to you like a barnacle. Why did you arrive with Therese in the first place?"

"I ran into her on the way to the lodge. I swung around to the Candy Cane Factory to speak to Martin. He'd already left, but Therese was there. Her vehicle broke down on the road."

"What was she doing outside of Tinkertown?"

"She told me she was going to apply for a job at the factory to earn her Claus stipend."

I tried and failed to imagine Therese toiling alongside the elves at the Candy Cane Factory. "She chose a nice interview outfit. What job was she going to do?"

"Receptionist, I think." He coughed in the way he did when he had something to say that he didn't relish telling me. "Actually, I recommended her for the job. Or I would have, but Martin wasn't there."

"So you were trying to arrange a job for Therese, were going to speak to Martin on her behalf on the same day she was coming in for an interview, and it just so happened that her snowmobile broke down in front of the Candy Cane Factory?"

"There's no reason in the world to be jealous, April. I would never do anything to hurt you. I'm not a Keith."

No, he wasn't like my first husband. Nick didn't have a devious bone in his body. "I'm not jealous; I'm just irritated by Therese's campaign to upstage me all the time. Next time, tell her to find another arm to drape herself on. And while you're at it, tell her not to cause scenes in my favorite coffee shop."

"She did that?" At my nod, he said, "You didn't say anything to me about it."

"It was just before Old Charlie was found. When I saw you that day, I had other things on my mind."

His eyes narrowed as he stared at the reindeer rumps ahead of us. "It's been an unusual few days. Everyone's acting a little peculiarly."

From what I could gather, Therese's behavior was perfectly in character. "Just so I know you're not going to throw me over for Miss Santaland Psycho."

He laughed. "No plans to do so at the moment." He took my gloved hand in his and gave it a bracing squeeze. "You're freezing," he observed.

I was always cold. "I'm fine," I said, and returned the

pressure on his hand. There was so much I wanted to ask him—and here we were, in perfect privacy if you didn't count reindeer. I doubted they were interested in what we had to say; besides, their jangling collars probably kept them from hearing us. "I need to talk to you about something difficult."

He looked over at me warily.

I rushed on, "About the snow monster hunt. I've been wondering what happened that day."

His shoulders stiffened. "You know what happened. Chris died. It was horrible."

"I'm so sorry to dredge up a bad memory. It's just that there's been talk, and if I could just piece together the events leading up to—"

He dropped my hand. I'd never seen Nick in a fury, but I was pretty sure that's what I was witnessing now. It wasn't red-faced, blustering rage, but something still and cold, like the world around us. The brittle silence before he spoke again was like a shaft of ice working its way up my spine.

"Why should *you* be trying to piece together what happened that day?"

"Because people are still saying—"

"I know what they're saying," he interrupted. "They're wrong. Don't you think they're wrong?"

"Yes, but I want to prove it. What if Chris's death wasn't an accident?"

"It was, April—a tragic accident, and not one I care to relive."

"I know." And here I was asking him to relive it. "I'm sorry, but what if—"

"You don't have to insert yourself into gossip or investigations," he said, cutting me off. "Nosing around is Jake Frost's business, not yours. We have to focus on Christmas now. That's the family business."

I understood that. He had worries—worries that had been

heaped on him unexpectedly when his brother died. As he tackled his first Christmas, the last thing he wanted to do was revisit that devastating event. Asking him to wasn't being kind, or supportive, or particularly helpful in healing up the little rifts and secrets that seemed to have crept into our relationship since the night after the ice sculpture contest. But nothing would strain our marriage like my husband being convicted of multiple murders and spending the rest of his life in the Santaland slammer. How could I explain that to him without sounding as if I actually suspected him?

His jaw set, and he pulled the reins taut to steer the final downhill curve toward the rear of the castle. With sleighs, sledding, skis, or anything involving ice, down was always more treacherous than up. The runners beneath us skidded and I braced myself. Sleighs, like murder investigations, seemed to take on runaway momentum all their own. And no amount of disapproval from Nick or anyone else would change my determination to steer toward the truth and steer the Clauses away from disaster.

# Chapter 12

It was impossible to insinuate the snow monster hunt and Chris's death into conversations with my in-laws. If Nick wouldn't talk to me about Chris's death, I doubted anyone else would open up to me, either. So I spent a day inserting snow monster questions into my interactions with various elves around the castle. Most of them thought I was as mad as Tiffany and sidled away from the subject, and me, as hurriedly as they politely could.

But with the gardener, Salty, I hit pay dirt.

"If you want to know about tracking snow monsters, there's only one elf you need to talk to," he said as he fixed a light on one of the trees in front of the castle. "That'd be Boots."

"Boots?"

"Boots Bayleaf. He was born in the Reaches. He knows all about abominables. He's led every hunt since I've been alive. It's what everybody says around here: 'Snow monsters? Ask Boots.' "

"Does he live in the Reaches now?" I asked.

Salty tugged his ear. "I don't know where he lives, exactly. He just shows up during troubles. He knows all about snow monsters, bears, snow leopards. That kind of thing. I'm sure he has a cottage somewhere, but I don't know where. I don't know who would—except Santa, of course. Your husband would know."

I couldn't ask him, though. He'd see through me at once, no matter how subtly I dropped Boots Bayleaf's name into conversation.

But I bet someone else in the castle knew how to locate the snow monster hunter.

I found Jingles in his lair, the butler's pantry, polishing silver. Most people in charge of a castle of staff would have hated this menial chore, but to Jingles, hiding himself away to rub valuable tableware to a sparkling shine was akin to meditation. Fat headphones covered his ears and he was rocking back and forth with a vigor that made me suspect he was not listening to Perry Como.

I tapped on his shoulder and he nearly jumped out of his skin.

The earphones were whipped off, a pulsing sound screeching out from the headphones before he managed to jab his finger at his smartphone screen and turn off the music.

I raised a brow at the headphones. "Cheery holiday tunes?"

You'd have thought I'd caught him doing something disgraceful. "I'm not a subversive."

I got it. "Everybody needs to flush the sugary residue of Christmastown out of their system occasionally," I guessed. It didn't seem very elf-like to listen to death metal, but then I remembered what Punch had told me about Jingles' mixed heritage.

He assumed his usual proud stance. "Is there anything I can do for you?"

I entered the narrow space—it was more of a deep closet than an actual room—and closed the door. "I need to find someone named Boots Bayleaf."

He nearly dropped the gravy boat he'd been polishing. In

the blink of an eye, his manner turned apprehensive. "What do you want with *him*?" He gulped. "Has there been a sighting?"

"No, but he led the snow monster hunt last summer."

"Are you still worrying about that?"

Jingles hadn't been very helpful when I'd raised this subject with him when he'd brought me my coffee this morning. If only he'd told me about Boots, it would have saved me a couple of hours of pestering the rest of the castle help.

"Boots might be able to tell me a little more about how Chris died."

"I thought you were looking into *Giblet's* death."

"Maybe Chris's accident relates to that. Tiffany seems to think so, and someone needs to check out her story. Giblet accused Nick of killing Chris. Until it's proved that didn't happen, he'll always have a cloud over his head."

"And you think you're the best someone to exonerate him?"

"Who else?"

"Well . . ." *Reluctant* didn't begin to describe the distaste with which he spoke the next words. "*I* could do it."

I remembered wondering why he'd sent me off with Quasar yesterday. He hadn't answered my questions about the snow monster hunts this morning, either, except with a vague shrug and to tell me he'd never been on one. Why would he want to question Boots in my place?

As if reading my mind, he said, "If it gets out that Santa's wife has been hunting down a character like Boots, people might start to ask questions. Elves would think you're trying to buy his silence about what happened on Mount Myrrh that day."

Maybe he had a point, but as long as I picked a time when I had no appearances to make, prizes to give out, or rehearsals to attend, no one would notice if I left for a few hours, much less that I'd met with Boots.

If I could find Boots.

"That's very kind of you," I said, "but hopefully no one will hear about my visit to Boots. I'm free tomorrow until the Reindeer Bell Choir rehearsal." This time I'd double-checked my schedule. "I just need to know where to find Boots Bayleaf. That's what I thought you might be able to help me with."

He nodded. "I know where to look."

Stealthily, we made our way to Nick's office. Outside the door, Jingles tapped lightly. When there was no answer, he cracked it open, peeked in, and then turned back to me, beckoning with his hand. The office was empty, but our being in there felt sneaky and wrong. I couldn't help thinking of the last time I'd come in here with Jingles and burned the message Nick had scrawled on the paper. *A VENOMOUS ELF.* That note, almost as much as Giblet's murder itself, seemed to be the beginning of this troubled time.

Jingles went straight to a corner of the room where a map was, and a table with a few large books below it. I took a detour by Nick's desk and grabbed a gumdrop from the bowl he kept there.

"For most places, Santa relies on the internet and GPS," Jingles explained, "but in Santaland we still find people the old-fashioned way.""

He reached into a cabinet and brought out what looked like the Santaland White Pages. It had been a while since I'd seen anything like it. He thumbed along the Bs until he reached Bayleaf, and then he started scrawling the address down. "This won't mean much to you," he grumbled. "I'll need to draw you a map."

"Thanks." I kept one eye on the door. If Nick walked in now, what would I say to him? I supposed I could tell him I was looking up Juniper's house, but after our talk in the sleigh yesterday I doubted he'd believe me. That was the sad state of affairs between us. In order to save my marriage, I worried I was wrecking my marriage.

"Okay, pay attention." On the map, Jingles pointed out the route I should take, his manner as serious as a toy shortfall. "This cottage is out almost to the border. It will take over an hour. The terrain is hilly, and if you get lost you might end up out of phone range to get directions home."

It didn't look that far, but I took his word for it and paid closer attention, leaning in as he determined where the trouble spots would be.

After Jingles had finished telling me the directions, it occurred to me that I had a bigger problem than not getting lost. How was I going to get there?

"I don't have a sleigh," I said. "And I would rather not have the entire castle staff know what I'm up to, which they would if I asked for a sleigh from the castle stables."

His lips turned down as he considered my dilemma. "I suppose you drove in your home country, before you came here?"

"Well, yes. But the conditions weren't exactly the same." Were any conditions like these, outside of Siberia?

"Good driving record?" he asked.

"Completely clean, except for a few parking tickets." What was he getting at?

Jingles hesitated before saying, "I *might* be able to help you out. If you promise to be very, very careful."

I wasn't sure what he'd come up with this time, so it was with curiosity and trepidation that I followed him down to his private quarters at the rear of the main wing. The little suite had its own entrance, next to which a small shed had been installed. He went inside the shed and then backed out a sleek new snowmobile, painted electric blue. The way the fat body of the thing hunched behind the protruding skis gave it the appearance of a mechanical grasshopper. Jingles ran his thumb along the shiny paint job and radiated smug satisfaction when his digit came away dust-free.

"Oh my," I said. That Jingles would be harboring such a vehicle—the Porsche of snowmobiles—amused me. It was clearly his pride and joy.

"What do you think?"

"It's . . . quite a machine."

He beamed like a proud parent. "I saved up for it for years," he explained. "It's got a power-boosting regulator, high-performing shocks, a comfort seat, and a fourteen-gallon fuel tank."

It definitely beat a pokey sleigh, but I'd never driven one of these contraptions. "Are you sure you want to lend it to me?"

His expression said he wasn't sure at all, but he swallowed his reluctance and said, "It's for a good cause. Our investigation. And I know you'll take good care of her." He caressed the metallic haunch, then frowned. "You *will* take good care of her?"

I assured him I would bring the vehicle back safely. It would save me time, that was for sure. "I'll leave tomorrow morning early. I shouldn't have any trouble getting back in time for the bell choir rehearsal."

Jingles gave me a brief demonstration and took me on a practice ride. It was like driver's ed on skis, with Jingles as a very nervous instructor. But I got the hang of it enough to feel that I could manage an hour-long trek.

I set off the next morning after breakfast, which would allow me ample time to find Boots Bayleaf's shack and get back in time for bell choir rehearsal. It was entirely possible that no one would even know I was gone, since Jingles instructed me to go out the castle's service road, which bypassed the main artery down to town. I skirted around Santaland altogether, passing few sleighs or other snowmobiles. Jingles had also lent me his helmet, so chances were no one would have recognized me anyway. The people who were familiar with Jingles' vehicle would have assumed it was Jingles behind the handlebars.

The snowmobile was fun to drive, but every once in a while I would feel it slide a little on the terrain and was reminded of the dangers of traveling cross-country over ice. In the course of investigating Chris's death, I didn't want to become a fatality myself. I sat stiffly, concentrating on the path ahead, looking for landmarks Jingles had alerted me to, and winced anytime I heard a rock or chunk of ice hit the undercarriage. I needed to bring the vehicle back to Jingles in pristine condition.

Most of the time I was more worried about the snowmobile than I was about the route I was taking. I lost my way when a road forked and didn't realize my mistake for almost a mile. Once I'd doubled back and corrected that mistake, however, it seemed Jingles' directions were fairly clear. It *seemed* that way, except when I got to the place he'd indicated Boots' cottage should be there was no cottage, just a barn. I buzzed by a few times before deducing that this was the only building in the area.

I stopped the snowmobile in front of the barn and approached it guardedly. There was no door at the front, except the timbered barn door. I knocked.

For a moment no one answered. Then I found myself in a bright spotlight. A voice directly above called out, "What is it? A bear?"

I craned my neck, squinting into the light. I could make out a man leaning out a window directly above me. He was wearing a down coat and holding a rifle. I took off my helmet.

"I'm a person," I said.

He snorted. "I *know* you're a person—I heard you buzzing by my house three times. You think I'm a bloomin' idiot? What is it you want to hunt?"

"I'm not here to ask you to hunt for anything, Mr. Bayleaf. I just need information."

He squinted down at me, then looked over at the snowmobile and whistled. "Holy macaroni! Is that a Snow Devil 1100?"

I followed his pop-eyed gaze to Jingles' vehicle. "I, uh, think so."

"Fourteen-gallon tank, Gator-gripper treads, and whisper-pro shocks?"

"And optional comfort seat." I was especially grateful for that padded seat after my hour-and-a-half ride.

He whistled again. "That's a fine machine."

"It got me here." I tried to turn his attention away from the snowmobile. "Mr. Bayleaf, I need to talk to you about the snow monster hunt earlier this year."

He frowned down at me. "What are you, some kind of journalist?"

"I'm the new Mrs. Claus. I married Nick Claus several months ago."

"Oh!" That gave him a jolt, and he lowered his rifle and tucked it out of sight. "'Scuse me—I didn't know. I'll be down in two shakes. Just let me get some pants on."

"Thanks." I certainly didn't want to interview an armed, pantsless man.

Boots took his time, and when he appeared again he did indeed have on pants and was still wearing his coat. The coat indoors struck me as odd until he beckoned me inside. The room was freezing and also, when he turned all the lights on, startling. The entire space was filled with taxidermy creatures—snarling wolves and ferocious polar bears, moose heads and snow leopards, and a large, sad-looking walrus head sitting atop a workbench. I couldn't help thinking of Norman Bates from *Psycho*.

"I hope there aren't any skeletons in your cellar," I muttered.

"No, just root vegetables and figs." He was fine with my thinking that he might have had a skeleton down there, though. "Got anything you want stuffed?"

I shook my head and burrowed deeper into my coat. How was it colder inside than outside? Although, given that there was a peculiar odor coming from that walrus, perhaps it was just as well that the heat wasn't cranked up.

"So you really came all this way just to ask about the snow monster hunt?"

"That's right. I heard you led the expedition, and I wanted to know—"

He held his hand up to stop me. "Just a minute, Mrs. Claus—"

"April," I said.

"Okay, April. I should let you know. I've been sworn to secrecy."

I drew back. "Sworn by whom?"

"Nick Claus," he said. "Your husband."

My old friend anxiety clogged my thoughts. Why had Nick sworn Boots to secrecy? It might not be an answer I wanted to hear.

"So before we get started and I agree to go back on my word, I got a question for you," Boots said. "Namely, what's in it for me?"

I blinked. Was this a shakedown?

"Boots Bayleaf wasn't born yesterday. Think he just runs his mouth for nothing? You think I built all this"—he gestured grandly about the room and its eerie display of lifeless wildlife—"by running some kind of charity outfit?"

"You mean . . . you want money?" Foolishly, I hadn't even brought any money with me.

He scratched his thick gray beard, which had a streak in it. A brown streak. Either it was a remnant of his real color or he'd dribbled coffee down himself. Repeatedly. I tended to think it was the latter.

He studied me intently. "It doesn't have to be money. There are other ways to pay."

A wave of heat crashed over me. "Now listen here—"

"Like a ride on that sweet, sweet Snow Devil 1100," he finished.

"Oh." My outrage, punctured, deflated. "I see."

What would Jingles think of this creature riding his beloved snowmobile? I knew the answer to that—he would probably just as soon Quasar take the controls. That wasn't the answer I needed at the moment, though.

"I *could* pay you," I said. "I'd have to go to town and come back, or if there's any way to send it to you by post . . ."

He spat on his floor, which was probably not the first time those wood boards had received a gob of expectoration. "Corn nuts! Money I got enough of at the moment. But not much opportunity to try out a Snow Devil."

That was really all he wanted? Just to test-drive the snowmobile? That didn't seem like much.

Except, again, it wasn't my snowmobile.

Noting my hesitation, Boots added enticingly, "I just might be able to tell you something about that snow monster hunt that nobody else knows."

What did he know? Temptation was an evil beast.

Jingles would kill me, though.

If he found out.

But he'd only find out if something happened to the Snow Devil 1100, so . . .

*No.* The pride with which Jingles had showed off his vehicle came back to me anew. "I just can't," I said. "It's not my—"

"Five minutes," Boots said.

"Deal."

*Pop quiz: When can five minutes feel like an eon?*

*Answer: When you're watching a grizzled mountain elf climb aboard the expensive snowmobile you borrowed from your persnickety steward and tear off into the white void, whooping with glee.*

I didn't want to look. But I couldn't not look.

Vehicle and rider raced up and down in front of the barn, then flew off-road, slaloming between trees, hot-dogging over hills, popping wheelies on the snowmobile's back tread, skimming in sharp turns that churned up curtains of snow. The engine faced each trick and hill with a sickly whine, like an overheated vacuum cleaner in its death throes. As I stood in horror, I could witness it all because the bright lights on the snowmobile lit every foolhardy maneuver.

My hands clenched into tight fists. At some point, Boots drove over a hill and out of my view, but I heard the Snow Devil shrieking like a giant strangled mosquito, in unison with its rider's cry of terror and glee. Fool sounded like he was on a roller coaster.

Then there was a crash, accompanied by branches snapping.

And then nothing.

Heart in mouth, I went running out in the snow, which sometimes drifted up to my knees. "Mr. Bayleaf!" I yelled, struggling up the hill I'd last seen him fly over. Cresting the top, I saw that he had simply flown, Evel Knievel–style, over a stand of snow-covered bushes. Only he hadn't cleared it. The snowmobile's skis and treads had landed on branches, wobbled off sideways, and then turned upside down in the snow.

I ran, fell, and rolled down the hill to the rescue. With my luck, the man would be dead, I wouldn't get my information, *and* I would have to explain to Jingles why his vehicle was wrecked.

But there was my luck and then there was the luck of Boots Bayleaf. When I dug into the snow, I found his coat and yanked him out by his shoulders. To my surprise, after he was pulled free he popped to his feet, shook snow off himself like a dog shaking off water, then let out another heartfelt whoop of glee.

"Son of a nutcracker! Now that's what I call a sweet ride!"

I groaned, and set about putting the Snow Devil upright.

"I gotta get me one of those," he said.

"I hope it's not damaged beyond repair." I attempted to brush snow off the comfort seat with my snow-encrusted glove.

"Damaged? After a little floopti-do like that?" He snorted. "This thing's a monster. Toss it off Calling Bird Cliff and it'd come out sparkling."

*Sure it would.*

"These things were meant to take abuse."

"That doesn't mean you have to abuse them," I said, unable to keep the scolding tone out of my voice.

He muttered something about prissy women who didn't deserve to drive sleek vehicles.

"Or crash them," I retorted.

But once the machine was de-snowed, it appeared to have come through its ordeal relatively unscathed. I pored over the surface for scratches—because God knows Jingles would—but I found not a flaw in the paint. And when I got on and turned the key, the engine jumped to life.

I drove us back to Boots' place—carefully. When we reached the barn again, I turned to him. "All right. You've had your ride. What do you know?"

"You'd better come have some cider. You might not like what I have to tell you."

Just that quickly, my stomach started gnawing again.

He poured cider out of a small barrel that had a rudimentary spigot poking out. The first sip made me choke. It was like apple juice crossed with ethanol.

"Good, right?" He laughed. "Got a kick!"

I coughed. "It's potent."

For what he was about to tell me, I needed something bracing.

"This isn't something most folks are supposed to know about," he said, "but I guess you're special, since you married one of them."

"A Claus, you mean?"

He nodded, then leaned back in his chair, which stood next to the stuffed wolf. He put his hand on the animal's scruff and petted it as though it were alive. "I never saw the monster we were hunting—didn't even know for sure if one had been sighted."

"You mean you don't know if there was a point to the trip?"

"All's I know is that someone reported spotting a snow monster track by Angel Lake. We can't have abominables making incursions that far into Santaland."

"You don't know who reported the track?"

"No, ma'am. And like I said, I never saw it myself. But I was gung ho to find the creature, and so were the other men. So off we went. We took sleighs halfway up Mount Myrrh, then started climbing. Treacherous terrain. We hunters say Mount Myrrh is the beast that contains beasts. You have to go careful. Everybody knows that. Most of the time, we were a rope team. But then Santa said he heard a snow leopard calling, and Amory and Santa—the old Santa, that is—went back to hunt it down, in case it was stalking us."

My eyes narrowed. Midge hadn't mentioned that Amory had backtracked with Chris. "Why Chris and Amory?" Although what I really meant was, *Why Amory?*

"Chris, because that's who he was. He insisted on going back himself—he loved danger, loved shooting. Nick volunteered to go with him, but Amory said no, they both couldn't go on account of both being Claus brothers. Sort of like they don't let all the royal family fly in one plane, he said. So Chris asked who would go with him, besides me, because he said I was needed to lead the monster hunt. Then, before anybody could pipe up, he sort of voluntold Amory to go."

"Chris *made* Amory accompany him?"

"Not in so many words, but there was a little dare in it."

"Surely Chris wasn't suggesting Amory was too much of a coward to go?"

"Nah, he was just razzing him a little. Chris loved to joke with people, and up on a mountain, in tough conditions, you need a little humor." Boots took a long swig and wiped his mouth with the back of his hand. "Anyway, that's when the party split up. And that was the last anyone besides Amory saw of Chris. They were supposed to catch up with us at our next camp, but Amory showed up alone, in a state. Said Chris had fallen. We backtracked to find him, but of course he wasn't there—just a yawning crevasse where Chris's tracks ended, and lots of Amory's tracks, too. Thing was, Amory had told us he didn't know where Chris had disappeared—said he couldn't find him."

"But Chris's footprints were in the ice by the crevasse. And Amory's."

"Plain as day."

One other thing didn't make sense to me. "How could Amory have lost Chris? You said the team was tied together—hooked together with a rope."

He scratched his beard. "Amory told us Chris thought that was a bad idea—for just the eventuality that happened. If two people are tied and one falls, it's easy for the other to get pulled down, too. There've been cases where the one above has to cut the rope and let the other drop to avoid falling himself." He stopped for emphasis. "The end of Amory's rope was frayed."

I froze at the implication.

"That's what your husband didn't want to get out, why he made us all swear not to talk, and so far's I know, nobody's uttered a peep about Amory."

"Because . . . ?"

"To save Amory's reputation, I guess. It's a helluva thing for a man to have to live with, letting his cousin—Santa Claus, no less—fall into the icy depths of Mount Myrrh."

It was hard to feel sorry for Amory just then. Suspicion crowded out my compassion.

Noting the gears turning in my head, Boots grinned. "Now, wasn't *that* worth a ride on your fancy vehicle?"

I didn't respond to that, but he wasn't expecting an answer. "You've told me this," I said, "but there's no reason to tell anyone else. Not if Nick asked you not to."

He drew back in offense. "Boots Bayleaf knows how to keep his lip buttoned."

Given that he'd just spilled the story to me in exchange for a joyride, I took those words with a whole block of salt. I stood, preparing to leave.

"Wait!"

"Do you have anything else?"

"Do I ever."

He hurried across the room and picked up something silver. Another clue?

"What . . . ?"

He turned, striking a pose. "Is there still a spot left for the

Skate-a-Palooza? My mama always said I had the best voice she ever heard."

And he proceeded to demonstrate how wrong Ma Bayleaf had been, by singing "Winter Wonderland" and accompanying himself on spoons.

# Chapter 13

Boots Bayleaf knew how to keep his lip buttoned. Unfortunately, I wasn't endowed with that skill.

As the snowmobile droned me back toward Christmastown, I mulled over what I'd learned. Had Amory killed his cousin, or merely covered up a dreadful deed necessitated by an accident? If he'd truly cut that rope and let Chris fall, that wasn't murder, necessarily, but something murkier. It would account for that PTSD Midge had mentioned.

One thing I was sure of: If Boots' account could be believed, it exonerated Nick. He clearly hadn't killed his brother. So why had he insisted on silence from everyone in the team, even as rumors about his own involvement flurried around Santaland?

This puzzled me, but like the old saying went: *Marry an enigmatic, overworked Santa in haste, spend the rest of your life's leisure moments in a frustrating guessing game.*

Okay, there was no old saying like that. But maybe there should have been.

The more I chewed over the situation, the more muddled I was over what my next step should be. The hum of nervousness in the back of my mind over bringing the snowmobile back to Jingles didn't help. I kept reliving that moment of seeing the machine overturned in the snow. I wanted to get it refueled and professionally cleaned before returning it to its finicky owner. There was a fuel depot past the Plumbing Works. And while I was in the neighborhood . . .

Getting answers out of Nick, especially on the subject of Chris's death, was like pulling teeth. I was pretty sure Amory would be an easier mark, even if he had something to hide.

The Plumbing Works office was housed in an industrial building partially hidden by a stand of trees. The concrete had been painted in cheery red, green, and white, but there was no disguising the charmless boxy shape of the hulking edifice. Poor Amory—having to leave his cozy lodge to come here every day.

The interior was more inviting than the exterior. I was led to a top-floor corner office with wraparound windows. The drapes were all drawn, shutting out what little natural light was available this time of year. When Amory's secretary ushered me in, it seemed strange to me that the one possibility of beauty—a view—was shut off. Unlike almost every other square inch of the Christmastown region, there were no decorations hung in Amory's office. No lights, wreaths, garlands. No banners wishing everyone a Merry Christmas, or cards or presents on display. No tree.

"April!" A long mahogany desk was centered close to the back wall, and Amory was leaning back in his chair, feet propped up, a pen nestled behind his ear.

"No one could accuse you of overdoing the Christmas fervor," I said by way of greeting.

His lips turned down. "I have a hard time feeling merry and bright about the sewer work your husband forced me into." He eyed me curiously. "So what are you doing here? Slumming?"

"This office isn't so bad."

He sniffed. "Not exactly Castle Kringle, though."

No, no one would mistake it for the castle. After standing awkwardly for a few moments, I sat myself down in one of the pair of leather chairs facing Amory's desk. "I have something serious to speak to you about, Amory."

He uncrossed his legs and took his feet off the top of his desk, and his lips turned down in an expression of mock seriousness. "Something wrong in your world? One of your elf choristers have laryngitis? Band lost a tuba?"

"It's nothing to do with musical events." I decided the best strategy would be to plunge right into the unpleasant truth. "I found out what happened on Mount Myrrh."

Amory's eyes bulged, and for a moment he looked as if he would profess ignorance of what I was talking about. But in quick succession he sagged in resignation and then stiffened again. "Nick told you, I suppose. Of course he did. I knew his noble silence was all an act."

"Nick said nothing. Someone else told me."

"Who?"

"Does it matter? Someone who was in a position to know what happened up there."

"*Nobody* knows what happened up there. Even I don't know. There was that damned snow leopard, or that's what Chris said. I'm not like my crazy cousins—I don't know one animal sound from another. So we formed a separate hunting party, away from the others. Big mistake."

"This person—my source—said Chris dragooned you into it."

He laughed mirthlessly. "That's a good way of putting it. Ever since we were kids he was that way with me. Oh, he was too jolly to be a real bully; he knew exactly how much teasing and pressure to exert to get you to do what he wanted. And I was never an excellent sportsman like the others."

That surprised me. "You mean Nick and Martin?"

"Sure. And Lucia, of course. She was better at sports than

all of us. Better at shooting, bow and arrow, harpoon, all those things. Though Martin was really good, too. He went out with Chris a lot when they were younger, after Lucia decided she was against killing anything."

"She's not against poisoning rats." I frowned. "But I think that has something to do with them passing fleas to the reindeer."

He nodded, and I realized I'd veered away from my purpose. "So you didn't want to go with Chris to find the snow leopard?"

"Of course not. We were almost to camp, where we could build a fire and eat, and rest a little. I volunteered to hunt a snow monster, not a stupid leopard. Who cared? Chris just wanted a pelt."

"Did anyone else volunteer?"

"Nick did, right away. Nick *should* have gone, but then Chris had said both of them couldn't because they were so close in line in the Santa succession. Well, what about me? I was fifth in line."

"So you went reluctantly." And probably resented every step that took him in the opposite direction of that campfire, and food and rest. In his place, I would have, too.

"I sucked it up," he said. "I'm good at that, thanks to a lifetime of having to do what I'm told. The orphan cousin, a minor Claus."

"What happened after you separated from the others?"

"Well, at first we just seemed to trudge forever, backtracking. Then Chris took us around a ledge that seemed too treacherous to me. He was always taking foolish chances! Yes, he had courage, but he was also a daredevil. Reckless and overconfident."

"So you reached a point on the mountain where you disagreed about continuing?"

"Yes."

"And you quarreled," I guessed.

"*I* tried to start a quarrel, for all the good it did me. I might as well have been talking to the glacier. Chris never listened to me."

"So he made you both go ahead."

He shook his head. "That's the thing that haunts me. I didn't go. He left me behind."

I shook my head. "He left you, or you insisted on staying where you were?"

"Okay, it was mostly the latter. But he could have listened to me, you know. I was right! The way he chose was too dangerous. It killed him."

Something in his story I couldn't quite buy. "You mean you were nowhere near Chris when he fell?"

"No, I wasn't. When he didn't come back for me, I went looking for him, following his tracks. I thought I'd found where he fell, but I wasn't sure."

"The person I spoke to said there were a mess of your footprints at the edge of the crevasse."

"Maybe there were. I was frantically trying to find my cousin. I wasn't being careful to lead a tidy line of prints. Do you have any idea how hysterical I felt that afternoon?"

"I can imagine."

"No you can't. I'm sorry, but you really can't. Not only was Chris gone—the most beloved Claus of our generation—but I knew how it would look to everyone. Like I'd killed my cousin. But why would I do such a thing? I *liked* Chris, on the whole. He could be a nitwit, and overly enthusiastic and sporty. It was like having Teddy Roosevelt for a cousin. But he was so likable, everyone forgave him his few faults. And they really were few."

"Were you ever jealous of him?"

"Honestly? Yes. But I never kidded myself that I would ever be Santa. Not really. Even if Christopher hadn't come along, Chris had two brothers who came before me in the pecking order. And frankly, I think Lucia probably would have tried to seize power and be the first female Santa before she ever let me near that red suit.

"Besides," he continued, "I had every reason to want Chris to stay alive. I knew all along that Nick had insane ideas about forcing us distant Clauses to work for our stipends. Believe me, if I could have climbed down into that crevasse and dragged Chris back up, I would have."

Everything he said made sense. Except one detail. "Your rope was frayed, someone said. As if you'd cut it."

"But not because I'd cut Chris loose and let him fall to his doom. When Chris and I unhooked ourselves, we noticed the rope around the catch had frayed. It was useless—dangerous, even—so he told me I'd be better off with bare rope rather than keeping a hook that wouldn't hold. After all, another person might not notice it, and use it at their peril. So I cut it off while he was gone. It gave me something to do."

Maybe that was plausible, but I still found Amory's actions suspect, if not on the mountain, then at least in the months since. "All this time, you must have known rumors were swirling around concerning Nick, and yet you said nothing to quash them."

"Why should I stick my neck out for Nick?" he asked. "What's he ever done for me?"

"He prevented an investigation into your actions that day. Otherwise everyone would be whispering that *you* killed the last Santa."

He grumbled at that. "Apparently some people are anyway. Someone blabbed a bunch of innuendo and lies to you, didn't they?"

"Someone told me the bare facts as he saw them up there," I corrected.

"And made it easy for you to extrapolate my guilt." He

crossed his arms. "Sometimes I think Nick's insistence on silence that day was partly to undermine me."

"How?"

"He knew I felt guilty. Maybe he thought I *was* guilty. He might have assumed it would all come out in a whisper campaign against me."

"Any whisper campaign seems to be directed at Nick. You couldn't have put any of those rumors to rest?"

Amory crossed his arms. "He swore us *all* to silence. He didn't say 'everybody but Amory.'" At my steady gaze, he bristled. "Do you think any of this has been easy for me? Imagine the guilt I've been living with. Not for Chris's death itself, but the fact that I wasn't there when he might have needed me."

"If it was an accident—"

"It was!" He thumped his fists on his armrests. "Are you saying you don't believe me?"

I raised my hands in surrender to calm him. "Since it was an accident, you have no reason to feel guilty."

He shook his head at my innocence, or ignorance, or both. "You don't know anything about how I feel. If I'd gone with him, he might be alive. We would have been tied."

"With a fraying rope?" I remembered what Boots had told me. "You might have both ended up at the bottom of that crevasse."

He slumped in his chair. "Maybe I would have been better off dying that day. All I've felt since is remorse, and anger, and doubt."

"Doubt?"

He banged his fist on the desk. "What good had it done to go back? Who knew if there really was a leopard stalking us? Chris said he'd heard one, and maybe one other person did, but we never saw tracks. No one did. That's why I thought going back was crazy. We should have all stayed together." He stood up and began to pace. "And all right, I shouldn't have let Chris go off alone, but he also left *me* alone to face that leopard."

"You just said there might not have been a leopard."

"Chris thought there was."

I nodded.

"Don't look at me like that!"

"How?"

"Like Nick, that day on the mountain. Like I really *was* guilty."

Maybe every syllable of his protestation of innocence was true, but he was as much of a wreck as he would have been if he had pushed Chris into that crevasse, or cut the rope. I felt sorry for him. A circular firing squad had set itself up in his conscience.

I stood up, and for a moment Amory ceased wearing a hole in the carpet. "I'm sorry I bothered you," I said. "I just needed to know. Nick would never have told me about what happened on the hunt."

"So you say."

"He wouldn't have. Nick isn't your enemy, Amory. People are blaming *him* for Chris's death, not you."

That fact didn't soothe Amory. "Nick, the martyr. Taking the blame."

I sighed. "Don't let this eat you up inside."

"I'm not," he said in a defensive tone. "What gives you that idea?"

"Your voice, your pacing, and the way you were when I came in, sitting in this dark, bare room, brooding. At least let some daylight in, for Pete's sake." I walked over and pulled the cord on the drapes before he could stop me. The drapes swung open, revealing a perfectly breathtaking view.

Of Mount Myrrh.

# Chapter 14

"Nice ride," Jake Frost said, startling me out of my wits.

I'd been lost in thought when I'd left the Plumbing Works, so it might have seemed natural that I didn't see him. Except how could you miss a man—or whatever he was—dressed head to toe in black in a snow-covered drive? Where had he come from, and when, and why was he here?

All my antennae were up as he circled Jingles' snowmobile. He was obviously as impressed with it as Boots had been, but he was too cool to let too much enthusiasm show. Whoops and exclamations weren't his style.

"How long have you had this?" he asked.

"It belongs to Jingles. And I've already regretted letting one person take a joyride on it today, so don't ask."

"Don't worry, I've got my own." He nodded to a black-and-white machine not far away, a less souped-up Snow Devil.

"What are you doing here?" he asked.

"I was wondering the same thing about you."

"I'm here to talk to Amory Claus."

I smiled. "What a coincidence. I just left him."

He buried gloved hands in his coat pockets. "Visit your husband's cousin often at work?"

"Nope. First time."

He studied me. I didn't avert my gaze. Nor did I offer up any more information.

"Did this visit have anything to do with what you learned on your outing this morning to see Boots Bayleaf?"

My jaw dropped. "How did you know about that?"

"I have my sources."

Sources, or sorcery? Both possibilities made me uncomfortable. "I don't like the idea of spies in the castle."

"That makes us even, because I don't like the idea of someone running a shadow investigation when I'm trying to track down a killer."

"Am I getting in your way?"

"People get weary of answering questions—if too many people come knocking, they can clam up. Also, there's the element of surprise. You lose that if you're the second person to question someone."

"Then you shouldn't let a mere amateur detective get the jump on you."

"Is that what you think you are? Nancy Drew in a snowmobile instead of a blue roadster?"

I laughed.

"What?" he asked.

"I've just had a vision of a young Jake Frost cozying up with a stack of Carolyn Keene books. Was that the origin of your brilliant career?"

"Dabbling in police work is no joke, April. We need to discuss this."

I swung my leg over the snowmobile seat. "Sorry, can't talk now." I turned the key and the motor buzz sawed to life. "I'm due at the Reindeer Bell Choir rehearsal in Mistletoe Park."

"After rehearsal, then!" he said, having to yell over the Snow Devil's motor.

I made no promises before I zoomed off toward town, but it didn't seem to matter. I knew he'd materialize again.

The Reindeer Bell Choir was Lucia's baby, and the only reason she would involve herself in anything musical. Reindeer were almost exclusively interested in food, the never-ending Reindeer Games, and keeping track of an always-shifting hierarchy among the herds. They were an energetic species, I had to give them that. But there were some reindeer who just weren't into the Reindeer Game culture, and for them Lucia had created the choir.

"They've got to have some way to connect with Christmas," she told me.

Walking up the hill where they were rehearsing, I was impressed by the gathering of twenty reindeer, all wearing "uniforms" of scarlet red and vibrant green that draped over their shoulders and backs. The white pom-pom balls edging their outfits bounced when an animal moved or twitched. The reindeer looked fantastic.

*Looked* was the key word.

The trouble was, they didn't seem to have any musical talent. Granted, "The Little Drummer Boy" was never one of my favorite songs, but this version seemed to go on and on, with a crescendo longer than Ravel's *Bolero*. The reindeer controlled the bells with their mouths or by having a bell strapped on their foreleg, but the rhythm was so off, the tune so muddled, I had a difficult time keeping my expression neutral as I listened to the slow but sure massacre of what little melody there was. Bells would be ringing in my ears for days.

I was so focused on the reindeer that I didn't see the flyer until a small gloved hand shoved it right at me. I looked down and read it:

*JUSTICE FOR GIBLET*

*A march down Turtle Dove Lane will be held December twenty-third to voice our concerns about the lack of progress in the investigation into the murder of Giblet Hollyberry.*

*Join us for this important, solemn vigil. Let's raise our elven voices for justice!*

A march? Through Christmastown? Were the Hollyberrys truly upset, or were they just trying to make trouble? The march was on the same night as the Skate-a-Palooza. They had to have planned it that way.

A whistle blew, and the elf who'd handed me the flyer stiffened in alarm. He looked behind him to see Constable Crinkles raise his fist. "Stop!"

The elf tore off.

Crinkles gave his nephew a push. "Run after him, Ollie!"

The deputy gave chase, but I doubted the malefactor would be caught. For that matter, I didn't see what the elf had done wrong. I approached Crinkles.

"Disgraceful!" he exclaimed. "I'm sorry you've come at this time, ma'am. Anyone would think we're . . ." He tugged at his chin strap. "Well, one of those places where people have marches."

"They'll calm down when there's an arrest."

"Yes, but until then, we'll have *un*rest—on streets that up to now have only seen happiness and parades. Santalanders haven't ever behaved like this before."

"They're just worried," I said. "Think of it as an Anxiety Parade."

He sighed. "I guess I better see where Ollie went off to. Dollars to donuts he let that rascally elf get away."

When he was gone, I tried to focus on the music again. The reindeer were finishing their last piece, a "Jingle Bells" that really stuck to your eardrums.

Lucia raced over to me as soon as the rehearsal broke up. "What did you think?"

She looked honestly interested in my opinion, which was a switch.

"Those outfits are fantastic," I said, wanting to be positive. "They really make the group stand out."

She smiled modestly. "I called in a favor with somebody in the order of seamstresses."

"Totally worth it," I said. "They sparkled."

"What about the music?"

I swallowed. "I could hear it all perfectly. I mean, wow! They were good and loud."

She crossed her arms, unsatisfied. "You came late—you missed 'Jingle Bell Rock.' That's our best number."

"Darn."

"It's only two nights before Skate-a-Palooza, April, and we still haven't been given our spot. What's the holdup?"

"I've been busy."

"Busy with what?"

I ignored the question. "I'll try to give them a good spot. But you know how many acts there are."

She buried her mittened hands in her pockets and kicked her toe in the packed snow under her feet. "Everyone just wants to hear Figgie and the Nutcrackers."

The local rock group had a big following. They were going to be the headliners. All the other acts had to open for them . . . or be tucked in after, when most everyone would be filtering out of the park.

"All the money goes to charity," I explained, "so we want a lot of people to come out." Figgie and the Nutcrackers would attract more ticket sales than the Reindeer Bell Choir, though I didn't want to make it sound as if all my calculations were financial ones.

"Why *were* you late?" Her gaze traveled down the hill to

the spot where I'd parked the snowmobile. "And how did you ever convince Jingles to let you drive that thing?"

"How did you know it was his?"

"Are you kidding me? He spends most of his days off polishing it. It's his baby—he barely even drives it himself for fear of its getting scratched. I can't believe he lent it to you."

"I needed to get somewhere fast."

"And he was probably trying to suck up to the wife of the new Santa." Her mouth twisted. "I wouldn't get too thick with him, if I were you."

"Who, Jingles?"

"I've had him turn on me. Who do you think squealed to Mom when Quasar's antlers got stuck in the curtains?"

"Wouldn't she have noticed anyway?"

"I'm just saying. Jingles isn't on anybody's side but his own."

"I never thought he was on my side," I said, but even as the words came out I knew they were false. I'd trusted Jingles enough to let him witness me destroying evidence and to confide in him about my investigation. "He's always been nice to me."

"Like I said . . ."

*Sucking up.* But why suck up to me? Before a few days ago, he always acted a little wary of me, as though I weren't worthy of my position. He called me *you* or nothing, not *Mrs. Claus.* Mrs. Claus was still Pamela to him.

To be fair, she was still Mrs. Claus to almost everyone, including me.

Why had he helped me at all? I thought back to when he showed me the note Nick had written that first morning after Giblet had died. I'd assumed Jingles' action had been out of allegiance to the family. But he could easily have burned the note on his own, without calling me into the library.

He'd wanted to make sure I saw it.

"You'll learn." Lucia glanced over my shoulder and her frown deepened. She lowered her voice. "Don't panic, but trouble's on its way and it's looking right at you."

I knew what I'd see even before I turned around. Jake Frost.

"You missed all the fun," I said to him in greeting.

"We couldn't have talked during the performance anyway."

I pivoted to Lucia to say something about her bell choir, but she was walking away. I ended gesturing awkwardly at her retreating back.

Jake watched her go. "Your sister-in-law seems to be in a hurry."

Yes, she did.

"But it was you I wanted to talk to," he continued. "We can go to We Three Beans if you'd be more comfortable there than outside."

"Who wouldn't?" The question answered itself, because the man in front of me seemed as comfortable wearing his loosely buttoned coat in the sub-zero weather as I used to feel walking around Oregon in a T-shirt and jeans. Was he immune to the cold? Did they bleed ice water out in the Reaches?

"I take it that's a yes," he said.

My eyes narrowed. "How did you know I liked We Three Beans?"

"I'm a detective. It's my job to find things out."

I wasn't comfortable being detected, though.

We Three Beans didn't have many people in it when we went in, and we were able to find an empty corner table. Nat King Cole sang "The Christmas Song," which went a long way to soothe the edginess I felt from having Jake Frost dogging my movements. I grabbed a gingerbread muffin to go with my latte. Jake ordered black coffee.

"All right," I said as soon as I'd had a few reviving swallows of muffin and caffeine. The baked goods at We Three Beans were to die for. Butter, sugar, ginger. Heaven. "What did you want to talk about?"

"I want to know what you think you're going to achieve."

I took another swallow. "There's a killer loose in Santaland. I intend to find him."

"Why?"

"Because I'd rather not live with a murderer on the loose."

His face registered barely restrained impatience. "But why *you*? You might have noticed that I'm here. I'm an experienced investigator."

"I've also noticed that my husband is a suspect. The Claus family isn't taking that seriously because, well, they're Clauses and they seem to think that everything will come up gumdrops and peppermint sticks no matter what, but I do take the accusations seriously. And personally. I'm sorry if you believe that we're working at cross-purposes, but I have every right as a citizen to talk to people and see what I can find out."

"You seem to believe absolutely in Nick Claus's innocence. Were you this trusting of your first husband?"

I put my cup down. "I suppose you've found out all about that. No doubt Therese sent you down that rabbit trail."

"A false trail—that became clear as soon as I contacted your old hometown for the records detailing your husband's car accident. His girlfriend at the time accused you of tampering with the car, but there was no evidence."

"I didn't even know she existed before the accident. I thought Keith and I were just going through a rough patch . . . for a lot of reasons. I was naïve then."

"And now?"

How could I use my gut feeling as proof when my gut had failed me before? Simple. Belief was all I had until I could gather better evidence. "Nick has a good heart. He loved his brother, and he doesn't swat a fly without feeling remorse, so I know he wouldn't go on a murder spree."

"Okay." He took a sip of coffee. "Then why not share information?"

Meaning he wanted me to tell him everything I knew, and he would probably tell me next to nothing about his investigation in return.

"If you're as experienced as you say you are," I said, "you'll probably find out what I've discovered on my own and then some."

"But why duplicate our efforts? Why not share?"

Why not? I didn't have an answer, except that there was something about the official investigation I didn't trust.

Or was it that I worried I'd incriminate someone I didn't want to be under the spotlight?

That note was on my mind again now. *A VENOMOUS ELF.* . . . Why had I burned it? I'd done so impulsively, almost reflexively, without considering whether it really had been written by Nick. An amateur mistake.

I *was* an amateur. How could I possibly find a killer on my own?

In any case, it wouldn't hurt to throw Jake Frost a bone and see what happened.

"This morning I've been looking into the snow monster hunt Chris Claus died on."

"I knew that."

I gaped at him. "You did?"

"Pretty obvious when you go to the trouble to hunt down old Boots Bayleaf."

"How did you find out about that? Did you follow me?"

"I didn't have to. I have sources."

Those sources again. Sources inside the castle? "Jingles?"

His lip curled up. "That's the thing about sources. You don't give them up."

Maybe it was Jingles. My mind raced through all my recent dealings with him.

That conversation I'd had with Lucia was making me mistrustful. I frowned. Maybe that was what she'd intended. In which case she was making me doubtful about her, too. Pretty soon I was going to be a mass of paranoia and they'd find me babbling to myself in the castle basement.

Maybe it was time to trust someone. Jake was there as an objective investigator, to find the truth.

I took a breath. "There've been rumors that Nick was responsible for his brother Chris's death. Giblet Hollyberry all but accused him of fratricide, and so did Chris's widow, Tiffany. But from what Boots Bayleaf told me, Nick wasn't anywhere near Chris when he died. The hunting team on Mount Myrrh had a snow leopard stalking them, and Chris and Amory backtracked to kill it."

Jake took a slow drink of coffee.

I leaned forward. He'd found something odd in what I'd said. "What?"

He shrugged. "Snow leopards are pretty stealthy."

"They must make *some* noise. Someone heard it cry, or call." Off the top of my head, I didn't know the appellation for a leopard sound. "You didn't talk about this with Amory?"

He shook his head. "Not in any detail."

So I knew things he didn't. "What did you talk about?"

"Where he was the morning Giblet died."

"Where was he?"

"In bed." Jake took another sip of coffee. "Who heard the snow leopard call?"

"No one's sure. Chris, and maybe one other of the party. But both Boots and Amory mentioned Chris."

"Any other sign? Prints, scat?"

"I don't think so. Chris fell—and then the snow leopard seems to have been forgotten."

"Understandably." I could see him mentally recapping our conversation. "So Amory was with Chris. And then . . ."

I explained the circumstances as Amory had told them to me. About his refusing to continue on with Chris right at the end and about his frantic search for him and how when he realized what had happened he'd gone back for the others. I also mentioned the frayed rope. It seemed the most damning element—I worried I was tossing poor Amory under the bus. But that wasn't the detail Jake zeroed in on.

"Your husband didn't want the details of Chris's death to get out?"

"No. He asked the others not to mention anything about it."

"Odd."

"Why?"

He shrugged. "This all should have been told to the constable as part of the facts of the case."

"Maybe Nick did tell Constable Crinkles, in confidence."

"Old Crinkles would've spilled that to me."

Didn't it just go to show . . . I'd worried about making *Amory* look guilty, yet whom was the investigator laser focused on? Nick.

"If you're just going to twist everything I tell you into a way to zero in on Nick, I'm done sharing. What else have you and the constable discovered?"

"There's the question of the button from Old Charlie's death. Madame Neige, the head of the Order of Elven Seamstresses, said that it was one that they used on the clothes made for the Claus family. But you knew that."

As I'd suspected, sharing information was a lopsided deal.

"Would you tell me if you knew more?" I asked. "If, say, you found something damning against my husband?"

"If I can count on your secrecy, certainly."

"I don't have any secrets from Nick."

*Except that he knows nothing about my investigating and wouldn't approve if he did.*

"That might be a problem, then."

"I won't narc on my spouse."

"Even if you began to suspect he could be a killer?"

I remembered Nick's having been out of bed half the night of Giblet's death and felt a flush. "Nick isn't guilty of anything."

"You just told me he covered up a possible murder."

"I don't know what his motives were for swearing the others to silence."

"You haven't asked him?"

"He doesn't know I'm—" At Jake's knowing smile, my throat cut off my words. "I just found all that out this morning. There hasn't been time to talk to him."

"I'll be interested to hear what he says when you do find time."

I pushed my mug away. "You won't hear it from me."

"Then I'll have to ask him myself."

And no doubt Nick would find out about my visit to Amory.

I scowled. "All right. I *will* talk to him. But I can promise you won't get the answers you're hoping for."

"I just want the truth, April." He slugged down the dregs of his coffee. "I wonder what it is *you* want."

# Chapter 15

Jingles examined his snowmobile as closely as possible without the aid of a magnifying glass. Even though I'd taken it through Walnut's Sleigh Wash by the fuel depot and had even sprung for the hand wax, I held my breath as Jingles pored over every square inch. If anything, his inspection became more meticulous once he'd twigged to the fact that I'd gotten it professionally cleaned.

When he finally nodded his approval, I let out a breath.

"Walnut's did a good job." He placed a hand lovingly on a handlebar. "Almost as good as I would have done myself."

"I wanted to save you the trouble. Not that there was anything wrong with it," I added quickly. "But Boots' place was a long drive. I hit a little muddy slush."

He winced at the thought of anything but pristine snow touching his beloved Snow Devil. "Did you learn anything?"

"Not much." After Lucia's warning not to trust Jingles, I hesitated to reveal more to him.

He scrunched his lips. "I'm surprised old Boots didn't try to extract some kind of quid pro quo to get something from you in exchange for information. It's about that crazy coot's speed."

I kept my gaze off the snowmobile that the crazy coot had been popping wheelies on. "He's a character, all right."

I left Jingles putting his vehicle to rest under plastic sheeting in his storage shed.

One person I could think of who would benefit from learning what I'd heard today was Tiffany. Familial relations in the castle could only improve when she found out her brother-in-law wasn't responsible for her being a widow. The testimony from both Boots and Amory about the snow monster hunt confirmed Nick could not have been responsible for Chris falling into that crevasse. Learning that she wasn't living under the same roof as her husband's murderer was bound to ease her mental distress.

I entered the castle through the side entrance to the lower west wing where Tiffany and Christopher had their quarters.

It was late afternoon and the hallway lights hadn't been turned on yet. One of the contradictory facts of life at the castle was that during winter afternoons, when there actually was a little natural light, the interior of the castle could seem darker than at night when all the chandeliers, lamps, decorated trees, and strings of lights chased out the winter gloom.

This part of the castle, the newest, had plaster walls, but Tiffany had had them all painted a gray shade called Stately Granite, which pretty much replicated the Frankenstein's castle dreariness of the Old Keep, only with a glossier finish.

Down the hall, Christopher was having a cello lesson. He complained about practicing, but listening to him and his professor playing a Bach Contrapunctus, I was impressed. *Maybe he should be playing at the skate night.*

I knocked at Tiffany's door but didn't hear an answer, so I rapped my knuckles a little louder. A few moments passed before the knob turned and the door swung open.

Tiffany was standing in a floor-length black velvet dressing robe, fitted to her torso like a corseted Victorian lady's dress. She wore four-inch mule slippers that brought her up to my height and she gripped a silver hairbrush in one hand like a weapon.

"I said come in," she huffed.

"Sorry—I didn't hear you."

Her steady gaze held mine. "What did you want?"

"To talk . . . if you have time?"

"I'm brushing my hair, but sure, come in."

She turned and crossed the cavernous bedroom to her dressing table, an ornate three-mirrored rosewood affair that was as wide as a classic Cadillac. The taste for modern decor—even modern vintage—hadn't reached Santaland. The castle was still packed with all the too-heavy, too-tall furnishings that had gone out of favor everywhere else: towering wardrobes that could crush a reindeer like a bug, dressers that required four elves to budge a few feet, and cabinets and tables so ornately carved that it took the better part of an hour to dust all the nooks and crannies.

One change had been made fairly recently in this room: The doors of a tall wardrobe had been replaced with glass, which created an oversized trophy case dedicated to Tiffany's figure-skating career. One of her costumes, dripping with blue and white sequins, hung in the center, surrounded by programs, skates, trophies, and clippings. Discreet yet focused lighting made everything visible—unmissable—in the dark room.

Of course I wandered over to look at the artifacts of Tiffany's former life. No one else I knew created shrines to themselves, but I hadn't met many people who'd been competitive on a world stage, as Tiffany had been.

Through the mirror, she saw me perusing the relics of her glorious past. "That's the dress I wore when I won bronze at Junior World."

"It's gorgeous—and so elaborate. I can just see you shimmering across the ice."

"I skated to a medley from *Beauty and the Beast*."

Looking at her seated on her cushioned, low-back chair in front of her vanity, petite but regal, I understood for the first time how she must have felt she'd found a perfect place for herself here. A princess of the ice became an ice princess for real—the center of attention, next to her handsome, charismatic prince. All the ceremonial duties that chafed at me probably seemed just right for her. And then, this year, her happiness had turned to sorrow.

Maybe I could take a scrap of that sorrow away.

I sat on the corner of the bed and watched her through the mirror. I'd never considered brushing one's hair to be an activity requiring much concentration, but Tiffany ran the fine-haired brush over her long dark locks as if it were an Olympian skill requiring as much dedication as perfecting a triple axel.

"I didn't dismiss what you were telling me that day we were on the roof," I said.

Her reflection showed no change of expression. "Why would you? You should know the man you married."

"I do. That's why I couldn't account for the disconnect between the good man I know and the terrible things you were insinuating."

Her hand dropped to her side and she twisted to face me. "Something happened on that mountain."

"Yes. Chris fell into a crevasse."

"He was an expert climber. A sportsman."

A reckless daredevil. I didn't say it, though—she was still holding that lethal hairbrush. "Anyone can have an accident, Tiffany. Chris did that day. I've talked to two men who were on the mountain, and they both confirmed that Nick was nowhere near the place where the tragedy occurred."

"Who did you talk to?" she asked sharply, as if this person had betrayed her.

"Does it matter? They were there and we weren't."

"Exactly."

I frowned. "Exactly what?"

"Those people can concoct any old story and according to you we'd just have to take their word for it."

"Because they were eyewitnesses to what happened that day. That's only logical."

Her eyes narrowed to withering slits. "Thank you, Mrs. Spock. It's also logical that you would coerce people to say anything to exonerate Nick."

"I didn't coerce anyone. And both people told me this independently of each other."

"Who were they?" she asked again.

I thought of Amory holed up in his office with the windows closed on the mountain that had borne witness to his lapse of either courage or stamina, which had resulted in his not being there to help Chris. If Chris could have been helped.

I decided to leave him out of it.

"One of them was Boots Bayleaf," I said.

She stared at me for a moment, then laughed. "That drunken geezer?"

"According to someone I spoke to, he's the best elf to have on a snow monster hunt."

"He didn't do my husband much good, did he?"

Unfortunately, I was unable to contradict her.

"Who was this other so-called witness?" Tiffany asked. "Nick, maybe?"

"I haven't said a word about this to Nick."

"Why not?" She studied me before a sly smile came over her. "Is the bride a little suspicious?"

"No," I bit out. "I was just trying to find out the truth, but you apparently don't want to know it."

"Three deaths." She held up three fingers. "Chris, Giblet, and Old Charlie. And believe me, there will be another. And if you keep poking around, it might be yours."

Was that a prediction or a threat? I got off the bed. "I don't know why I bothered," I said in disgust. "I felt sorry for you."

"Save your pity for yourself. I married a man who was killed. You married a man I wouldn't trust for all the gumdrops in Sugarplum Mountain."

As if she put any value on gumdrops. I doubted one had ever passed her lips.

"If you're determined to be wrong and miserable, I can't stop you," I said. "But at least let Christopher be free of your delusions. He's a happy kid, except his worries about you. He loves his family, but he wants more freedom, a life outside the castle. Don't you remember what that was like?"

She rose now, too, like a panther ready to pounce. "Don't I? You have no idea what my life was like—oh, sure, it was hard, but have you ever skated across the ice, twirling, leaping, with the eyes of an entire arena on you?"

"No, of course not."

"That's real freedom, but it only comes after laying the groundwork. After dedicating your life to an avocation and putting in the effort. That's the kind of freedom I want for my son, in whatever he chooses to do." She gave me a dismissive head-to-toe scowl. "You wouldn't know anything about it."

"All I'm saying is that Christopher deserves to cut loose a little, like a normal kid. And he wants to see you happy again, too."

She bit her lip, seeming to consider my words, but then her gaze hardened again. "Don't worry about Christopher and me. The happiest day of my life will be when he turns twenty-one and Nick has to step aside. *If* Nick makes it that long."

What was she implying? "Is that some sort of threat? Nick

is looking forward to that day, too." We'd talked about moving back to Oregon most of the year once his responsibilities here were over. It was still ten—now more like nine—years away.

"Nick can't get away with things forever."

Lucia was right. Crazy as a bedbug.

I left Tiffany in her Ice Capades museum of a room. In the hallway, my phone let out a "Fa-la-la-la" jangle in my pocket. I flipped it open and glanced at the screen. The preview of a new text message flashed:

**D. SPROAT: I WON'T FORGET THIS.**

I sank against the shiny gray wall and heaved a breath, letting the warm cello sounds floating down the corridor soothe my taut nerves. *Forget what?* What was Damaris fuming about now?

I'd just been thinking about retiring to Oregon as a light at the end of the snow tunnel. A text from Damaris Sproat was a timely reminder that there were crazy people everywhere.

I was punching in the first number of my PIN to phone my friend Claire when someone called out.

"Hey there!"

I looked down the long, dark hall. "Hello?"

No answer, although I thought I could hear the sounds of someone running. An elf, probably, hurrying about his or her business.

I glanced back down at my phone screen, which had gone black again. I pressed the start button and began keying in my PIN again.

"Hey there!"

The voice, enthusiastic and beckoning, drew me down the hallway, past the room where Christopher's music lesson was taking place. An irregular corner led to the front section of the castle on the right, and on the left it joined up with the Old Keep.

"Hey there!"

Of course the person shouting was in the Old Keep. I took a breath, walked cautiously to the old winding staircase foyer, and peered down.

Was someone trapped in the cellar? I couldn't see anyone. "Hello?"

I cautiously descended a few steps.

"Hey—!"

This time the shout was cut off, almost as if the person calling out had had a door slammed on them.

I hurried down and paused in the dank corridor to look around. I hadn't forgotten about the wooly rats. I whipped out my cell phone and turned on its flashlight, studying the narrow passage. There was a wine cellar down here, part of Jingles' bailiwick. All the rooms were locked, as far as I knew. But today one of the oak-and-iron doors stood slightly ajar. I eyed it anxiously.

"Hello?" I called out again.

No answer.

A cold knot formed in my chest, as if some unknown terror lurked on the other side of that door. *Don't be silly.* This wasn't Transylvania; it was Santa's castle at the North Pole. A few rodents were about all there was to be afraid of.

I straightened and walked toward the open door. If someone was in distress, I was doubly foolish for being afraid of my shadow. The door opened with a push—albeit also with an ominous creak—and I stepped inside.

The stone floor was so cold I could feel the chill through the soles of my shoes. My breath puffed in front of me in the illumination of the phone's light. And then I started to see the eyes.

Glassy eyes. Dead-looking stares. I turned in a circle; I was surrounded by faces. Bodies too, but it was the faces that leapt out at me—porcelain, plastic, wood, cloth—doll faces.

Scary old dolls in tattered dresses with outstretched arms and dead stares. Clown dolls that had probably launched a million nightmares and a couple of Stephen King books. A baby doll with a face painted as a Pierrot. Marionettes with rictus grins hanging from the ceiling. A Charlie McCarthy ventriloquist dummy lay in a box as if it were a coffin.

I forced myself to breathe. Dolls. Just dolls. Old, creepy dolls, but—

*Click, click, click*—

I barely had time to register the noise behind me, like a winch being turned. I pivoted just in time to see a man leaping out at me, holding a knife.

"Hey there!"

Shrieking, I dropped my phone and ran. Without a flashlight, I stumbled into a pile of what looked like knock-off Raggedy Anns with messy yarn hair. Scrambling, I got to my feet and shot toward the sliver of dim light coming through the door. I hurtled up the stairs, not even realizing I was still yelling until I plowed right into someone's chest.

It was Nick.

"Oh, thank goodness!" I threw my arms around him. "Someone tried to kill me."

His arms around me loosened and he drew back, studying my face. "Who?"

"That demon down there!"

His expression screwed up in disbelief. "Was it a person or an elf?"

"I don't know, but he had a knife!"

Nick let me go, turned, and took a step down. I gripped his shoulder to stop him. "Don't—he's deranged. Send Jingles."

Nick laughed. "I won't tell Jingles you volunteered him for demon slaying."

"I mean, send anybody else."

Christopher appeared at the top of the stairs next to his music tutor, Mr. Merriman. Merriman was a basketball-shaped elf in a dark green velvet suit and black booties with Pilgrim buckles. Thick spectacles perched over beady eyes.

"What's going on, Uncle Nick?" Christopher asked.

"April saw something down here."

"Can I go with you?" Christopher hopped down several stairs.

I stopped him with my outstretched arm. "Don't. There's a maniac down there. With a knife or something. He attacked me."

"Right here in the castle?" Mr. Merriman exclaimed. "Good heavens!"

Christopher ducked under my arm and ran down to join Nick. Groaning, I followed at a safe distance. Even more reluctantly, Mr. Merriman fell into line behind me, holding his cello bow in front of him like a sword. Much good it would do him against the knife-wielding fiend.

When we reached the door, there was more light coming from inside. Nick had found the bare bulb hanging from a ceiling timber and pulled the chain.

All the dolls were still staring at me. So was my would-be assassin.

Nick pivoted toward me. "Is this who jumped out at you?"

My attacker was a jack-in-the-box. A large one, but still . . . a toy. The papier-mâché head was attached to a narrow spring-loaded body. The toy wore a shiny jester's cap, and in his hand was a stick bearing a miniature copy of his head, also in motley. The knife that had terrified me.

My fear ebbed, quickly overwhelmed by a tide of embarrassment.

Christopher howled with laughter. "You were screaming bloody murder because of a jack-in-the-box?"

"It looked different in the dark," I said weakly. The light *had* been bad.

Even the cowardly cello instructor eyed me with equal parts pity and mirth.

"Hey, April," Christopher taunted. "Boo!"

He tossed an old troll doll at me and I caught it one-handed. Handball had given me good reflexes. If only it could have had lasting beneficial effects on my eyesight, or my courage.

Nick leveled a shaming stare at his nephew.

"What is this place?" I asked, before Nick could scold the kid for teasing me, which I richly deserved.

"It's rather creepy," Mr. Merriman said, shoving his glasses up his nose as he inspected the Pierrot baby doll I'd noticed before.

Super creepy. I was finally beginning to breathe easier and look around the room objectively. There were boxes piled up to the ceiling against one wall and other stacks of various heights elsewhere. Some boxes had been opened, some overturned. I saw a few dolls that looked as if they'd been shredded by an animal. Could rats do that?

"Why are all these dolls down here?" I asked.

"It's the doll cellar," Nick said. "Where the outdated ones are stored."

There were an awful lot of them. I wondered if selling them online would be permissible, although the postage cost from the North Pole alone might discourage buyers. Unless Nick could just toss them off his sleigh Christmas night, like Santa does in—

"Wait a second." I frowned. "So these toys are misfits?"

"I guess you could call them that," Nick said.

"So why not send them . . . ?"

Nick's eyes went wide—the facial equivalent of flapping

his hands in warning that I was about to say something very stupid.

Mr. Merriman, unfortunately, picked up on my unspoken blunder. "Good heavens, you aren't one of those people who think there's actually an Island of Misfit Toys!"

"It's like when I wanted to go to school at Hogwarts." Christopher bleated out a laugh. "Only I was eight."

My face burned. "Is it really so outlandish?"

The three of them exchanged anxious looks on my behalf, which was rich. I was living in a land so fantastical I couldn't even tell my best friend about it for fear she'd think I'd gone off my rocker, yet *I* was the crazy one for believing one little part of the Christmastown myth. Right.

"Toys are inanimate, April," Nick said.

*And reindeer are wild animals, and elves are tree-dwelling cookie bakers on TV commercials.*

Mr. Merriman nodded. "Nothing animated here except a jack-in-the-box."

As I leaned down to pick up my phone where I'd dropped it, I took another look at the creature who'd scared me so. He was silent now, as if to make my mistake seem all the more foolish. What, or who, had wound him up? "When I was upstairs, I heard the thing calling, 'Hey there!' at—well, not at me, obviously. I didn't know that at the time, though."

"That's what he's programmed to say," Nick said, not understanding.

"But why was he working five minutes ago but not now?"

"Maybe he has a wonky battery," Christopher said. "Sometimes I think one of my electronics has run down, but then I turn it on and it'll work for a minute."

Nick nodded, then raised a brow at me. *See?* his expression seemed to say. *Even an eleven-year-old has a more rational brain than yours.*

Would I sound paranoid if I mentioned the footsteps I'd heard from the hallway? Probably—I couldn't even say for sure where they'd come from. Even without jibbering about mysterious footsteps, I sensed that I'd already sunk a little in the estimation of the three people in the room.

"I don't really believe toys are alive," I insisted.

Christopher snorted. I so wanted to beg him not to tell Lucia about this. Martin, either. But of course he was going to tell both of them. He'd probably be spreading this tale all over the castle. What kid could resist?

Something in the corner caught my eye. One of those chalkboards on an easel had been set up—a long time ago, probably. Someone had drawn up two columns: "Naughty" and "Nice." I squinted, unable to make out everything in the shadowy light.

Bored now, the others headed for the door.

"You coming, April?" Nick asked.

"In a minute," I said. "I'll lock up when I'm done."

He looked perplexed. "I thought you'd want to get out of here."

"Yeah," Christopher said. "You were screaming so loud we thought somebody was killing you."

*So did I.*

"I'll just tidy up a bit," I said. "Hate to leave a room in disorder."

Christopher piped up with the enthusiasm of a kid who'd just figured out a legit way to skip out on schoolwork. "I can help."

"You've got another few bars of Bach to master, young man," Mr. Merriman said, pointing toward the door with his cello bow.

Dragging his feet, Christopher moaned, "Back to Bach." He laughed at his wordplay and followed his teacher.

Nick lingered with me. "What's caught your eye now?"

I turned on my phone light, aimed it at the blackboard, and then began to pick my way over to it. "Look at this."

| *Naughty:* | *Nice:* |
|---|---|
| *Chris* | |
| *Nick* | *Lucia* |
| *Amory* | |
| *Martin* | |

Though all the lettering had faded over time, I could still tell that Lucia's name, under "Nice," had been gone over several times to make it stand out.

"Not hard to guess who was playing Santa that day," Nick said.

I imagined a diminutive Lucia stuck inside on a blizzard day, coming down to this room to hide or just play by herself. Instead of reindeer, she would have been able to herd old dolls and boss them to her heart's content. Her captive audience.

"What's all this stuff being saved for?" I asked.

He shrugged. "It's just where overflow got shoved at one point, generations ago, and no one bothered to clear it out. Most families have a jumble closet or an overstuffed attic, don't they?"

"Not with creepy dolls and demonic jack-in-the-boxes."

Nick's reply was cut off by the ringing of his phone. "Nick Claus," he answered. As he listened, letting out a series of increasingly distressed grunts, I studied my nemesis, Mr. Jack-in-the-Box, with his frozen smile and his shiny cheeks. He was silent now, and still as stone. What had set him off?

Or who.

Nick hung up the phone, a worried look on his face.

"Trouble?" I asked.

"Someone at the Workshop warehouse misplaced a carton of Candyland."

"An emergency, then." Five-year-old me would have thought so, at least.

As we shut the door on the storage room, an ice rat skittered past and dived into a pile of boxes. I swallowed a shriek. Lucia's poison obviously hadn't worked.

I remembered the last time I'd run through this door screaming in terror. Nick had been right at the top of the stairwell.

"What were you doing here?" I asked as we climbed the stairs. "It seems a strange coincidence that we both happened to be in the Old Keep."

He smiled distractedly. "I was looking for you, actually. I thought I had an hour free, and hoped we might be able to have a little time together to grab a coffee or something."

"I was hoping that, too," I said. "I have something I want to talk to you about. It might not be something you want to go into, though." In fact, I knew it wasn't. Especially right now. Hard to discuss the details of a fateful snow monster hunt and his brother's death when his mind was occupied with Candyland.

"I'll see you at dinner," he said.

We went our separate ways. I was still mulling over all that had happened in the doll cellar. First the jack-in-the-box had frightened me, and I'd run out of the room and up the stairs and collided with Nick. Then Christopher and Mr. Merriman had appeared. They were just down an adjacent hall, so it made sense that they'd heard me yell.

Another person had been down that same hallway, too, and was bound to have heard me. Tiffany. But she hadn't come running, or even walking. Strange that she would be so incurious about shrieks of terror happening so close to her own bedroom, and so close to where her son was.

Unless she'd understood exactly what was going on down there.

# Chapter 16

The next time I went down into Christmastown for band rehearsal, I felt as if I were the most popular person in Santaland.

"Hey there!" people called out to me along the street.

Everyone seemed to be smiling at me. Smiles were contagious, and I grinned and waved back at them all. The good cheer felt like a promising change from the tension I'd sensed lately, especially from elves. Perhaps the march for Giblet didn't mean all of Christmastown would turn against the Clauses.

A snowman on the edge of a playground hailed me as I passed and nearly dislocated his midsection slipping down a snowbank. "Hey there."

Snowmen didn't usually waste their energy moving just to greet someone.

"Hello," I replied warily, though I tried to shake off the uneasy feeling. *Nothing weird about a snowman saying hello.*

The air of Christmastown was crisp and redolent with cinnamon, which wafted out of half the storefronts. Groups of young elves scampered and tumbled everywhere during morning recess from school, and a one-man band stood on the corner playing "Jingle Bells" with all the bells and whistles and drums at his command.

In the band hall, Smudge grinned at me as we were setting up the percussion. "Hey there!" he said brightly.

It all made sense then.

I dropped my triangle. "Very funny."

I'd underestimated the gossip grapevine. Word of my making a fool of myself had traveled faster than a reindeer relay, and now I was the grown woman who mistook jack-in-the-boxes for ax murderers and who learned geography from *Rudolph the Red-Nosed Reindeer.*

Never mind that there were red-nosed reindeer all around us. Oh no, *I* was the crazy one.

"Don't listen to them." Juniper sidled by me with her euphonium. "Everybody gets punchy in mid-December."

"December's a sort of catchall excuse around here," I grumbled.

"An excuse for what?" Martin asked, slipping between Juniper and me. He grinned. "Hey there."

"Not you, too." I leveled a withering stare on him. "We're relations. You're supposed to be on my side."

"I am, I am." He winked at Juniper. "Anyone in the family that makes me seem less like the family dunce has my eternal gratitude."

Juniper's mouth dropped open. "How can you say that!" Before I could thank her for sticking up for me, she finished in a rush, "No one would ever think *you* were a dunce, Martin."

I cleared my throat. Friendship versus Infatuation? Infatuation wins.

Martin laughed at my expression. "Thanks, Juniper. That's the nicest thing anyone's said to me in hours."

"I meant it. Everyone thinks you're clever."

Martin didn't seem to know what to do in the face of perfect sincerity and admiration. But I could tell he found it irresistible. Who wouldn't?

Luther Partridge tapped his baton on his stand, bringing

us to order. Martin scrambled over to his seat, and I scooted back to my position next to Smudge. "New love," he muttered in disgust.

I glanced over at him. "What are you talking about?"

He nodded between Martin and Juniper. "Those two."

"They barely know each other," I said.

"I think that's about to change."

*Huh.*

I would've liked to mull over the pros and cons of having the only real friend I'd made in Christmastown getting involved with my brother-in-law, but the rehearsal required most of my concentration. What with my investigative activities lately, and finalizing the Skate-a-Palooza schedule at last and posting it on the community hall bulletin board, I hadn't had time for practicing. And now in addition to all our Christmas songs we were going to play at the Peppermint Pond event, the band had decided to go forward with "Requiem for Giblet," which required crash cymbals and timpani, neither of which I'd had experience with. Given the ill feeling among many of the elves, I didn't want to be accused of not doing my best for the Giblet tribute.

After rehearsal, I hurried to gather my things.

"We Three Beans?" Juniper asked.

"Can't. I have to get back to the castle early today. It's croquembouche day."

"Oh." Juniper looked disappointed until Martin sauntered up with his sax case.

"Did someone mention coffee?" he asked.

"April can't go," Juniper said. "Your mother's giving her a baking lesson."

"I'm the pastry chef's helper," I reminded him.

"Just because April's playing Julia Child doesn't mean we can't get coffee," he told Juniper.

"Really?" Juniper asked, then tried to compose herself

into some semblance of cool disinterest. "I mean, I guess I have time for a cup."

"Good," Martin said. "Let's go."

Juniper sent me an ecstatic smile. "Sorry you can't come with us—enjoy your baking lesson!"

She was out the door like a shot.

Martin winked at me.

I didn't know what was more astonishing—the fact that the two of them were actually pairing off or that Smudge had realized which way the wind was blowing before I had.

Another blow to my self-confidence as an investigator.

Speaking of blows to self-confidence, I had to hurry to go meet my mother-in-law.

"It's not enough to be just a baker. You have to be an architect," said my mother-in-law as she filled round pastry puffs with rum-infused cream from a pastry bag.

We were wearing matching aprons proclaiming *Baking Spirits Bright!* across the front in glittery red and green letters. Matching, that is, except for the fact that hers was pristine and mine was spattered with egg yolk, batter, and cream. I wasn't completely hopeless in a kitchen—I'd fed guests at the Coast Inn for years. In the inn's guest book, someone had even written that my cloudberry blondies, my own recipe, were to die for. But the croquembouche was not just any normal dessert. It was a power tower of flour. We'd been baking cream puffs half the afternoon; the filled dough balls were the bricks that would create the castle Pamela was building.

Most croquembouches were pyramids of cream puffs made to look like a Christmas tree—or, for normal occasions, simply a pyramid shape. But Pamela's confectionary ambitions couldn't be limited to simple trees. The plans for the pastry replica of Kringle Castle covered in a dome of spun sugar had been rendered on the Plexiglas board, where the dessert would be constructed, although a paper copy of the blueprint had also been pinned to the kitchen wall for reference.

Turns out, it takes a lot of cream puffs to build a castle. Not to mention patience. We had plenty of the former, but my patience was in short supply. Especially when I realized the same Christmas music mix was cycling through for the third time. It was Pamela's, so very heavy on Johnny Mathis and novelty songs, which she seemed to think were chuckle worthy every time. At the third repetition of that Chipmunks song my temples began to throb.

"April, dear, you're sagging," Pamela said. "We still have puffs to stuff."

I got back with the program, though I couldn't help noticing that the dough balls were taking up most of the counter space in the castle's substantial kitchen. "This is going to be kind of big for a dessert, isn't it?"

Pamela, concentrating on her work, barely looked up. A stray lock of gray hair had escaped her bun, which was the most disheveled she'd ever allowed herself to appear in my presence. "It's not just dessert—"

"It's architecture," I finished for her. "I'm just curious how big a piece of real estate it's going to take up."

She gestured to that large piece of double-stacked Plexiglas on the kitchen island, dusted with powdered sugar. "It's going to be the centerpiece of the dining table for the All-Guild charity luncheon tomorrow. My dessert is always the highlight, and every year people look forward to what I'm going to come up with next."

I tried to concentrate on my work, but squirting cream into pastry puffs left too much of my brain free to think about other things. Like that chalkboard I'd seen in the basement. Something about it still niggled at me. The "Naughty" list, maybe. *Chris, Nick, Martin, Amory.*

*Amory.* What had he been doing on that list?

"Did Amory visit the castle much when Nick and the others were little?" I asked.

Pamela, concentrating on constructing a wall using rose water–flavored syrup as mortar, didn't look up. "He wasn't a visitor. He lived here."

This was a news flash to me. "The whole family used to live in the castle, you mean?"

"Not his family, just Amory. We don't talk about it much—unpleasant subjects are so, so . . ."

"Unpleasant?" I guessed.

In Pamela's lexicon, *unpleasant* was just about the worst thing you could say about something, or especially someone.

She lowered her voice. "Amory's parents died in an avalanche. They'd taken all the Claus children skiing up by the lodge. It was a miracle they weren't *all* killed. Lucia, the oldest, was looking after them all on the bunny slope, or whatever you call it, when the avalanche began a little farther up the mountain. Somehow she managed to keep a cool head and made the boys run to the side, out of its path. Apparently when most people see an avalanche, they try to out-ski it by going down the mountain, but Lucia's instincts kept all the children safe. Amory and Chris ended up under a little snow—just the fringes—but she dug them out. Unfortunately, no one could save Amory's parents."

"Poor Amory." To have seen what happened to his parents, and then to also have been there the day Chris met with his fatal accident. I believed Midge's account of his PTSD now.

"He coped very well, considering. For all his prickliness, he's very resilient and always has been."

Was he really?

I tried to imagine what that day must have been like for a group of children—watching a mass of snow coming down a mountain, crushing lives of adults they knew and loved, and almost killing them, too. Then the aftermath, trying to get help. And then discovering that Amory's parents couldn't be saved.

"We were happy to have Amory here with us," Pamela continued. "The house brimmed with life back then. You can imagine—three little boys."

"And Lucia."

Her brow furrowed. "Yes, and Lucia." She sighed. "I always wanted a little girl."

*But what I got was Lucia. . . .*

She didn't say it, but her thoughts rang out loud and clear.

"Lucia's a singular person," I said.

"Oh yes, I'll grant you that. And she was always her father's favorite. When she was little he'd always take her riding on his sleigh with him." She frowned. "I suppose that's when she developed her mania for reindeer."

Or when she decided she deserved to be Santa?

"Your husband must have been happy when Chris came along, though," I said.

"Oh yes—you couldn't ignore Chris. Everybody loved him." She shook her head, and tears trembled in her eyes.

Regret shot through me. "I'm sorry. I shouldn't have mentioned him."

"Don't be sorry," she said quickly. "So much of the time everyone's trying not to mention Chris, but I love to think about him. I crave it, in fact. Only . . . maybe not when I'm making the croquembouche."

She gave the pastry her undivided attention again.

I began to fear the thing would never be finished. Slowly but surely, though, progress was made. When Pamela stepped back, looking done, I wouldn't say the dessert resembled Kringle Castle in every detail, but it did look like a large building with a tower. Maybe that was the closest you could get by stacking cream puffs on top of each other.

"Looks great." I wasn't lying. Even if it wasn't photo perfect, it was impressive.

She gaped at me, aghast. "It's not finished! We've still got to do the most important part. Waldo, bring the dome!"

Did I mention preparation? As it turned out, what we'd been doing was the least of it. Pamela and Waldo had been dreaming up this confectionary tower since the year before, and now a special glass dome was wheeled into the kitchen.

"Wow," I said. "That'll fit over the castle perfectly." My gaze narrowed on the glass. "Although maybe we should clean it first. Something's smeared all over it."

"That's butter," Pamela said. "We're going to make *la cage.*"

I'd forgotten the spun-sugar cage—*la cage*— that was supposed to go over the final creation. Now I could barely suppress a groan. My feet were achy, and I longed to shower the flour coating off of me and scrub the sticky syrup off my hands.

My lack of enthusiasm wasn't lost on Pamela. "This is the best part—and it only takes a few minutes."

Right.

Actually, she was only off by an hour. By 6:00 p.m. we had drizzled the hot golden sugar over the buttered glass, let it harden, and then carefully—very carefully—pulled it up in one delicate piece and placed it over the cream-puff castle.

Now it looked impressive, like a shiny, lacy sugar web over the dessert. "I can't imagine actually eating this," I said. "It's so beautiful."

Not to mention, it had been so much work.

A sense of accomplishment filled me when I looked at that castle resting under its spun-sugar dome like a pastry snow globe. In spite of all the intense labor it required, I felt pretty proud of what we'd done today.

Pamela, who'd been pacing around her creation and inspecting it critically, finally allowed herself to look pleased. "Eating it's the best part, actually. You cut into the sugar cage, and it all crackles apart like shattering glass and the crunchy bits are caught by the sticky parts below."

Waldo and two of the castle's kitchen elves wheeled the confection away.

"They'll keep it in the walk-in freezer till tomorrow morning," Pamela explained. "Then it will be thawed out by luncheon."

"Smart." The castle "freezer" was a large storage room off the kitchen whose windows were kept cracked up. Keeping things frozen in Santaland was a low-tech affair.

"Now do you think you could make one next year on your own?" she asked me. At my horrified look, she laughed. "I was just ribbing you, April. Of course I know you couldn't. It takes years to master the croquembouche." She patted my arm. "But you've made a good start."

That was probably the most praise I was ever going to get from her. I decided to quit while I was ahead. "I need to clean up before dinner," I said after we'd tidied up most of our mess in the kitchen.

"Very well. Thank you for your help today," she trilled out to me politely as we parted ways in the hall. As if I'd merely dropped off a package or something. To me, exhausted and drooping, it felt as if we'd been through a war together. A croquembouche war.

I dragged back to Nick's and my room, ready to slip my tired feet into my soft lamb's wool slippers. It took my last ounce of effort to push open the heavy door and close it after me.

A figure on the bed caused me to gasp.

"What are you doing here?" I demanded.

Therese smiled at me. "Don't worry. I wasn't waiting for Nick. Just for you."

I rolled my eyes. As if I'd actually thought she and Nick would have a rendezvous in our bedroom. "How did you even get up here?"

She laughed. "I know this place better than you. I also know all the people who live here better than you do."

I crossed to the bellpull to summon Jingles or one of his helpers. I was too tired for this nonsense. "I get it. The detectives dismissed the malarkey you tried to whisper in their ears about me, so now you're trying to intimidate me this way. It's not working."

Therese lifted her head. "You can have me tossed out now, but you know I'll be back. Permanently, someday. Look at yourself." Her eyes traveled up my flour- and batter-coated person, and my ridiculous apron. "You're a mess."

"I just spent five hours in the kitchen with Pamela."

It was the wrong thing to say. Her face reddened. "It's croquembouche day. Do you know who's been helping her with that for the past three years?" Her tone of betrayal gave me a good guess. "Not Lucia," she said, "not Tiffany. *Me.* But did she even ask me this year?"

There was something wrong with this woman. I kept tugging the sash. *Hurry, Jingles.* "Therese, there's a whole world apart from this place. And there are millions of men besides Nick."

She jumped to her feet. "Then why didn't you take one of them? Why did you have to come here and steal him from me? All this was supposed to be mine!"

In a millisecond she was in front of me, her thin hands around my throat. I was so shocked I didn't know how to respond—and then I realized I couldn't respond even if I'd wanted to. My windpipe was squeezed shut by her long-nailed claws. Who knew she was so strong? My head grew woozy from both the pain and the increasing lack of oxygen.

*My god, I'm going to die right here in Kringle Castle.* Another

Santaland casualty. Would Jake Frost think Nick was responsible for this, too?

*Three deaths. . . . And believe me, there will be another.* Maybe this was what Tiffany had meant.

Seconds went by, maybe minutes. All I could see was Therese's face, then a moment of darkness, and then I was dropping to the hard stone floor. My vision came back just in time to witness Lucia hauling back and decking Therese with an uppercut to her jaw. The woman went down in a heap—much as I had. Only I was still conscious and Therese was out for the count.

Lucia towered over me. "Are you okay?"

Just then, Jingles skidded into the room. "What was all that ringing abou—" The last word morphed into a sharp intake of breath as he gawped at Therese lying there, and then at me. "Did you kill her?"

Lucia laughed. "Guess again. Therese almost killed April. Help me get April up. Then we need to call Constable Crinkles."

"No," I croaked.

Lucia looked at me as if Therese's choke hold had strangled my wits. "You'd let her get away with attempted murder?"

"I want to talk to Nick," I said.

"You think he'd be okay with someone trying to kill you?"

Jingles took my side. "It's to avoid a scandal," he explained to Lucia. "Think how this would look—two women catfighting over Santa in his bedchambers. During Christmas week, no less. Heaven knows there's enough talk already."

Lucia looked disgusted. "It looks bad because it *is* bad. Therese is a maniac."

"She's definitely disturbed," I said. "She needs help. She needs to get away from here."

"Yes," Jingles said, ringing the bell. "And right now *I* need help. How do we explain Therese being out like this?" Neither Lucia nor I had an answer. After a moment of thought, he answered his own question. "We could tell the rest of the staff that Therese ate something that didn't agree with her."

Lucia was skeptical. "And how do we explain away the welts around April's neck? 'Therese ate a bad clam' isn't going to cut it."

We debated different lies we could tell, and then settled on saying nothing. I would wear turtlenecks until the red marks calmed down.

I was in the en suite washroom while Jingles and his helpers finally hauled Therese away.

Lucia knocked when they were gone. "Coast is clear."

I came out. I'd jumped in the shower and was wearing my robe and slippers. It would have been bliss except for the fact that it felt as if someone had stomped on my neck with a work boot.

I sank onto the bed and looked up at my sister-in-law. "Thank you for saving my life."

She shrugged modestly. "It was nothing."

"I'm not the only one in Santaland who owes my life to you, I've heard."

Her expression grew wary.

"The avalanche," I prompted.

"Oh, that." She said it as if it were nothing. "People say I did something great back then, but I was just the oldest left in charge of the kids. When the avalanche happened, my instincts were to run."

"You ran in the correct direction."

"That was just luck. It wasn't as if I'd devised a survival plan. Mostly, I was thinking about saving my own skin."

"You protected them all."

"Well, they were littler and cuter then—even Amory."

"So Amory lived here through most of his childhood?"

"Yeah, he was a little twit sometimes—still is—but he was okay. All of them were."

"That's not what you thought when you were a kid, though, was it?"

Her eyes narrowed. "What are you talking about?"

"I saw a little chalkboard on an easel downstairs in the doll cellar. You'd written two columns—'Naughty' and 'Nice.' Chris, Nick, Martin, and Amory were all listed as naughty."

Her breath caught. "I'd forgotten all about that chalkboard. I used to try to teach the dolls about hockey plays."

I laughed. "I'd imagined you trying to teach them how to read."

"So how did you know it was me?" she asked.

"Yours was the only name under 'Nice.' I figure it had to be you."

She frowned. "Weird. I don't remember doing anything like that."

"Go look—it's still down there. You'd probably recognize your handwriting."

She shook her head. "That wouldn't prove anything. We were all forgers."

"What?"

"We thought it was hilarious to copy our dad's handwriting and leave 'Naughty' and 'Nice' lists that we'd made up on his desk. Then we started doing it to each other—copying out homework assignments badly to get one of the others in trouble with our tutors. One time Chris wrote a story about a kid poisoning an English tutor and signed Martin's name. Martin was furious."

"Did Nick do this, too?"

"Oh sure. He was the most serious of us, but even he indulged in hijinks every once in a while." She tilted her head. "Why do you ask?"

"Just curious."

"You could talk to Nick about it, you know."

As if he didn't have enough troubles.

"Talk about what?" Nick asked from the doorway.

Lucia and I turned.

He was standing in the doorway, looking at us with concern. "What do we have to talk about?" he asked.

Lucia and I exchanged glances; hers was apologetic.

"For one thing," she said, "you need to talk to April about Therese. That crazy woman attacked April right here. Nearly strangled her—look."

She pointed to my neck.

Whatever Nick had been feeling about my discussing our marriage with his sister, it changed now as he looked at the angry red marks on my neck.

"Therese did this?"

I nodded.

"April wouldn't let me call Crinkles. I still can't figure out why. Therese is a menace. April was about to lose consciousness when I found them."

"Thank heavens you came in when you did," he said.

He put his arms around me, and I leaned into him. Despite months of eggnog and carbs, he was no less in shape than he was last summer. I breathed in the evergreen scent of his aftershave and a rush of reassurance flowed through me. I really was safe now.

Lucia backed toward the door. "If Therese had tried to strangle me, I wouldn't want her running loose in Santaland, waiting to ambush me again. But hey—maybe that's just me. I'd prefer not to be murdered."

After she was gone, I looked up at Nick. His face was drawn with worry.

"You need to get Therese help, Nick. She's miserable here. Send her south; give her a new start. Most of all, get her counseling."

He nodded. "This place seems to be hard on people when they're alone."

"Don't I know it," I said.

He drew back, surprised.

Why had I said that, and in that sarcastic tone of mine? "In the U.S. we have football widows. I feel a little like a Christmas widow some days. I know you've been busy. I understand that. I'm just trying to navigate a new world here."

"You're doing fine," he said. "Has anyone said anything to you?"

"Not really." I laughed. "Aside from your mom. I spent the afternoon with her. Baking and supposedly bonding, although I'm afraid we might be immiscible, like oil and water. But we did get the croquembouche done."

"Anyway, better that you're baking instead of carrying on some half-baked investigation."

"Half-baked?" I swelled in offense until a vision of myself running in terror from a jack-in-the-box flashed in my mind. Don Knotts, detective.

"Let's make a deal," Nick said. "I'll talk to Therese tonight if you promise just to drop your snooping. Things are bad enough without having to worry about you chasing a murderer—and, worse, a murder catching on to what you're up to."

I felt the sore ring around my neck from where Therese had tried to strangle me. He was right. I'd almost been killed—and I didn't even think Therese was the one who'd been causing mayhem in Christmastown. The real killer might be more effective at eliminating me. And poor Nick was supposed to be acting his jolliest while I interrogated everyone who'd talk to me. Even him. I just couldn't bring myself to try to bring up the snow monster hunt with him. He had too much to worry about already.

I had so much to do in the coming days that I wouldn't

have time to put much thought into who killed Giblet Hollyberry and Old Charlie.

Besides, Jake Frost was on the case.

"Okay," I said. "I'll leave the investigation to the detective for a while."

And I meant it.

Honestly, I did.

# Chapter 17

The evening after my husband's ex-not-really-a-girlfriend's attempt to kill me, I tried to resume normal life. Nick slipped out to talk to Therese, while I played a game of Scrabble with Martin and Christopher. As usual, I got trounced by Zs and Xs on Triple Letter Scores. After that, I took myself off to bed. I might even have nodded off for an hour or so.

But when I woke up, Nick wasn't there next to me. The last time I'd awakened in the middle of the night and found Nick's side of the bed empty had been right before they discovered Giblet dead in his cottage.

*A sampling of two is not a pattern*, my brain told me. Nick was probably in his office, catching up on work. I could get up and check.

But if I checked, it would look as if I didn't trust him. I did trust him. Therese, on the other hand . . .

He probably wasn't even with Therese at all. Maybe he'd fallen asleep reading in his study.

Right.

The point was, I just didn't know where he was. And if there's one thing that drives me crazy, it's not knowing.

I sat up. If I wanted to find out whether Nick was in his office, I should just go look. A good spouse would tell him to come to bed and get some sleep. Or, if he insisted on working, I could fix him some hot spiced tea.

I rose, shrugged on my robe, and headed down to his office. There was enough glow from the lights strung along the hallways to feel comfortable strolling around. Nick's office, however, was dark. I turned on the ceiling lights just long enough to confirm he hadn't fallen asleep at his desk.

So much for bringing hot beverages to my workaholic husband. Now I felt I needed something myself.

There were no strings of lights in the cavernous kitchen, and I didn't see a light switch. I crossed the room and bumped into the butcher-block island.

Strange. I'd never been in the kitchen when it was empty. In fact, I rarely was in it at all. In just a few months I'd become so used to being waited on that I no longer knew my way around my own kitchen. I'd never lived in a place where I couldn't even find a box of tea bags. Cupboard after cupboard revealed practically any ingredient or gadget a person could hope to find in a kitchen. Except a simple tea bag.

I pushed through a pair of thick swinging doors and entered a frigid room that had me pulling my robe more tightly around me. This insulated room served as the walk-in freezer. I gave the swinging doors another look to make certain there was no way to get locked in. There wasn't, at least not that I could see.

Squinting, I scanned the shelves. All manner of dairy was kept here—butter and ice cream—anything needing to be preserved that could be frozen, and things I wouldn't have expected, like bread. The castle made fresh bread several times a week, and yet they had a shelf of loaves right here, pre-made.

I was studying an adjacent shelf when I heard a scream.

Where had the sound come from? I was disorientated. I couldn't say for sure if the scream had been outside or inside the castle.

More important, *who* screamed? Or had it been an animal?

There was a window high on the wall, and I scrambled up on a worktable to get on my tiptoes and look out. I suspected the sound came from outside. But when I peered out, I could see nothing but the lit trees and ice sculptures that dotted the grounds. Nor could I detect any telltale footsteps in the snow.

A banging noise sounded in the next room. Someone was running—loudly, clumsily—almost as if they were fleeing. Trying to escape. But they weren't familiar with the kitchen, either. Another crash made my heart leap a foot in my chest. I could hardly hear for the rushing of my pulse in my ears. Who was out there?

Whoever it was, they were coming closer. I grabbed the first object I could find, what looked like a frozen pheasant, and gripped it like a baseball bat. I wasn't sure how much damage frozen poultry could do against a panicked assailant, but it felt better than nothing.

I had just enough time to position myself, Babe Ruth–style, when the doors swung open with a crash. I yelled, and so did the huge flashing thing that came after me.

Quasar and I were both braying at each other, shock in our eyes. He dug in his front hooves and then hopped back awkwardly, mirroring my own reaction. A split second later, the sound of glass shattering filled the room. I almost yelled at him to be careful, but I caught myself. Now was not the time to point out that he might have broken Claus heirloom crystal. He was already one freaked-out reindeer. His one remaining antler made him look even more distressed and off-balance. His nose fizzled once and then went out, as if his nerves had drained all the power out of him.

"D-did you hear the scream?" He was screaming himself. "I bet it was Lucia!"

I only had to think about it for a moment. "It couldn't have been her. Too high-pitched."

"But she isn't in our room. Where is she?"

Quasar looked as if he might burst into tears. Could reindeer cry? I patted the thick fur on his neck and did my best to calm him down. "Maybe it was just an animal outside."

His lopsided head waggled. "I-I don't know."

"What is this racket?" Jingles yelled, pushing through the doors. He stopped, arms akimbo, dressed in a calf-length flannel nightshirt, pointed-toe booties, and a long candy-striped-pattern nightcap with a fluffy green pom-pom at the tip. "Do you two want to wake up the entire castle?"

"Quasar and I heard a woman screaming. Or maybe it was an animal."

"Lucia might be in trouble!" Quasar insisted.

"No one would touch Lucia," Jingles said. "Not without getting hurt plenty in return."

No doubt we were both remembering how she'd dealt with Therese.

"Maybe it had something to do with what happened this afternoon," I said.

"Therese, you mean?" Jingles sounded skeptical. "Why would *she* be screaming?"

I didn't want to tell him that Nick had gone off to talk to her and had never come back. I didn't want to drag Nick into this at all.

"We sh-shouldn't be talking. We should be looking!"

For once I agreed with Quasar, and so, to his obvious astonishment, did Jingles. "Right," he said. "Let's split up and search to see if we can find what happened." He looked at the reindeer. "Quasar, go outside, circle round the grounds, and report back if you see anything. April and I will look in all the rooms to make sure everyone's where they should be."

I knew at least one person who wasn't where he should be, but I said nothing for the moment. I couldn't decide how to shield Nick from suspicion . . . or if I should.

Quasar was reluctant to go outside, so I convinced Jingles I could look after the inside if he accompanied Quasar investigating the perimeter of the house. After Jingles went to slip on his coat and snow boots, I returned to the living quarters of the house.

Now I wouldn't have to make excuses for why Nick was not in our bedroom and, as far as I knew, was still absent from the castle entirely. I checked our bedroom again—he was still gone—and then made my way to the west wing. Christopher was sound asleep, and when I peeked into Tiffany's room she was also in bed. One floor up, Pamela was flat on her back wearing both a satin sleeping mask and a nightcap, and some sort of earphones over her ears. No mystery why she wouldn't have heard anything.

As I was sneaking back out of her room, Martin opened his bedroom door across the hall. He was wearing his robe and slippers, and his hair was pushed every which way, as if he'd been tossing and turning all night. He squinted at me through bleary eyes. "What are you doing?"

I finished closing Pamela's door as quietly as I could. "Quasar and I thought we heard someone screaming."

He frowned. "You two staying up all night together now?"

"No . . . well, it's a long story. I just wanted to check on everyone."

"*I* didn't scream," he said. "Though I might if I can't get back to sleep."

"I'm sorry. I just need to check on Lucia and I'll be out of your hallway."

He drew back, puzzled. "You think Lucia's running around the castle shrieking in the middle of the night?"

"Quasar said she wasn't in their room."

Curious now, he led the way down to the end of the corridor. The minute he opened the door to Lucia's room, the earthy scent of hay wafted out at us. There was a trodden-down pile of it in the corner—where Quasar bedded down, I presumed. The nearby four-poster was conspicuously empty, although the covers were pulled back. She'd at least made the attempt to sleep there tonight.

We proceeded to check every room in the castle from top to bottom. I peeked into the servants' quarters, counting the sleeping elves. I even braved going back down to the doll cellar. Nothing.

"Maybe Quasar's right to be worried," I said.

Martin shook his head. "Lucia's okay. She's probably got a perfectly good explanation for that noise, and it won't be what you think. It never is."

I bit my lip. Should I wake up more of the staff and organize a search party? Should I call Constable Crinkles?

"Besides Lucia, is everyone else in the castle accounted for?" Martin asked.

"Yes," I lied.

"Good. I can go back to bed, then. Good night."

Before he could leave, I hooked his arm. "Wait. Maybe Quasar and Jingles found something outside. Don't you want to find out?"

He arched a brow. "You sent that dynamic duo to do the outside check? Now I'm curious."

We all congregated back in the kitchen.

"Nothing," Jingles declared of the search outside. "At least nothing that we could find that looked lethal. There were some footprints and odd paw prints in the snow."

"Odd, how?"

"Too big to belong to a snowshoe hare or a rodent, too small to be reindeer. Whatever it was made Quasar jumpy, though."

"I-I wasn't scared," the reindeer insisted.

I remembered Starla Winters. "Could it have been a wolf?"

Quasar choked, then made a reflexive hacking sound. Guess he didn't like wolves.

"That wasn't a wolf howl I heard, though," I said.

Jingles tilted his head. "But if a wolf got hold of someone and was killing it—"

"Good grief!" Martin said. "Could you two be any more gruesome?"

I shook my head. "If a wolf had attacked someone right outside the house, I'm sure it would have sounded different. And there would be evidence." Bowing to Martin's sudden sensitivity, I didn't say the word *blood*.

"Is there a snowman nearby?" Martin asked. "Maybe he could have seen something."

Quasar shook his head. "No snowmen at the moment. All the ones who'd been on castle grounds retreated after what happened to Old Charlie."

Though it showed a lack of faith in the Claus family, who could blame the snowmen for decamping into the forest? They felt vulnerable. Any maniac with a blowtorch could reduce them to a puddle in nothing flat. And Nick was the only suspect anyone had spoken of.

Just then, Lucia sauntered in through the back door into the kitchen. "What is this?" She pulled off her hat and gloves. "The midnight snack club?"

"Where have you been?" I asked.

"Out for a stroll. Is that a crime?" Nonchalantly, she extended a long arm over to a bowl of fruit, picked out an apple, and crunched into it. Her parka puffed her up to twice her bulk, but she was still so tall and lean, it didn't seem to matter. She was the only person I knew who looked svelte in a puffer coat.

"We heard a scream," Quasar said. "I was worried."

"Aw, I'm sorry," she said, chewing. "I just got restless and wanted to stretch my legs."

I had a hard time believing her. "You were out there and you didn't hear anything?"

Her eyes widened. "Not a thing. Sure you weren't just dreaming?"

"I was awake."

"A-and I heard it, too," Quasar said.

Martin frowned, then looked down, crooking his ankle to inspect the bottom of his slipper. "What's this sticky stuff on the floor?"

I remembered the sound of the glass shattering after Quasar and I had surprised each other. "Something broke in the freezer room. Be careful where you step."

"Broke?" Jingles' eyes bulged in alarm. "What broke?"

He pushed through the swinging doors into the freezer room, flipped the light switch, and let out a yelp. He nearly flattened us coming right back out again just as we were going in. It felt like we were all in a Three Stooges sketch.

"We're dead," Jingles declared. "We might as well toss ourselves off Calling Bird Cliff."

"What are you jibbering about?" Martin asked. "Who'll notice something broken in this place?"

"Amen," Lucia agreed. "This castle has more glassware than Santaland has snowflakes."

Jingles shook his head frantically. "It's not glass. It's the croquembouche."

Frozen, we exchanged shocked glances. Then, as one, we stampeded through the doors. And skidded to an abrupt halt.

It was a tragic sight. Pamela's beloved *cage* had shattered into a thousand sugary shards. The castle itself hadn't fared much better. The half closest to us was squished, with the crushed cream puffs creating a gloopy mess. The remaining walls and the tower leaned precariously.

"Judas Priest!" Lucia cried.

"What happened?" Jingles asked.

"I startled Quasar earlier and he lurched backward," I said. "He must have fallen on the croquembouche."

"Sat on it, you mean," Jingles said.

This was a disaster. Come morning, someone was going to have to break the news to Pamela, and I did not want to be that someone.

None of us did.

"I'm going back to bed," Martin and Lucia said in unison.

"Cowards." I rounded on them. "You can't run out on us now. We have to try to fix this."

Martin's laugh contained a hysterical edge. "Fix it how? The dessert has been crushed by a four-hundred-pound reindeer's butt. There's no coming back from that."

For once, Lucia agreed with her brother. "Especially if you're a pastry."

"I didn't mean to," Quasar said.

"No one's blaming you," Lucia said.

"*I* am," Jingles said.

I leveled a stern look on him. "It was an accident. No one did this maliciously."

"I don't understand," Quasar said. "Can't we still eat it?"

We gaped at him, and he understood. "Humans sure are f-finicky."

"So are elfmen—or at least this one is," Jingles said. "What's more, I value my life. I say we dispose of the whole mess, break a windowpane, and announce that there was a robbery."

A cowardly plan, but I couldn't deny its appeal.

"A croquembouche thief?" Lucia shook her head. "That's a new one."

"So's a serial killer in Christmastown," I said, "but we have one of those."

Jingles snapped his fingers and looked at me. "You helped Pamela make the croquembouche. Maybe you can repair it."

I thought of the hours of labor that went into constructing

that elaborate dessert and then looked at the heap on the floor. "The key word is *help*. I didn't do it myself."

"You don't have to do it all yourself now," Jingles said. "At least, not from scratch. You just have to fix it."

How?

"It wouldn't look the same. Pamela would know right away."

Martin shook his head at me. "You're selling yourself short. I bet you could fix this, April. Why not try? It's better than the fictitious dessert thief idea."

I wasn't so sure about that, but I was inclined to at least give it a shot. What could it hurt? If we announced to Pamela that her greatest creation had been sat on by Quasar, there was a chance Quasar would be diced into reindeer jerky. "All right," I said, not without reluctance. "But I'll need assistance."

Quasar offered. The poor animal wanted to make amends, but I told him he should get some rest. Mostly, I wanted him as far from the kitchen as possible. The last thing we needed was another accident. Jingles stayed with me. He at least seemed to know the rudiments of creating this dessert. The first order of business was to make more of the puffs. When we were opening up the pantry and checking that we had everything we needed, I found a covered bowl with a sticky note on it that read *Leftover Custard*.

I could have cried with happiness. "It's like yesterday's sent me a gift."

"I wish yesterday could drag me back an hour and tell me *not* to try to find out what that scream was," Jingles grumbled. "I'd still be in bed asleep right now."

I wouldn't have minded being in bed, either. But I still wanted to know who had screamed. I'd heard it, as had Quasar. Jingles too. The reindeer had been in Lucia's room at the end of the hall above, nearest the kitchen, where I was at the time. Jingles' quarters were down the corridor past the kitchen. The scream had sounded loud—to me. But perhaps the reason for that was the location of the person making the noise. It had to be close to the kitchen.

Jingles and I were making more *pâte à choux* for the cream puffs. To achieve a light, fluffy result required arm-tiring labor, especially beating egg yolks by hand into the thick dough. We were too chicken to turn on the industrial mixer, which made enough noise to raise the dead.

While the puffs were baking, I prepared caramel for the "mortar." I burned the first batch into crystallized sludge and had to start over. And then Jingles and I started making a new *cage*.

When we finally had everything ready to start the renovation of the crushed castle, it was already getting quite late . . . or early, depending on your perspective. We had to rush to assemble everything before the kitchen elves came down. Jingles had done a fairly good job of cleaning and salvage: The Plexiglas had been wiped clean, the crushed puffs cleared away, and as many shards of the shattered sugar *cage* picked out as he could manage. It was a real Cinderella-with-the-lentils kind of task, but he'd managed to get almost all of them.

Much of Pamela's blueprint—the one she'd drawn in icing sugar on the Plexiglas—was now gone. We had to improvise, and while our results weren't perfect, they weren't terrible. Jingles did a good job remembering which details of the castle Pamela had tried to replicate in dough. When we were done, we both stood back, bleary-eyed, and tried to study our presentation objectively.

"She'll never notice," Jingles predicted.

"Let's hope."

We hauled the croquembouche into the freezer and took ourselves off to our respective rooms. The still-empty bed gave my heart a jolt. All the frenzy over the croquembouche had driven worries about my wandering husband temporarily out of my head. At the sight of his unslept-on side, the worries came roaring back.

I crawled into bed, looked at the time—4:36 a.m.—and wondered where Nick had gone. And what this meant. He'd gone to talk to Therese. *And that took all night?* My thoughts churned. I'd never be able to get to sleep. Which made me angst more. Tomorrow evening was the Peppermint Pond Skate-a-Palooza . . . not to mention the elf march. It was sure to be a long day, and even longer if I was exhausted.

But somehow I managed to nod off.

In my dreams, I was back home in Oregon, stringing lights everywhere. Brilliant electric streaks flew out of my fingertips, as if I were a sorceress. I strew lights all over my house and then proceeded to do up the whole town. When I finished, Cloudberry Bay was gorgeous. Everyone hailed me as a genius. Even Damaris had to concede to my decorative superiority. If Christmas spirit was a competition, I'd trounced her.

*"I'm no genius,"* I said with elaborate modesty. *"I'm just Mrs. Claus."*

Someone was pushing me. Shoving my arm.

"Stop!"

"April!" Jingles' voice was pure distress. "Get up. Please, you *must* wake up."

I forced one eye open, and it felt as if my eyelid were being raked across sandpaper. A blurry Jingles loomed right over me, his expression frantic.

"Mrs. Claus—the dowager Mrs. Claus—is threatening to fire all my people. She thinks *they* messed up the croquembouche!"

So much for fooling Pamela. I was dead tired and, come to find out, staying up to almost five had done us no good whatsoever. "She must have sniffed us out right away."

"Something . . . happened to it," Jingles said, his expression twisting as though he was recalling a horror, "and now she's blaming Waldo!"

"You should tell her the truth." But even as I said the words, I realized how weaselly they sounded. Jingles wouldn't think it was his place to rat me or Quasar out to Pamela. The responsibility for preventing Waldo and the others from bearing the brunt of Pamela's indignation was mine alone.

I got up, put on my robe and slippers, and followed Jingles down to the kitchen.

Poor Waldo. He was standing at attention, practically quivering yet trying to remain calm in the face of accusations of pastry demolition and counterfeiting. The rest of the kitchen elves were upset and showed various expressions of disbelief, dismay, and even resentment.

As I arrived through one door, Nick appeared from the outside door. He was wearing his scarlet coat and matching hat, but that was the brightest thing about him. His face looked drawn, tired, and strangely dark. "What's going on here?" he asked.

Everyone turned to him for justice, speaking at once.

Pamela's voice carried better than anyone's: "This elf destroyed my croquembouche and tried to pass a sham off as mine!"

"Santa, I swear I had nothing to do with this! I left Mrs. Claus's—the dowager Mrs. Claus's—croquembouche right there in the freezer. It was straight and beautiful!"

I stepped forward and took a good gander at the rebuilt croquembouche. In the cold light of day it resembled Pamela's fanciful creation about as much as a log cabin resembled Versailles. The walls—I could have sworn they'd been perfectly straight last night—now slanted at odd angles, and bits of the tower had plopped down into the icing sugar snow overnight. What had gone wrong? Had someone sabotaged my fix? Then I remembered the difficulty we'd had with the caramel burning. I'd been overly cautious with the second batch—it had been rather runny. Maybe too runny to cement my cream puffs into place. Also, *la cage* lacked the lacy delicacy of Pamela's original, so it did little to mask the disaster happening below.

I cleared my throat. "It wasn't Waldo or any of the kitchen elves," I said, projecting loud enough to be heard above the din. "It was me. I did it."

All eyes were on me now, including Pamela's shocked, outraged gaze and Nick's disappointed one.

*"You?"* Betrayal mingled with indignation in my mother-in-law's voice. "Why would you destroy what I tried so hard to teach you to make?"

"I didn't destroy it. That is, I didn't mean to." This was tricky, because I definitely didn't want to get Quasar in trouble with Pamela. "There was an accident. Something must have fallen, because the croquembouche cage had collapsed in the middle of the night. So I attempted to fix it."

Pamela aimed a skeptical gaze at my efforts. "And you couldn't do any better than *this*? After all I taught you?"

"I guess I don't have your talent," I said. "So you see, it's nothing to do with Waldo or anyone else." I turned to the kitchen elves. "I'm so sorry. I went to bed last night after fixing the mess . . . or thinking I'd fixed it. I never dreamed anyone would be blamed for my shoddy pastry repair."

They all nodded—even Waldo—though I'm not sure they were entirely appeased. It's a horrible thing to be falsely accused. And, looking at the situation from Pamela's perspective, it was also terrible to have lovingly labored over the creation of something wonderful and then see your work destroyed, or at least diminished.

"I can't apologize enough, Pamela. I should have told you what had happened, but it was the middle of the night and I was just focused on trying to make things right. Instead, I just seem to have compounded the wrong."

She was somewhat mollified . . . but only somewhat.

"I'd like to make this right," I said. "I know the party is this afternoon. . . ."

She gave her head a mournful shake. "I don't see *how* you can make this right. There's no time to make another croquembouche."

I grasped frantically for a solution, or at least a peace offering. Finally, I thought of something.

"I can make a mean cloudberry blondie," I said.

# Chapter 18

"What happened last night?"

Though he tried not to show it, I could tell Nick was irritated. We'd escaped the others and were closeted in his office. I sagged into an overstuffed chair, trying not to feel annoyed that he blamed me for something that wasn't my fault. Not entirely, anyway.

"Quasar sat on the croquembouche. It was an accident. I just couldn't tell Pamela that or she'd be serving reindeer flambé to her guests this afternoon. We tried to repair it, but it didn't quite work out—"

"And you let the elves take the blame."

"No—I stepped in as soon as I heard what was happening. Unfortunately, I overslept. I didn't get to sleep until almost five." I crossed my arms. "Although I assume I got more sleep than you managed."

"You assume right."

I was glad to turn this conversation smack around where it belonged, focused on Nick's actions, not mine. "I only went down to the kitchen because I was looking for you. I thought you were in here, so I was going to bring you some tea."

"That would've been nice. I could have used some hot tea last night."

"Why? Therese doesn't do tea?"

He blinked at me, confused.

"The last time I saw you, Nick, you were off to give Therese a talking-to. Is telling your old girlfriend not to attempt to kill your wife an all-night activity?"

His expression turned from confusion to astonishment. "You think I was with Therese all this time?"

"I don't know. You certainly weren't in bed."

"Because I was at a fire. One of the cottages in Tinkertown burned down. A family of six."

"Oh." Shame filled me, especially when I remembered how tired Nick had looked when he came in. "Do they need a place to stay? There's plenty of room here."

He shrugged. "They're living with relatives until they can rebuild."

"You were fighting the fire?"

"I pitched in."

"I'm sorry." I seemed to be apologizing to everyone this morning. "I didn't know."

"I should have sent word to you," he admitted. "But it was the middle of the night. I assumed you were asleep."

"It was hard to sleep last night. At least for some of us." Most of his family seemed to have managed pretty well. "While I was downstairs, I heard a scream—it might've been a woman, I thought. Quasar thought so, too. That's why he got so nervous. He worried it was Lucia."

Nick frowned. "Was it?"

I shook my head. "She came sauntering in from outside, later, after we'd already checked every room in the castle."

"You mean you went around the castle doing a bed check?"

"I had to. What if it was somehow connected to—"

Too late, I noticed his face darken and I remembered I'd promised to leave off investigating. "Just because I'm not trying to solve Giblet's murder doesn't mean I shouldn't look into suspicious things happening around me. Therese tried to kill me yesterday afternoon. What if that scream was actually the sound of someone else being attacked?"

"It was probably just an owl or something."

"Maybe." But I had my doubts.

"At any rate, there's nothing we can do about it now." He leaned back, shaking his head. "Spiders, mysterious screams, people attacking each other. I swear to you, April, this was a peaceful place before you got here."

"You think I brought chaos with me?"

He laughed. "No, but I don't want you to think I was selling you a bill of goods when I told you what a wonderful place Santaland was."

"It *is* wonderful. Cold and slightly homicidally inclined at the moment, but wonderful."

"I think I'd go mad if all this was going on and you weren't here with me."

I tilted my head. "Even if I am the croquembouche destroyer?"

"I tried to tell Mother how good those blondies were."

Despite my offer of cloudberry blondies, Pamela and the elves had opted to make a sheet cake. Without my assistance. After all that had happened, I couldn't really blame her. I wasn't a great pastry chef's assistant, and bars weren't really fancy luncheon fare.

But Nick had sampled the blondies in Cloudberry Bay, when he was a guest at the Coast Inn. The memory of those summer days washed over me like a balm. Our gazes met and held, and I felt my heart swell a few sizes. Would we ever get back to that intimate, carefree feeling we'd had last summer?

"I wish I had time to catch a few Z's now," he said.

I wouldn't have objected to crawling back into bed, either,

though I don't know how much sleep either of us would have gotten.

"You should try to nap at some point," I said. "Right now, I need to get to town to start preparations for Skate-a-Palooza."

He straightened stalwartly. "You're right. Christmas week."

"How's your Podgy Pooper problem coming along?"

"Pudgy Puppers," he corrected. "They upped production at the Workshop. I think we'll be fine. But you know. No rest in December."

This was practically the winter mantra of the Clauses: *no rest in December.* I wondered if wives of guys with firework stands felt about July the way I was beginning to feel about December.

"I need to go check to see how the decorations down at the pond are coming along." I was halfway to the door before I turned and asked, "What *did* you say to Therese?"

"I asked her not to attempt to murder you again."

I smiled. "I appreciate that."

"Figured you would. And then we discussed perhaps sending her to live somewhere else for a while. She said she wouldn't mind going to Arizona."

*Arizona!* "That's quite a change. Not that I'm complaining." Anywhere far away would do.

"She said she wants to live somewhere completely different."

"I suppose she expects the Clauses to bankroll her."

"She's not asking for much. I'm inclined to give her what she needs to resettle."

Of course. Nick would give people the Santa suit off his back.

We parted ways as if it were just another morning . . .

instead of the start of what would be an extraordinarily awful day for the Claus family.

I changed clothes and went down to the park, intending to oversee things for about an hour or so. As soon as I got there, I was beset by problems. The temporary bandstand was still unfinished, so that the elves hammering and the elves in charge of decorations were clashing. I suggested the decorator elves let the construction people finish, then despaired as the construction elves took a long lunch. Musicians arrived early, adding to the pileup. I couldn't speak for anyone else, but having a little girl warming up her "I Saw Mommy Kissing Santa Claus" while hammers pounded wasn't putting me in the Christmas spirit.

Meanwhile, Gert's Pretzels and Hoppie's Hot Drinks argued over the placement of their stalls.

"Gert's has had this spot for three generations," Gert said.

Hoppie was having none of it. "How can that be? You're Gert and you're only thirty-two."

Hands on her hips, she stood inches away from him, red-faced. "My grandmother was Gert, too, and my mother should have been called Gert, but she changed her name to Rainbow because she was a hippie. But it's the same stall and you know it, and it's always been *right there*, by the entrance to Peppermint Pond."

I was supposed to be mediating, but for a moment I was too distracted. "There were hippies in Christmastown?" Somehow all this snow didn't seem conducive to Summer of Love type situations.

"Not many," Gert admitted. "It's hard to let it all hang out when the temperature never gets above freezing."

It took a good half hour to convince Gert and Hoppie to coexist peacefully—each moving ten feet away from what they considered the optimal spot.

As soon as that fire was put out, I had to deal with a tilting bandstand, bands badgering me about the lineup, and Tiny Sparkletoe of the Christmastown Community Guild, who was concerned about the number of trash receptacles on hand. By the time I'd run to the hardware store and come back with two additional cans, the ever-popular Swingin' Santas, the first band slated after the little elf girl, were already playing and skaters had taken to the ice.

The tunes they played provided a jaunty counterpoint to the drumming and chanting approaching slowly from the other side of town.

No sooner had I directed elves where to set up the cans than I spotted Juniper gliding around on the pond. She was doing figure eights with an ease I envied. I was still awkward on skates.

She waved at me and sped over. "Guess who's meeting me here this evening."

"Martin?"

She turned pink. "It's like a dream come true! I never thought he'd ever look twice at me. I think I owe some of this to you."

I didn't get it. "Me?"

"He only started noticing me after you and I became friends, even though we've been in the band together for two years."

"Maybe you seemed more approachable to him when you became the friend of someone he knew."

She nodded. "That's what I mean. I owe that to you. You'd laugh if I told you all the ways I used to try to capture his attention—even self-defeating things like dressing funny or playing bad notes in rehearsal. I thought, if he just *looked* at me, maybe I'd have a chance." She shook her head. "I even did some things I'm ashamed of now."

One minute I was listening to what she was saying, and the next my attention was totally riveted on the pond.

Juniper followed my gaze. "What is it?"

"Tiffany," I said.

My sister-in-law had donned one of her old exhibition outfits, which made her look like a red, sparkly slash across the ice. All eyes were on her, and not only for her sudden transformation from woman in widow's weeds to merry widow. I'd never witnessed anyone doing the things she was doing outside of televised skating competitions: jumps, and one-legged glides, and dizzying spins. My mouth dropped in astonishment.

She executed a leap I'd only seen attempted by skaters on television. "Holy flip!" Juniper exclaimed. "That was a triple Salchow!"

The people around the pond clapped and cheered, and more ice was cleared to make way for her. I'd known she was a onetime medal winner, of course, but I'd never seen her in action. And what was even more surprising was the outfit she was wearing—a bright red flirty version of a Santa suit. The band—the Swingin' Santas—was doing an upbeat version of "Santa Baby" and she was hamming and vamping it up as if they'd practiced the routine for months. Hard to believe that this was the same woman I'd known since coming to Christmastown.

What had come over her?

"I've never seen her like this," I said, having to speak loudly over the beating of drums from the Giblet march, which was growing closer.

"She's a natural!" Juniper said.

She was, and the crowd was eating it up, whooping and clapping with each move she made. But her talent and star quality weren't foremost in my mind. Her mental state was what concerned me.

For a moment I was reminded of myself in my first year of

widowhood. I'd been miserable for so long, locked up alone in my house, binge-watching TV shows without actually seeing them. I watched one British mystery show twice in a month and didn't remember whodunit the second time through. My brain had been incapable of holding information—just that Keith was dead and he had cheated on me; that fact took up most of the space in my head so that nothing else could get through.

But then one day I'd been passing by an outlet mall and stopped. Two hours later, I drove home with the loot I'd purchased in a mad shopping spree. When I came down from this manic episode I had to take most of the stuff back. My spree had been a release.

That's what Tiffany's mad skate struck me as—someone pushing a release valve. I looked around for Christopher, worrying about what he'd make of this. I couldn't spot him in the crowd, which was huge and growing. Some of the people watching by the pond were leaning on *Justice for Giblet* signs. They'd trickled away from the march to watch the last Mrs. Claus's exhibition skate.

"The worst moment was when I went to the Candy Cane Factory after his brother died," Juniper said.

It took me a few moments to realize that we were back to talking about Martin. "Why did you do that?"

"To offer my condolences, nominally." She shook her head. "But really it was just a pretext for talking to him. Isn't that terrible?"

"I'm sure he was glad to accept your sympathy," I said.

"Maybe he would have been, but I never got a chance to find out. When I got to his office, right after I'd heard about the hunting accident, they said he'd taken the day off."

"Well then, you certainly have nothing to feel ashamed about. You didn't even say anything to him."

"Yes, but if it's the thought that counts when it comes to good things, shouldn't bad thoughts be black marks on our conscience?"

Someone tapped on my elbow. "April Claus?"

I turned and looked down into the red face of Noggin Hollyberry. "Hello, Mr. Hollyberry."

"I knew you Clauses had gall, but this beats everything." He pointed toward Tiffany. "Having that sparkly lady making a spectacle of herself while we're trying to have a solemn march. As if the noise from the band wasn't bad enough!"

"The Skate-a-Palooza was on the calendar all year, long before the march. It's not my fault your trying to disrupt our event backfired."

He quivered. "We aren't disrupting anything!"

Tiny Sparkletoe hurried over to us in a flutter. "What's the matter?"

"That music and that skater!" Noggin said. "It's making our marchers peel away to watch."

"Well," Tiny observed, "they seem to be enjoying themselves."

"They're not supposed to enjoy anything! This is for Giblet!"

My phone rang, and I took the call without looking, worried that there would be another problem to troubleshoot. "Hello?" I said.

"April."

It was Nick. He sounded relieved to hear my voice. Who else did he expect to answer my phone? "What's wrong?"

"Is Tiffany there?" he asked.

"Um, yes." I cupped my hand before speaking into the phone again. "She's skating."

"Get her away from there and back up to the road as quickly and quietly as possible. There's a sleigh coming to pick you both up."

I frowned into the middle distance, watching as Tiffany executed an elaborate spin to *ahs* from the audience. She looked like a sparkly top. "I'm not sure she'll want to go." I wasn't keen to leave, either, but something important must have come up if Nick had gone to all the trouble to send transportation for us. "Why the sleigh?"

"There's been an accident. Christopher is very ill. The doctor's here."

"Oh my god. What's happened?" How could it be both illness and accident? There was something Nick wasn't telling me. Blistering cold swept through me. "Is he going to be all right?"

"We're not sure. Christopher—" His voice broke, and he had to stop, take a breath, and start again. "He seems to be unconscious now. The doctor says the success of his recovery will depend on the poison that was used."

My heart slammed against my ribs. "Poison?"

"We think Christopher ate a poisoned gumdrop."

# Chapter 19

"I never should have left him," Tiffany said. "I knew he was in danger."

We were burrowed under blankets in the back of the sleigh Nick had sent for us. Despite the fact that she'd been skating, spinning, and jumping until just ten minutes ago, my sister-in-law's face was pale as chalk. I didn't know what to say to her. I'd already told her the bare facts that Nick had given me over the phone.

I had hurriedly pulled her off the ice, telling her to stay mum about the reason. Nick didn't want news of what had happened to Christopher to cause a panic. The Hollyberrys thought I had capitulated to their request that we not outshine their Justice for Giblet march, but it was probably only a matter of time before word of what had happened at the castle filtered out to the population at large.

"I've been worried for months. Ever since Chris—" Tiffany's throat choked off her words.

*Please let Christopher be okay.* A gumdrop. It sounded so insignificant. How much poison could be put in a little piece of candy? And why would anyone do such a thing? Perhaps the poison hadn't even been meant for Christopher. Whoever had done this could have been trying to kill someone else—or just creating mayhem at random.

"Christopher's strong," I said, trying to reassure her.

She was in no frame of mind to receive comfort, least of all from me. "Of course he's strong—that's why he was targeted. Chris was strong, too, and look what happened to him."

As much as I told myself not to jump to conclusions, I couldn't help thinking about Amory. I'd let my natural sympathy for what he'd been through in his childhood color my view of the story he'd told me about what had happened on the monster hunt. Maybe he really did lie about what had happened. Now I imagined him on that mountain, cold, exhausted, and eaten up with decades-long resentment, seeing the opportunity to push Chris into the abyss.

But did he resent Chris so much that he would try to kill Christopher, too? And how would he have gotten those deadly gumdrops in the house?

"We don't know what happened," I said aloud, an admonishment to myself as much as to Tiffany.

"I do." Her eyes flashed as she turned to me. "I was on guard, watching my boy for all those months, and then *you* came along. Telling me I was smothering him. 'Ease up,' you said. '*Freedom.*' I should never have listened to you. Especially given who you're married to."

Anger rose in me at the unfairness of her accusations, and where she was placing the blame. She'd already convicted Nick. At the same time, while her son's life hung in the balance I couldn't fault her for lashing out. She was living the mother's nightmare.

"Nick had nothing to do with this. He's distraught over Christopher."

She sent me a withering look. "Sure he is."

"If you could have heard how worried he sounded when I spoke to him on the phone . . ."

Suspicion flickered in her eyes. She straightened. "Maybe he has reason to worry. Maybe he realizes that you're the poisoner."

I knew she harbored bitterness toward me, but I hadn't expected this.

"Look what's happened in Christmastown since you arrived here," she said. "Two murders. And now my son."

My mouth dropped open. But then I remembered what Nick had said to me just before I left: *I swear to you, April, this was a peaceful place before you got here.* He'd been joking, though.

He *had* been joking, right?

Nothing about any of this seemed funny now.

"I promise you, I had nothing to do with what's happened to Christopher." Or to Giblet or Old Charlie, but I doubted she cared about them.

I might as well not have spoken at all.

"You think I don't see your endgame?" she asked. "I was in your position, you know. I married Chris and he whisked me away to his grand castle in the north, where I was treated like a queen."

I couldn't say that I ever felt like a queen in Santaland, but I was too curious to see where she was headed with this argument to stop her.

"And I gave Santaland a prince," she continued, "a perfect little boy who was going to be Santa someday. But then Chris died, and you came here to displace me."

"I wouldn't—"

"You might be queen now, April, but Christopher *will* take his rightful place, and then you and Nick will be out of power, a footnote in Santaland's history."

"Good," I said. "That's what Nick and I both want."

She was too busy speculating about my motives to hear me. "Maybe you didn't realize this until it was too late. So you decided to do something about it. Make your own children the heirs."

I shook my head. "Nick and I have no children."

"Yet."

"We won't have." I hesitated. This was really no one's business but mine and Nick's, but perhaps by divulging our secret I could put her mind at ease . . . at least about this. "I can't have children, Tiffany. It caused my last marriage to crack up, even before my husband died."

"Maybe that was your husband's fault."

I shook my head. "I discovered Keith had gotten a girlfriend pregnant before he died. She came to the funeral."

"And you didn't know this before then? What did you do?"

"I retreated like a wounded animal, cursed and broke a few things in the house, and then put part of the insurance settlement into a trust fund for the kid. After all, it wasn't the baby's fault."

Her eyes widened. "Does Nick know about all this? About your not being able to conceive, I mean?"

Did she think I would marry him without telling him? "Of course. I told him the whole story last summer, even before he proposed." Before he told me who he was, actually. "I reminded him of it after he asked me to marry him, and he said it didn't matter to him. And when I asked him how he could be so sure, you know what he said? 'Because I have a nephew, and he's like a son to me.'"

Tiffany absorbed what I'd told her but said nothing for a long time. That was okay. I hadn't been looking for sympathy, and if it put thoughts of Nick as a serial killer out of her mind, so much the better.

Finally, she huffed impatiently. "Why are we going so

slow? What's the point of having these special reindeer if they're going to be so pokey?" She leaned forward and yelled at the two pulling us, "We're in a hurry! Can't you make this thing fly?"

They were already running.

The animal on the right shook his head, sending a jangling of bells ringing through the still night. "We have orders not to be conspicuous."

"Orders from whom?"

"Santa."

She turned to me with a glare. "Do something, Mrs. Claus."

I hesitated. Nick would have urged caution to avoid talk about the emergency at the castle spreading and possibly starting a panic. A fear of poisoned candy around Christmas would cast a pall over the season.

On the other hand, Nick wasn't a mother worried about getting to her son's sickbed.

I thought I remembered seeing a blaze on one of the reindeer's flanks. "On, Comet. Fly us home!"

I was unsure if that's all I had to say. I barely knew how to drive a sleigh, much less how to command reindeer to fly.

There was a hesitation, and then the gait of the animals in front of us changed from a trot to a loping, surging bound. With a stomach-turning lurch, the sleigh left the earth and climbed over the treetops. Was I really flying?

The speed at which we seemed to be rushing up at the eerie northern lights told me I was. Terror, along with a strange, sharp jubilation, surged through me.

Still holding the reins, I pushed myself against the side of the sleigh for dear life. We had no seat belts, and the sleigh was hardly a jetliner. We caught every breeze and bump in the air, wafting about like a kite. Or so it seemed to me.

I hazarded a glance over the side of the sleigh at the world below. The lights of Christmastown blazed behind us, especially around the pond. The sound of Figgie and the Nutcrackers carried on the wind from here, and some of the skaters on the pond were carrying candle torches, creating a shimmering light show. It was probably striking on the ground, but from here it was breathtaking.

Not that I had much breath. Sleigh flying is swift and rough, and I couldn't quite dislodge my heart from my throat. Did Nick actually intend to go around the world in one of these contraptions? I was going to have to sit him down between now and Christmas and have a serious talk about safety belts.

We closed in on the castle fast, and the sleigh began to plunge toward the earth much too fast for my liking.

"Careful, Comet!" I couldn't help calling out as we seemed to be on a collision course with the castle's side portico.

I expected a crash, but the sleigh came to a magically peaceful landing and abrupt stop.

Tiffany was ready to hop out but turned back to me, I assumed to thank me for countermanding Nick's orders.

Instead, she said in a low voice, "Those are Dashers, not Comets. You *really* haven't learned much about this place, have you?"

From the wind and stars and dizzying flight, we entered a castle that was still, dark, and silent. The west wing living quarters were as still as poor Christopher himself, lying across his bed in his room, the walls of which were decorated with stencils of airplanes, rocket ships, and—oddly, yet appropriately—reindeer-pulled sleighs. I only took a quick peek at his duvet-covered form before retreating to the family quarters.

A somber group had gathered in the west parlor. Jingles came through with a pitcher of eggnog and set it down without a word, but with a mournful look at me. Lucia leaned against Quasar, who was staring into the fire. There was something odd about his appearance, but I couldn't put my finger on it. I chalked it up to his subdued demeanor. He knew better than to chew on decorations during this time of crisis, or fall into a snoring sleep. Even his fizzling nose had gone respectfully dormant.

Martin sat upright in his favorite chair, uncharacteristically somber. I couldn't help noticing he was dressed in what he'd probably intended to be skating attire—a plaid sweater, corduroy pants that hugged his legs below the calves, and a deep red scarf. He must have been on his way out the door to go to Peppermint Pond when he'd heard about Christopher. And Juniper was probably still waiting for him. I hadn't felt at liberty to divulge what Nick had told me, just that Tiffany and I needed to return to the castle. I hoped she didn't think that Martin was standing her up and that her unlucky romantic streak was continuing.

The only sounds around us were the muted crackling of the fire behind its great screen and the clicking of Pamela's knitting needles.

I hadn't seen my mother-in-law since this morning. The croquembouche caper seemed an eon ago. I settled next to her and looked around me. "Where's Nick?"

*Click, click.* "In his office, talking to that loathsome detective."

She had to mean Jake Frost. Nobody would have called Constable Crinkles loathsome. Or a detective.

"What happened?" I asked.

Martin looked surprised I hadn't heard. "I was about to take Christopher down to Peppermint Pond when he felt violently ill. He said he'd eaten a gumdrop or two."

"Where did the gumdrops come from?" I asked, but I already knew.

"Nick's office," Lucia said. "Nick always kept some out because he knew Christopher liked them. Especially the licorice ones."

I shut my eyes for a moment, wanting to block out how bad that sounded for Nick. No wonder Jake Frost was interrogating him. I thought I'd convinced Tiffany that Nick had no motive to poison her son, but in the face of damning evidence it might be harder to persuade the law of his innocence. Yet that wasn't what really mattered now.

"You seem worried, April," Lucia said.

Martin sent her a withering look. "Of course she's worried. Christopher's fighting for his life. We're all worried."

"But is April worried about Christopher, or Nick?"

He rose up. "Isn't it bad enough that we have detectives crawling around the place without you doing their speculating for them?"

She blinked, surprised by the vehemence of the attack. "What did I say? That April is worried about Nick? Why shouldn't she be?"

"It was what you were implying," Martin said.

"I was just talking," she argued.

"You were being a snake in the grass," he shot back.

*"ENOUGH!"*

The room fell silent again, and we all stared at Pamela in shock. Tears rolled down her cheeks, and her hands were trembling around those knitting needles. Her unflappable matriarch demeanor had fallen away, leaving the worried grandmother raw and exposed. "Will you two stop bickering for once in your lives? At least until Christopher gets better. Now more than ever, we need to stand together as a family."

The siblings glared at each other, but Lucia retreated back to her place by the fireside.

The knitting needles resumed their clicking. "April, why don't you pour everyone some eggnog," Pamela suggested, her voice returning to a determined calm.

The thought of drinking eggnog now of all times nauseated me, but it would be something to do with myself for a minute. Any distraction was welcome. How long would we all be sitting here like this, I wondered. I was willing to sit forever if that's how long it took Christopher to recover, but how long would it be until we knew if he was out of danger or not?

On the tray, there were more glasses than people present in the room. Who else had Jingles expected to be here?

"Has anyone sent word of what's happened up to the lodge?" I asked.

Pamela stilled, thinking. "Oh dear, I didn't think to."

"Amory and Midge were just here, weren't they?" Lucia asked.

"Midge was here." Pamela frowned. "I didn't see Amory."

I'd forgotten about the reception. Good grief, a herd of people had paraded through the castle today. I found that news strangely comforting in terms of Nick—the list of possible suspects besides him had just grown by at least a hundred—though daunting for what it meant to the investigation into who had poisoned those gumdrops.

As I was passing around glasses—no one seemed any more interested in the eggnog than I was—the door swung open and Nick came in. He crossed the room and lowered himself onto the sofa next to his mother.

"Have you heard anything?" I asked.

"The doctor said Christopher's condition is the same," he announced.

Disappointment made the rounds on everyone's expressions, followed quickly by a shadow of relief. The same meant no worse, at least.

As I handed Nick a glass, he told me, "You'd better go to my office. Jake Frost wants to talk to you."

I studied Nick's face for any indication of how he felt about this, but his expression betrayed no specific worry, or warning.

As I entered the study, Jake Frost stood with his hands in his pockets in front of the large map on the wall. I cleared my throat and he pivoted.

"They told me you were watching the skating at the pond." He said it almost as if I were somehow callous to be away while Nick's nephew was being poisoned.

"I had a hand in planning the event," I said. "I was expected to be there."

"And you missed the luncheon here at the castle."

"I couldn't be two places at once." I crossed my arms, already impatient with circling around the heart of the matter. "I'm not sure what my being at the pond has to do with what happened to Christopher." I nodded to the desk, where a now-empty candy dish sat. The gumdrops were gone. Seized as evidence, I expected. "Is it true he was poisoned?"

"We are still checking the gumdrops—Dr. Honeytree will be able to tell us—but according to the boy himself, it was the gumdrops that made him sick. Specifically the gumdrops that always sat on your husband's desk."

"Lots of people knew Nick kept them there."

"Yes, I was told he kept them because Christopher liked them."

"Nick did not poison Christopher. The suggestion that he would do such a thing makes me ill. Your trying to connect my husband to Giblet's and Old Charlie's deaths seemed absurd to me, but somewhat understandable, given the circumstances. Still wrong, mind you. But Nick loves Christopher. He wouldn't harm a hair on his head." I took a deep breath. Having told Tiffany, I might as well explain it to the law. "We can't have children. *I* can't," I specified. "Christopher is the closest Nick will ever come to having children, unless Martin and Lucia also have children someday."

Jake Frost took all this in. His solemn silence stood in for his condolences to me. I preferred that, to be honest.

"It's not just for an heir that your husband might want to do away with his nephew," he said.

Those words made my heart sink. Of course I'd known he suspected Nick, but he'd obviously thought this through very hard.

"Why then?" I asked.

"So he could be Santa himself, for life."

That idea had never occurred to me. Maybe because I knew Nick didn't relish his position as, say, Chris had. Santa was never a title he craved, and as far as I knew, he'd never resented his older brother having it in the way that, say, Amory had.

I shook my head. "If you knew Nick, you wouldn't say that. He's not ambitious."

"You're right," Jake said. "I don't know your husband. I'm just a detective, looking at the evidence from two murders and one attempted murder. And all that evidence points heavily to your husband."

"Just circumstantially."

"Circumstantial evidence is evidence," Jake said. "What's more, this homicidal cluster paints a picture of ambition—the ambition of one man who is busily getting rid of any impediment."

I gaped at him. "Nick?"

"Yes, Nick. First, there was his brother's death."

"Nick didn't cause that," I pointed out.

"No—we're still unsure about the circumstances surrounding Chris Claus's death. And why are we unsure?" He didn't wait for me to answer. "Because at the time, your husband issued an edict to all the men on Mount Myrrh not to talk about what happened that day. If more had been known about the suspicious circumstances, maybe there could have been a more thorough investigation.

"Now I have two sure murders and one attempted homicide on my hands. And we know that Giblet Hollyberry was pointing the finger at Nick, implicating him in Chris's death."

"Giblet didn't know what he was talking about."

"Yet the very next day someone went out of his way to silence him. And just hours later an old snowman, who many believe had witnessed something unusual at Giblet's cottage, was melted into a puddle of ice."

"I know. I saw it."

"And that's when we start to have a very real connection to your husband."

"The button," I said. "A button that could be found on any number of garments in this castle, or even on hand-me-downs that the Clauses have given away over the years."

"Could have, but we know the same buttons were used on Nick Claus's clothes. And now, having gotten rid of his brother, the man who knew he killed his brother, and the witness to the second murder, he has also tried to do away with the boy who would take his position away from him."

"Ten years from now," I said, incredulous. "Why on earth would Nick go on a homicidal spree now when he could sit back for the next decade and see what happens?"

"See if something else befell his nephew, you mean?"

"No—of course not. I just mean he gets to be Santa for ten years and then he can retire. He has the best of both worlds. I have an inn in Oregon. We're going to return there and run it and let Christopher take the reins. Nick can't wait to move to Cloudberry Bay."

"He never once mentioned that to me."

I was brought up short. "He didn't?"

The detective shook his head. The grand bargain I'd made

with my husband obviously was more prominent in my mind than Nick's. I searched for the most likely reason. "Well, it's December."

"I beg your pardon?"

"It's the busiest time of year for the Clauses. Oregon's probably the farthest thing from Nick's mind right now. He's got a world of children to deliver packages to."

Jake nodded, but I could see something in his expression. *You poor deluded fool*, that look said. He hadn't pitied me when I told him about my inability to have children, but it was clear he thought I was a sad creature now.

"Are you going to arrest Nick?"

"As you say, everything at the moment is circumstantial. And we're still testing the gumdrops found in this room. It could be tomorrow before we discover if they were really what poisoned Christopher."

If Christopher said they were, I held out little hope that it could be otherwise.

"One question," Jake said, turning and picking something off the floor. "Can you tell me where this might have come from?"

The jagged object in his hand looked like a branch at first until I realized it was an antler. And then I remembered why Quasar had appeared so odd to me in the parlor. He'd lost his lopsided look. He'd shed his remaining antler.

"Where did you find it?" I asked.

"Right here," he said, pointing to the carpet. "On the floor by the desk where the bowl of gumdrops sat." He scrutinized my face closely. "I repeat, do you know where this could have come from?"

I shrugged. "Some reindeer, I guess."

# Chapter 20

"How should I know how his antler got there?" Lucia said when I sought her out in her room. "Ask Quasar."

An old NSYNC poster was pinned to the wall, which never failed to make me do a double take. Hard to imagine Lucia at any age mooning over Justin Timberlake in *Tiger Beat*, but apparently that was a thing that happened. The poster still held pride of place next to a "Best Fishing Lakes of Alaska" pullout from *Field & Stream*. Teen dreams die hard.

I stayed close to the door. Quasar was fairly clean for a reindeer, but there was still a strong musky whang in the air.

"I-I can tell you how it got there," Quasar said, not waiting for me to ask. "I was looking for Lucia this afternoon. I thought she might be in the study napping."

"And your antler just happened to fall off there?"

"I guess," he said. "I'm glad it's gone. It kept bumping into things."

"I can't believe that stupid detective can't find anything better to ask questions about than Quasar's antler," Lucia said.

"It was right in the room, next to the gumdrops," I explained. Why I felt compelled to jump to Jake Frost's defense I had no idea.

"All right, so it was there—it doesn't mean Quasar was

guilty of spiking the gumdrops with poison. I'm not even sure he could. He's not the most dexterous creature, if you haven't noticed. The smarter thing to ask would be if Quasar saw anybody in there."

We both turned to him.

"I-I didn't see anybody. But I was looking for you, Lucia," he reiterated. "I don't know why you wanted to exercise in the middle of the night?"

"I wondered that myself," I said.

She sighed and answered as though I were dragging it out of her. "All right, I'll tell you. Quasar snores."

I gaped at her. "*Quasar* snores?"

She nodded and then turned to him apologetically. "I'm sorry, friend, but it's true. Some nights you saw away so hard I can't get a wink of sleep."

It was surprising that the two of them sleeping in the same room didn't set off tsunamis.

I was afraid I was going to laugh, which would antagonize her more than she already was. So I waited for Quasar to point out the obvious, but that didn't seem to occur to him. Instead, he was mortified. "I'm sorry! I-I should probably be put out in the barn, I guess. I never knew I was *that* bad."

"So there's your answer," Lucia said impatiently. "Quasar dropped his antler in the study, and I went walking because I couldn't sleep. Nothing particularly noteworthy or suspicious in any of that, is there?"

"No." Except that I doubted she was telling the truth. I remembered what Quasar had told me about how her behavior had changed recently. How she'd become secretive . . . how she even smelled different. She was hiding something. "There's the matter of a package that came here for you. Live animals. A SPEX agent told me about it."

"That's got nothing to do with Christopher," Lucia declared, as if her denial should be the last word. But her agitation at the mere mention of the package convinced me I was on the right track.

"So you did receive a package like that."

Fear showed in her eyes. "It's none of your business."

"It is if it had anything to do with Giblet's death."

Her jaw dropped. "Giblet! That's crazy. Lynxie wasn't—"

Her mouth clamped shut. Both Quasar and I were riveted now. "*Lynxie?*" I asked. "Who—or what—is Lynxie?"

Her face reddened. She crossed her arms and huffed out a breath. "What do you think? He's just a pet. He had nothing to do with Giblet's death."

"A pet lynx?" I asked.

"A cat-lynx cross," she corrected. "He wouldn't hurt a fly. I can't even get him to kill the ice rats. I've been trying to train him for over a week." She shook her head dolefully. "It's just not working."

Quasar and I looked at each other. "Where is this . . . Lynxie?" I asked.

She kicked her toe, angry that her secret was out. "In the old stables."

"Why are you keeping him out there?"

"You heard Mother—she said she didn't want any more animals in the house. But I already had Lynxie. I ordered him special from a place that responsibly breeds lynx crosses. I thought it would be best to have a cat that's used to the cold. Poor guy. For a night or two I tried keeping him in the castle on the QT, but he was a little destructive . . . to everything but rodents."

"Let me guess. You had him in the doll cellar."

Her eyes widened. "How did you know?"

"He shredded a few dolls."

"Lethal to inanimate objects, but terrified of rats." She

shook her head again. "He's in the old stables until I can civilize him a little, and train him up. Then Mother will appreciate him."

I doubted that.

"Th-that's why I smelled danger," Quasar said. "Do lynx kill reindeer?"

"No! That is . . ." Lucia sent me an uncomfortable sidewise look, then repeated, "No! Of course not. He's very sweet." She added in a lower voice, "When he's in a good mood."

"Is *that* what we heard outside last night?"

She nodded. "He lets out yowls sometimes, just like a housecat. I *really* think Mother will like him once she gets to know him. I even thought about asking if we could bring him into Christopher's room. The purring of cats is supposed to be very beneficial in healing."

"I might hold off on that," I said. "You said you were home this afternoon during the big luncheon today. Did you see any of the guests around Nick's study?"

"No, but I'm not sure I would have paid much heed to someone loitering there. Nick's study is a natural place for visitors to be curious about, and if I had seen someone near the door I would've assumed that Nick would be in there welcoming them."

"But you said you *didn't* see anyone."

"Not that I recall, no."

So neither she nor Quasar witnessed any of the luncheon guests sneaking around in a way that would have allowed the person to slip into Nick's office and replace the gumdrops with poisoned ones. I tried to hide my disappointment.

"Whoever did this to Christopher is a real fiend," she said. "Who could hate Christopher? He's the nicest kid in Christmastown."

"Maybe they just hate what he represents—the Santa torch

being passed to the younger generation. The killer might think Christopher's unworthy."

"Why? Christopher's a good kid, and conscientious. He'll make a great Santa—but that's ten years away yet." Lucia frowned. "Why try to do away with him now?"

"Jake Frost has a theory about that. He thinks Nick is power hungry and will stop at nothing to retain the position of Santa."

"Well, that's a load of bull spit," Lucia declared. "He obviously doesn't know Nick."

"That's what I said." I asked tentatively, "But what if someone else *is* ambitious?"

"Like who?"

"How about Amory?"

She looked as if she was going to argue, but then her mouth snapped closed. She tilted her head, considering. "You mean he was jealous of Christopher?"

"All Clauses." Bitterness ate at him, I could tell. Bitterness and guilt, and . . . I wasn't sure what else was going on in that man's head.

Lucia looked grave. "Does the detective really think a Claus did this?"

"He thinks Nick did it."

"And you think . . ."

"I think it was a Claus," I said. "But not Nick."

She scowled at me. "So it wasn't Quasar you came up here to interrogate, was it? It was me."

I wanted to say that I couldn't cross anyone off my suspect list at the moment, but that would have sounded ridiculous. As Nick had pointed out to me time and again, I wasn't a detective. Mrs. Claus wasn't supposed to have a suspects list.

Well, I wasn't a typical Mrs. Claus.

"What makes you suspect me?" she asked. "I love Chris."

"One of my very first conversations with Nick was about

you. I asked him why, if you were the oldest, you were never in line to become Santa."

"I've asked that my whole life," she said, "but so what? Them's the breaks. If I hadn't accepted that by now, I'd be mad or living out in the wilds like Boots Bayleaf. I wouldn't be sitting here in the castle eating my heart out for what I couldn't have."

"You're the one with the poison, though."

Her face screwed into a frown. "You mean that stuff for killing rats? It's strychnine powder. Any kid who'd eat a gumdrop of that stuff without spitting it out would have to be nuts. You can't stick strychnine powder into a gumdrop without someone noticing."

I nodded, taking her point. What I knew of poisons came mostly from streaming *Poirot*, where Agatha Christie's poison victims always died in a quick and telegenic fashion.

"Have you seen Amory today?" I asked.

"It's a workday. He's probably down at the plant."

I stood.

"You're going there now?" she asked, as if my leaving the castle would be unseemly. Lucia, of all people, was suddenly concerned about appearances. "With Christopher still as sick as he is?"

"That's why I'm going—who knows where all this will end?" It was the same thing Tiffany had said to me days ago. I'd thought she was unhinged; instead, she'd been prescient. I owed her an apology; not that she'd care at this point. Her suspicions about Nick were wrong, but she'd been right to suspect foul play. And right to warn that there would be further violence touching our family.

The least I could do for Tiffany now was to try to find who was culpable for all this tragedy.

Lucia gave me an assessing look. "I'd call Amory first. The Plumbing Works would be a long way to go for no reason."

I took her advice and called ahead. Amory's secretary informed me that he hadn't been at work all day. "He's out sick today," she said.

I should have called Kringle Lodge first, too, but I wanted to check for myself whether or not Amory was there.

When Mistletoe announced my arrival, Midge fluttered out to greet me. "What a surprise! It's so nice of the castle to send someone to ask about Amory," she said. "But you shouldn't have bothered, April. It's just a cold."

He hadn't been malingering, then.

But even if he actually was sick, "just a cold" wouldn't necessarily preclude Amory's nipping out to poison Christopher. True, in my quick survey of the elves at the castle I'd conducted before I'd left to come here, no one remembered seeing Amory that day. Yet the luncheon had taken up part of the afternoon. Amory could have snuck in at the height of that event without anyone noticing.

"Would it be possible to say hello to him?" I asked.

"The personal touch—how kind," Midge gushed. "He's been cranky all day, poor thing. Seeing a friendly face might cheer him up."

I wasn't sure how friendly he'd consider my face to be. If I'd been thinking more clearly, I would have brought some flowers or fruit or something appropriate for giving a sick person. Either Midge didn't notice my lack of an offering or else she was too polite, too obsequious, to let on.

We went upstairs and she knocked timidly on the door. "Amory, dear, are you up?"

"Yes, blast it," came the testy reply.

Midge shot an anxious sidewise smile at me. "Mrs. Claus is here—April, I mean."

"Good grief, what does that nosy idiot want?"

She cleared her throat. "April is *right here.*"

A short, awkward silence ensued.

"Oh! Well, better have her come in then."

I turned the knob, fully prepared to let some accusations fly, but a loud, juicy sneeze stopped me in my tracks. Some colds are trifles, but a single look was enough to see that Amory was in the grips of one of those full-blown, red-nosed, sneezy, stuffy affairs that make the moniker *cold* seem insultingly insignificant. The poor man was adrift in a sea of used tissues, his eyes bagged and droopy, the rest of him bundled against chills, even though the room was stifling from the fire blazing in the hearth.

"Hi, Amory," I said, standing well back. Whatever he had, I didn't want to catch it.

"Whaddya doing here?" Now that I was in the same room, I could hear that his stopped-up nose was making his consonants indistinct.

"I just wanted to see how you were. Your secretary told me you'd called in sick today."

"Oh yes," Midge said. "Amorykins has been in bed all day. He's the worst patient you can imagine. He pestered the servants all afternoon long, especially while I was down at the castle for wonderful Pamela's fabulous party."

If he'd been pestering servants all day, then that would be plenty of elves who could attest that Amory—Amorykins!—hadn't left his sickroom.

A perverse disappointment shot through me. I started to feel like a ghoul. As if I wanted to believe that Amory would plan such an evil attack against his own relative.

And yet . . . someone had done it.

"April?" Midge prompted.

"Sorry," I said. "Wool-gathering."

"It was a perfectly splendid party your mother-in-law hosted today. Of course the sheet cake wasn't as magnificent as her croquembouche, but she said there had been some kind of calamity. . . ."

Right. Quasar and I were the calamity. "It's a shame it didn't work out this year," I said.

Midge nodded sympathetically. "Well, this has been the year for calamities, hasn't it? What's next? I often wonder."

I shifted uncomfortably. In my hurry to find out Amory's true state of health, I'd forgotten that the news about Christopher probably hadn't reached the lodge yet. Midge had left the castle before he'd fallen ill, and Pamela said no one had called.

"Actually, a terrible thing happened just today." Their eyes widened in disbelief as I explained about the poisoning.

"Someone's tried to kill *Christopher*?" Amory asked, aghast and outraged. "Why?"

"No one knows yet."

He and Midge exchanged looks, and then Amory sat up and swung his legs over the side of the bed. He was wearing solid blue flannel pajamas, but there was something about his big bare feet that made me turn away. "I'd better get down to the castle," he said.

"No," I answered quickly. "You're not well, Amory. I doubt Tiffany would thank you for spreading germs around her son."

I could tell from his woozy expression as he contemplated standing up that he would rather not make the journey down the mountain at night in the snow. "You're probably right," he said, collapsing back against his pillows. "Tell everyone at the castle that Midge and I are really concerned for the boy, though."

"I will," I said.

"Yes—send our love," Midge said. "And you'll keep us updated on Christopher's condition, won't you?"

"Yes, you must tell us if—" Amory's words cut off. "Well, let us know if he gets better."

*Or doesn't get better*, he didn't need to add.

"I will."

Midge showed me the door quickly after that, although she pumped me for more information all the way down the stairs. I had precious little to give. In parting, I promised again to keep them up-to-date on Christopher's condition.

Then, after she'd let me out the front door, I circled back around to the side, to the lodge's kitchen entrance. I wanted to double-check with the staff to see if Amory was telling the truth about being in bed all day. After speaking to a few people, I realized he must have been. His cold was not a put-on. He really was sick, and as terrible a patient as Midge had said. He'd tossed orange juice at one of the elves and yelled at two of the others. There was mutiny in the air in that kitchen.

I thanked them all for speaking to me and went back to the sleigh. My phone *fa-la-la-la-la'ed* with a text:

**JUNIPER: Have time for a coffee?**

Did I? Probably not.

**ME: We3B in twenty minutes.**

I might have gotten there a little later than that, but Juniper wasn't on time, either, probably because of the difficult-to-navigate streets due to revelers from the Skate-a-Palooza. My event, and it had practically gone off without me. So much for making a meaningful contribution. I'd missed most of the acts. I'd even missed playing with my own band.

We Three Beans was in its last hour of service, and the pickings at the counter were woefully slim. I grabbed a red-and-green Rice Crispies Treat in cellophane and a drip decaf and went to a table in the corner. Juniper arrived soon after, wearing her band uniform. She didn't have it in her to look truly miserable, I suspected, but neither did she seem her usual happy self. "Bohemian Rhapsody" was blaring on an overhead speaker and she didn't even sing along as most of the other elves were doing.

"Is everything okay?" I asked, suddenly worried about what I'd missed. "Was there any problem with the acts tonight?"

"It all went like clockwork, right down to the fireworks."

I'd forgotten about those. "I missed those, too."

"You left in such a hurry," Juniper said.

"I got a phone call from Nick. It was an emergency."

Her eyes went saucer wide. "It wasn't Martin, was it?"

I started to say no, but she cut me off. She looked stricken. "Here I was wishing all sorts of terrible things on him all night for standing me up. But what if he was really sick all that time?"

"He wasn't sick," I said. "Christopher was."

"Oh no." She looked as pained for Christopher as she was relieved for Martin. "What's wrong with him?"

"He was poisoned by a gumdrop. Now he's in bed, unconscious. That's why Martin didn't show up for your date."

"It wasn't a real date," she said, as if she didn't care. "Gosh, of course he stayed home for Christopher." Her eyes registered surprise. "Why aren't you there now?"

"I had some things to check out."

"You mean the festival?" she asked. "I could have done anything you needed me to—shut things down, tidy up . . . anything."

"It's okay," I said. "There's a cleanup crew."

"I feel just awful. You must think me so selfish for asking you to come all the way down here just so I could whine at you."

"You haven't whined. Did you have fun tonight?" I asked.

She shrugged. "I skated around a little with Smudge."

"Smudge skates?" It was like imagining an alley cat on skates.

"Everyone who grew up here does."

All of the sudden, it felt as if there was another stampede down the street. Weren't the Reindeer Games over? Out the snow-frosted windows, I could see lights flashing and people running. Then sirens sounded as a police vehicle, a motorized wagon on skis, tried to get through the crowd. The hum that went through the crowd penetrated even the walls of the coffee shop, and I stood on tiptoe to see over the heads on the sidewalk. In the back of the police wagon, which was driven by Deputy Ollie, I could just make out the forms of Constable Crinkles and Nick.

An elf dashed into the cafe, out of breath and holding his cap. The bell over the door tinkled with a cheeriness that was completely out of sync with the dread pounding in my heart. Everyone in the coffee shop was watching him.

"They're taking Nick Claus to jail," he announced. "Santa's been arrested for murder!"

# Chapter 21

Now that the worst had happened I felt strangely calm.

Except it wasn't actually the worst, since, thank heavens, Christopher was still alive. I knew Nick wasn't a killer, and now all I had to do was convince these thickheaded elves in the constabulary of his innocence.

As I waited on a bench by the fireplace while Crinkles and Frost interrogated Nick, my phone received a text. My heart froze, but the message wasn't from the castle. It was from Cloudberry Bay.

To be perfectly honest, I hadn't given Cloudberry Bay a thought since my last text from Damaris. What had she said? *I WON'T FORGET THIS.* Oh dear. I opened Claire's message with a feeling of trepidation. What had I done, or failed to do, now?

Claire didn't mention that. She'd simply taken a photo of the Coast Inn.

Only it didn't resemble the Coast Inn I'd left at the end of summer. Every angle of the house was lined with white lights. In front, someone had twined strings of colored lights through the tree branches and decorated my young cedar as if it were a Christmas tree. A few feet away from the Christmas tree was an inflated snowman, bigger than life. On the inn's roof, a tableau of Santa's sleigh, Santa, and his nine-reindeer team pranced across the shingles. Each of the three windows across the front had *Ho* spelled out in blinking lights. And, most amazing of all, in the front yard a train manned by stuffed elves and filled with gifts drove around a circular track.

Of course the elves didn't look exactly like real elves, but whoever had created the display had come surprisingly close.

**CLAIRE: Merry Christmas! You now have the most Christmassy house in town!**

It was hard to shift gears, back to concerns about my old life. I had to remind myself that Claire knew nothing about the world I was living in, or all the terrible events taking place here.

**ME: Has Damaris seen this?**

Of course she had. Cloudberry Bay wasn't exactly Los Angeles. In Cloudberry Bay, if you've seen two streets you've seen them all. Literally. That was what Damaris had been texting me about—she'd seen people decorating my house and realized her fit about my lack of Christmas spirit would come to nothing.

**CLAIRE: Seen it? She's already filed three complaints with the town council. Something about decoration by proxy not counting . . .**

**ME: Excellent!**

A smiley face winked at me.

**CLAIRE: You see? All your troubles are over.**

If only.

"All right, Mrs. Claus," Crinkles said, interrupting my texting. "You can talk to your husband now."

I snapped my phone shut and hurried over to the room where Nick was being held. It was a tidy little bedroom with an en suite washroom. Hardly Alcatraz. But I still didn't like the idea of him being cooped up here. Two nights before Christmas, no less.

As soon as the policemen left us alone, Nick and I embraced. He was wearing a black fisherman's sweater over his red Santa pants tucked into black boots.

"Is there any word about Christopher? The detective wouldn't say, and he seemed to be telling Crinkles that they should keep me in the dark."

"He's the same, as far as I know."

Nick sighed. "He's got to get better. If anything happens to him, it would destroy poor Tiffany. Mother, too." He shook his head. "All of us."

"The doctor said he needed rest. In the meantime, we need to get you out of here."

He sent me a clear-eyed look. "From what Crinkles told me, that's not going to happen. I just hope they find the real culprit before he or she harms anyone else."

I didn't hold out a lot of hope that Constable Crinkles would flush out the guilty party. But I felt growing confidence that I could.

"Nick, where did you go the night of Giblet's murder?" I asked. "You weren't in bed."

His eyes looked as if he was casting back months ago instead of just one week. "I thought I'd heard a noise, so I got up and just walked. I couldn't sleep."

I wondered if the noise had been Lynxie. I hadn't even seen him yet and that cat had already caused a lot of problems. "You were gone a long time."

"So were you," he said. "When I returned to our room to go back to sleep, *you* weren't there. I looked for you but gave up and finally went back to bed."

I pictured us both bumbling around the castle, narrowly missing each other in hallways. Like a Mr. and Mrs. Abbott and Costello at the North Pole.

"While you were up and about, did you write a note about Giblet and leave it on your desk?" I asked.

"I don't remember being at my desk at all that night."

"So you never left a note about a venomous elf on your desk?"

His face screwed up into a perplexed look. "Why would I do that?"

That was the question I should have asked myself. Instead, I'd let Jingles put the idea in my head that Nick had been plotting Giblet's demise. And then I'd destroyed evidence that might actually have helped him.

I gave Nick another hug, noting that his stomach wasn't as big as it had been even a week ago. Stress made for skinny Santas. "I'm so sorry," I said.

"What do you have to be sorry about?"

"I doubted you at the wrong moment."

He drew back and looked into my eyes. He knew what had happened after Keith's accident, about my having to absorb a betrayal I hadn't even suspected while my first husband had been alive. He knew, and I also saw that he understood why doubts would be hard to tamp down.

"But you didn't really think I'd killed Giblet and Old Charlie," he said.

"I knew you couldn't have . . . and yet incriminating evidence kept popping up that I couldn't explain." I mentioned his middle-of-the-night walkabout, the note on the blotter, the button. "And then there was the whole question mark surrounding Chris's murder."

Nick combed his hand through his thick hair and let out a ragged sigh. "I should have satisfied your curiosity about that topic instead of letting you imagine the worst."

"You found it upsetting to talk about. I understood that, so I spoke to Amory and I have a better handle on what took place that day. I think one of two things happened: Either Amory was too cowardly to continue on with Chris to kill the snow leopard, so he hung back and wasn't there when

Chris fell into the crevasse. Or maybe tied together, the two did go back, and when Chris fell, Amory felt he had no recourse but to cut the rope or fall over the ledge himself and then lied to cover up what he'd done. Am I right?"

"Those were the conclusions I came to," he said. "I wouldn't have faulted him for either."

"But you thought others might," I said. "So you swore the others to silence, even as rumors spread that you had somehow caused Chris's death."

He nodded. "I grew up with Amory. I was there when the emergency workers dug his mother and father out of the snow after the avalanche. It was devastating. Amory wasn't the same kid after that. How could he be? He has a lot of faults, but I don't hold them against him. I know he probably wakes most mornings thinking of that avalanche. I did for years, and it wasn't my parents who died."

"When Giblet hurled the accusation of murder at you, you stayed silent because you didn't want to throw suspicion on Amory."

"I never blamed Amory for whatever happened on that mountain, but other people might not have been so forgiving."

"Other people like Tiffany?"

"That frayed rope might have upset her," he said. "I thought it best just to try to let it all die down."

I wasn't sure I thought his attitude was the right one. He'd played policeman, judge, and jury. Perhaps because of that, a killer had escaped.

"The only way to put the rumors to rest and all of this behind us is to catch the real killer," I said. "Do you know who it is?"

"I don't have a clue." He looked down at me with equal parts affection and amusement. "But you have this all figured out, don't you?"

It was the second time I said "I do" to my husband.

He looked as if he dreaded the answer. "It will break my heart if it's Amory."

"It's not." I sighed. "But prepare to have your heart broken anyway."

# Chapter 22

After Nick's arrest, the mood in Castle Kringle took an even darker turn. Poor Pamela appeared to have lost heart. The knitting needles had stopped clicking, and she just sat forlornly on her sofa with a half-finished sweater in her lap. I understood every thought that was going through her mind, every careful gesture, yet I wanted to give her a bracing hug. I didn't, though. We had a tacit agreement to—as she always said—keep up normal appearances.

"How could they take Nick away?" she asked. "We've always been so good to the constabulary. We paid for their new vehicle last year."

The wagon they'd carted Nick away in, she meant.

Even in sorrow, Lucia's sense of ethics rose up in protest. "So because we donated money, Crinkles should just let us get away with murder?"

She was on her third eggnog in an hour and grew more voluble in her opinions with each slug. Martin hadn't hidden the fact that he'd spiked the nog liberally with brandy. Who could blame him? Pamela said nothing about the eggnog, and I was sticking to coffee. Now more than ever I had to keep my wits about me.

"Constable Crinkles told me that they were holding Nick partly for his own protection," I said.

"And you believed him?" Lucia leveled an incredulous gaze on me. "Did you also believe your parents when they told you the dog had been sent to a farm in the country?"

"Now, you can't blame April for holding out hope that Nick's not the poisoner," Pamela said. "We all should. It would be terrible if there really was such an evil person among us in the castle."

But there was, and she knew it.

As if on cue, Tiffany appeared. Gone were the sequins; she was back in head-to-toe black, her face unspeakably grave. I knew the words that were about to come out of her mouth, words no mother should ever have to say, and my heart ached for her.

Jingles stood behind her, head bowed.

"It's over," Tiffany announced.

Pamela looked up, tears trembling in her eyes. "You mean . . . ?"

Tiffany shook her head. Jingles lifted a handkerchief and blew his nose.

Pamela's straight back gave way, and she collapsed into the couch cushions, sobbing. "I can't believe it."

Lucia jumped to her feet. Some people cried in grief; Lucia got blistering mad. She strode right up to me, bending to get right in my face. "If Nick did do this, I'll never speak to him again. He can rot in that jail." She swung toward her mom. "And I swear, Mother, if you so much as knit him a pair of socks I'll never speak to you again, either!"

"L-Lucia . . ." Quasar lumbered to his feet. By the time he was standing, Lucia had already slammed out of the room. Tiffany slipped out after her quietly.

"L-Lucia is upset," Quasar announced.

"We guessed that," Martin said.

"I-I better go after her."

I nodded.

Only Pamela, Martin, and I remained in the room. And Jingles, who stood silently in the corner. I tried not to look at him.

"I can't believe what's happened to my family." Pamela turned to me. "It's as if I've lost three of my boys in one year."

"Two," Martin said. "Chris and Christopher."

"Isn't Nick lost to me, too?" she asked. "At least, the Nick I always thought my son to be."

Martin rose to his feet. I'd never seen his face so solemn, never heard his voice so grave. He was stepping up as the head of the Clauses, and taking up monumental duties at the most difficult time. "This is a mournful time for our family, but it's also December. Christmas will come, and Santaland and the whole world look to us to do our jobs." He buttoned his jacket. "I'll do all I can, Mother, to the best of my ability."

She nodded, unable to speak. I squeezed her hand.

"I suppose I shouldn't waste any time," he said. "I'm going to the factory to see that everything is in order. Then I'll come back here and try to sort out Nick's business."

Pamela lifted a handkerchief to her eyes. "That's very helpful of you, Martin."

"Yes, thank you," I told him.

He looked at me with aching sympathy. "I know this puts you in an awkward position, April. But I want you to know that no one here blames you for what Nick's done—and we won't forget you, either."

Pamela turned to me, too, with a very believable expression of hope. It was as if, on the darkest day of her life, she'd pinpointed one bright spot. "Yes, I suppose you'll want to go back to that place you're from. You never liked the weather here—you're always shivering. Now you can return to that motel you run and get back to making those what-you-call-'ems—blandies?—for your guests."

"Blondies." I bit my lip. "I'll have to think about what my next step will be."

"No hurry," Martin said.

"Of course not," Pamela agreed.

"You're very kind," I said. "Both of you."

"Well," Martin said, "I should get going. We don't have much time before Christmas, after all."

He kissed his mother's cheek, and she held him for a few moments before letting him go. As soon as he'd left the room, we both stood.

Pamela's face was strained but not unkind. Today she'd received both the best news and worst news a grandmother and mother could hear. I felt so sorry for her, but I don't think I'd ever admired a person's strength as much as I did hers then. She'd played her part perfectly.

"You'd better go," she said. "Quickly."

Jingles stepped forward and pulled a helmet out of a bag he'd been holding. "You'll be careful, won't you?" he asked as he handed the headgear to me.

I assumed his concern was more for his snowmobile than for my head. "I will."

He gave me a long look, and his eyes were full of something I'd never seen in them before. Was it respect? If so, I hadn't earned it yet. "Good luck, Mrs. Claus."

"Thank you, Jingles." I turned to Pamela. "Maybe you should break the news to Lucia."

She nodded. "It felt a dirty trick, keeping that kind of secret from her. I'll have to make it up to her some way. I don't know how."

"Lucia will think of something," I assured her.

* * *

I'd wondered how Christmastown would react to Santa Claus's arrest. I'd expected that there might be pandemonium, or another impromptu march. I'd envisioned Hollyberrys with torches storming the constabulary. But what actually happened was even more disturbing.

The town had gone dark. Silent and dark.

I'd never seen Christmastown without all its lights blazing. Most of the cottages and timbered houses were shuttered, so that not even candles flickered in windows. Everything was closed, even the coffee shop, the pub, and Sparkle's Corner Store. It was a good thing the snowmobile had a strong headlight, because without the Christmas lights draped like bunting everywhere, the streets were inky dark.

A sharp wind didn't help. Candy wrappers blew across the snow road, along with a few *Justice for Giblet* flyers. My cleanup crew had given up. It looked like the whole town had.

Giblet's accusations had been one thing; he was a bad-tempered kook. I doubted even most of the Hollyberrys had believed him. But hearing that Santa was actually arrested for murder was the worst blow possible to Santaland's collective psyche. Especially two days before Christmas.

Would there be a Christmas? The elves were probably wondering. Driving past all the dark cottages, I wasn't sure myself. I just knew I was going to do my part to make it all happen.

When I arrived at the Candy Cane Factory, it too looked almost deserted from the outside. The windows were dark except for a corner office on the second floor. Martin's modest sleigh, harnessed to a single depressed-looking reindeer, was parked in front. Down the block I could see the other vehicle I was looking for. I pulled Jingles' pride and joy right up to the front of the building.

The door was open and unguarded. To my own ears, my footsteps seemed to echo around the entire factory, which had let its employees go for the night. It still smelled strongly of peppermint candy, though. You never think of sweet as a smell until you're in a building where sugar is boiled all day long. Just a minute in that place was all it took for the oppressive sweetness and the sharp mint to soak into my pores.

For all that we were relatively alone in the factory, Martin didn't hear me coming. Small wonder. I didn't recall exactly how to get to his office, but all I had to do was follow the sound of Elvis singing "Here Comes Santa Claus" blaring down a corridor. It grew louder as I approached the closed door with Martin's nameplate on it. I stopped and peeked in.

There was my brother-in-law in a red Santa hat and matching coat over his black suit pants, boogying down to the King. The music was cranked and Martin sang along—*"Right down Santa Claus Laaaane!"*—as he shimmied around his office. He paused once to twirl around with a coatrack; then he let his ersatz partner go, spinning dizzily, wildly, laughing with joy.

A happy dance. A victory dance.

I stepped into the room and looked around. A Christmas tree stood in the corner, and various plaques and certificates hung on the wall. A large shellacked fish was mounted on a board—it reminded me of Boots Bayleaf, and might have been his handiwork. There were odd juxtapositions: Candy cane sample cases were displayed next to a primitive harpoon-like implement. A small collection of windup toys stood next to a well-stocked bar.

I cleared my throat.

Martin whirled, his eyes bugging in surprise. "April!" He lunged for the record player and hit the needle arm, which skidded across the vinyl with an ear-jarring scritch. We both winced.

"What are you doing here?" he asked, suddenly sober again.

"Just came to talk. I never really offered condolences to

you about Christopher, did I?" I looked him up and down. "But . . . you don't seem to need them."

He whipped the hat off his head, as if by doing so he could erase what I'd just seen. "I was just blowing off steam. You know."

"Yes, I know exactly what you were doing."

"Everyone reacts to grief differently," he said defensively. When I didn't respond, he shifted gears and became the perfect host. "Well, as long as you've traveled all this way, come in and sit down. Would you like a drink? I don't have any grog, but—"

"Do I look dumb enough to accept a drink from a man who poisoned his own nephew?"

His reaction was a perfect combination of surprise, hurt, and pity. "You can't be in that much denial, April. You know that Nick—"

"Nick is innocent. Of everything. But you've been on a months-long killing spree and setting him up to take the blame for it all."

He laughed. "I don't have the slightest idea what you're talking about."

"All right, let's start with the death of your brother Chris. He was your first victim."

"Have you lost your senses? Chris died on a snow monster hunt. I wasn't anywhere near Mount Myrrh that day. I was here, minding the factory."

"So you claimed. Yet I spoke to someone who said they came to see you on the day of Chris's murder. You weren't here."

He shrugged. "Well, maybe I wasn't here the *entire* day—"

"Exactly. You weren't here the *entire* day. You shadowed the group up the mountain. Tell me, Martin, was there ever even a snow monster sighting, or was that a whisper campaign you started? You knew your brother, a gung-ho risk taker and sportsman, would be the first to volunteer to go up the mountain. And while you said you would stay home—good old Martin, plugging away at the factory—you followed them, and then separated Chris from the rest by imitating a snow leopard's call."

"How did you come up with this wild theory?"

"For months I've watched you horsing around with Christopher. You can mimic any animal. A while back, Amory told me that you used to go hunting with Chris. Maybe you'd been on Mount Myrrh with him before, on that very pass.

"You'd known Chris would be the one who insisted on going back to hunt the leopard, but you really lucked out when Amory was too afraid to follow Chris for that last bit. Chris found you instead, didn't he? Or maybe he didn't. Maybe you just managed to hide out and push him at just the right time. That's probably more your style. Then, when the rest saw all the footprints at the place Chris had fallen, they all assumed the worst—that Amory and Chris had had some kind of tussle, or that Amory had been tied to Chris and cut the rope."

"Amory is a weak idiot. He shouldn't have gone up that mountain anyway. He was always terrified of skiing and climbing after what happened to his parents. And the fact that he went back to hunt with Chris was nothing but Chris being his usual horrible self."

"Horrible? Chris?"

His face reddened. "You didn't know him! I lived in the shadow of that idiotic arrogant jock my whole life. Do you understand? My. Whole. Life."

"Everybody liked him."

A bitter laugh snarled out of Martin. "Oh sure, he was the golden boy. He played sports well, yukked it up and knew everyone's names, and he married the pretty ice princess. Of course he was in a good mood all the time—he was born to the best job in the world. He got the suit and all the glory while Nick, Lucia, and I did all the grunt work for him."

"Did you look him in the eye when you pushed him down that crevasse? Or did you sneak up on him from behind?"

"What do you think? I'm not an idiot, nor am I some snarling villain who needs to have the last word. One short, sharp shove was all it took. No fuss, no fanfare, just do the work. That's the Martin Claus way." He shrugged. "It was just the first step in a larger plan anyway. Nothing to gloat over."

"And then Nick told the others to say nothing about what happened on Mount Myrrh, which played right into your hands, didn't it? In the void left by the lack of a police investigation, rumors started to percolate. The whispers all focused on Nick."

"I can't help it that people don't like him as much as the rest of us," Martin said. "Nick's never tried to be popular."

"No, but you have. You play in the band and hang out at elf bars, and you even started a flirtation with an elf recently. A real man of the people."

He lifted his shoulders in a modest shrug. "Santaland's had a traumatic year. I wanted them to feel good about the person who finally ended up as Santa."

Even though *he'd* been the one inflicting all the trauma.

"I don't know where you got that spider, but you killed Giblet. You fired him once from working here. Maybe you bumped into him at the Tinkertown Tavern, made sure the whispers about Nick reached his ears. My guess is that you visited his house to discuss hiring him back at the factory. And that's when you slipped the spider into his stocking in his room. And then, when you were sure he was gone—after the messenger arrived at the castle—you slipped an incriminating note onto Nick's desk. It was written in Nick's handwriting, which puzzled me until Lucia told me that you'd all been forging each other's writing since childhood."

"What happened to the note?" he asked.

"Jingles and I destroyed it."

Judging from the understanding that flashed in his eyes, I'd just given him the answer to something that had been puzzling him for days. He made a *tsk*ing sound. "Destroying evidence in a murder investigation. Not very law-abiding of you, April."

"I shouldn't have," I agreed. "And I shouldn't have been so suspicious of Nick at first when they found Old Charlie with that button of Nick's next to him. You killed the poor old snowman because he saw you at Giblet's. As soon as you heard he'd been in the vicinity, you took a blowtorch and ended his life." My gut twisted at the memory of that sad, frozen puddle. "It's my everlasting shame that *I* was the one who told you about Old Charlie that day after rehearsal."

Martin crossed his arms and sat back against the edge of his desk. "I gather you've told our venerable Constable Crinkles any of this? Or maybe you told Jake Frost. You and that detective seem awfully chatty. Maybe when they put Nick away, you can become Mrs. Frost."

I didn't let his mockery distract me. "Chris, an elf, and an innocent snowman. It all seemed disconnected, but then you poisoned Christopher, and your motive became clear. The police thought that Nick killed his brother, then the elf who suspected him in that killing, and the snowman who witnessed him killing the elf, and then his nephew, clearing the way for himself to be Santa forever. But his getting caught cleared the way for you."

"With no evidence, you'll have a hard time proving any of this. Who's going to believe you? You're just a wife desperate to exonerate her husband, the serial-killer Santa."

I smiled. "But I do have evidence. You see, you had me so worried about Nick that I left a nanny cam device in his office. I have video of you going into Nick's study and switching out the gumdrops. I have a recording of you, just before you were to head out to Peppermint Pond, telling Christopher that a fresh batch of licorice ones was on the table."

His expression darkened. "Then let's see this evidence. Let's hear it."

"I transferred it to my phone."

He held out his arm and snapped his fingers. "Hand it over. I'll believe it when I see it."

"My mother didn't raise a nitwit. I'm not going to bring my phone here with you, alone. Anyway, I intend to let the police see it first. Unless . . ."

His face froze momentarily, but in the next instant he smiled. "I get it. Blackmail, is it?"

"Your mother's right. I really should go back to Oregon, but I wouldn't like to go empty-handed. I ought to deserve *something* after spending months in the freezing cold."

"Aren't you clever," he said flatly.

"Not as clever as you, pretending to be my ally all these months."

"I *am* your ally, April. You're clearly not fit for the position you've found yourself in, just as I'm wasted here as a glorified factory foreman. Look at me." He stuck out his ample belly and gave it an affectionate pat. "Can you honestly say I wasn't made to be Santa Claus?"

"You *look* the part."

He drew up. "I *am* the part. Born to don the suit—as opposed to that serious stick, Nick. He's just not up to the role; we all know that."

"You think the spirit of Saint Nicholas lives on in you, a man who frames his brother for multiple murders?"

"Are you worrying about Nick?" he asked. "Don't. The

North Pole doesn't have the death penalty. Yes, he'll just be kept in that jail forever, but it's a cozy cottage. He can live out his life there reading, or studying languages if he wants, or doing the constabulary's books. That's more his speed anyway. Nick'll be fine. Happier, in fact. And I'll be doing what I was born to do."

"What about Christopher? Wasn't he born to be Santa, too?"

A shadow—maybe the last vestige of Martin's conscience—crossed his face. "I'm sorry about him. Truly."

I'd witnessed how sorry he was earlier. The kind of sorry that Snoopy dances with joy after hearing that his nephew's died.

He rubbed his hands together. "The question now is, what do *you* want, April?"

I arched a brow. "What do you think?"

"Ah! Money." A smile quirked his lips. "Then follow me. There's gold in our vaults, you know."

"I didn't know." I really didn't.

"Then let me show you." He led the way out of the office, holding the door for me like a perfect gentleman. He was still wearing his Santa coat. I followed him out of the office wing and up three flights of stairs. We were both slightly winded when we reached the top. He pushed two industrial double doors open, and suddenly we were on a kind of catwalk over the Candy Cane Factory floor.

"What is this?"

"The syrup room," he said.

I leaned over the railing, peering into one of the massive tubs below. The syrup bubbled gently. "You keep it boiling all night?"

"Just warmed so it won't be hardened solid when the elves come back in the morning."

I wondered how long I needed to go on with this charade.

Certainly I had enough on Martin now to show that he was responsible for every major crime that had occurred in Santaland this year. What more did I need?

One thing I *didn't* need was what happened next: The "Fa-la-la-la-la" sound of a text arriving on my phone, which was hidden inside my coat.

My heart sank. I thought I'd turned off my notifications.

Martin froze in alarm. "Your phone. You *do* have the evidence on you."

Not the evidence he thought. Everything I'd told him had been a bluff. But now there actually was something on my phone I needed to preserve. I tried to keep my face neutral, but he saw right through me.

"You've been recording."

"No," I lied. "Why would I? I'm blackmailing you, remember? Do you think I want proof of that floating around?"

Martin was vain, he was rapacious, but he wasn't stupid. In a split second he closed the gap between us. His hands closed around my throat. "Give me that phone," he said.

I couldn't shake my head. This was the second time in as many weeks that I'd been choked, and the feeling wasn't any more pleasant the second time around.

"Give it to me!" His grip tightened. "Or I'll drop you in the syrup along with the damn phone."

Before I knew what was happening, he'd grabbed me around the waist and was hoisting me up and over. I grabbed the edge but felt myself dangling over five hundred gallons of peppermint syrup. I had to hang on for dear life, or else some kids would get a big surprise this Christmas: life-sized peppermint-coated Mrs. Claus.

Under these circumstances, I didn't have much choice. "In my coat pocket," I gasped.

He reached into my coat and grabbed it.

"All right, Claus!" Jake Frost yelled from the door. He held something at his shoulder—the harpoon from Martin's own office. Behind him stood Constable Crinkles, trembling like a uniformed jelly. "Hands up, and step away from the rail."

I looked back at Martin as his predicament dawned on his face. And then he looked at the phone. The phone with the evidence against him. He held out his arm, dangling the phone over my head. Now it, like me, was suspended over a vat of hot peppermint syrup.

I saw what he would do. "No," I said.

He grinned at me, opened his hand, and the phone slipped from his grip.

I shot out one hand, grabbing it. My reflexes shocked him.

"Handball," I grunted.

He was still smiling. "Value your hands, do you?"

In the next instant, his foot sank down on my other hand, the one that was around the rail.

I yelled and looped my elbow with the phone around the pole.

I heard Nick yell, "Let her go!"

Nick?

Above me, Martin fell backward, but I was too relieved to have the pressure off my hand to care what happened to him. I struggled to pull myself up. Upper-body strength was never my strong suit, and my Mrs. Claus pounds weren't helping any. If I lived till January, I was definitely going on a diet.

Luckily, in the next instant I felt two hands hoisting me up. Jake held one hand, Nick the other.

Jake glanced over at him. "We thought you might like to see a friendly face."

Back on my feet, I stumbled toward Nick and threw my arms around him. "It's over," I said.

But he was looking at Martin, who was moaning on the

floor and gripping his leg, which had a walrus harpoon sticking out of it. His whimpering echoed around the empty factory. "Help me!"

No one seemed in a hurry to.

Nick let me go just long enough to shake the detective's hand. "Thank you for believing in me."

"Not you, Santa," he said. "Mostly I believed in your wife's belief in your innocence."

"Someone help me," Martin whined again.

"I'll help you," I said. "You only have three murders on your hands instead of four. We lied to you. Christopher survived your attack on him."

His eyes rolled back in his head. "I'm glad. I never felt right about those gumdrops."

"You're an idiot," I said. "An evil idiot. Did it never occur to you that someone would eventually realize that the person who poisoned the candy was the man in charge of making it?"

# Chapter 23

My gray sweater with the little tinkle bells sewn in made me resemble a jangling lady Sasquatch, but I was too happy to care. Nick was back from his first Christmas trip, and he was relaxed and happy now that the big event was over. Also that the troubles of the pre-Christmas weeks were concluded.

It was a subdued celebration. Nick was free, but I doubted the Clauses or Santaland would ever be the same place again. Still, on the night after Christmas we gathered in the big parlor to sing carols, open gifts, and sample all the goodies the kitchen elves had made for us. As Pamela said, in times of crisis, customs take on more importance than ever.

Christopher, who'd bounced back from his lethal gumdrop ordeal, was excited about his latest toy—a new sled and a team of four huskies who were creating canine chaos in Pamela's well-ordered castle. And what was Pamela saying about it? Not a word. Nor was Tiffany, who had already agreed to let her son go driving into town to meet some of his friends who also had sleds. They were going to be the new town terrors, probably, but I couldn't help being happy for him. He deserved a little fun. And who could resist a small pack of rambunctious young dogs and puppies?

The little huskies seemed unable to leave Quasar alone.

They had herded him into a corner, where he nervously munched on a pile of lichen, my and Nick's gift to him. Occasionally he would butt the head of the smallest dog, still a puppy, who was a little too pushy.

"They are cute little things," Pamela was forced to admit.

Lucia's eyes brightened, and she saw her opening. "Not as cute as a kitten. Wouldn't it be nice to have a kitten, too?"

Unsaid was that the kitten in question was a forty-pound half-wild hellcat.

"No," Pamela said. "Absolutely not."

Wisely, Lucia deferred the bad news till later.

On the whole, we were as happy as a family could be after it had lost two of its members. For Tiffany and Christopher, we drank a toast to Chris's memory, and for all our sakes, none of us mentioned Martin's name. The less said of him the better. He was in the Christmastown jail awaiting trial, but Jake Frost had informed me that, if convicted, Martin could be sent to live out the rest of his life in a facility in the Farthest Frozen Reaches. That idea comforted me. I wanted him as far away from the rest of the Clauses and myself as possible.

After Jake told me this, he'd whisked himself off toward home, somewhere in the Farthest Frozen Reaches. I wondered whether we'd ever see him again. Now that the Christmastown crime spree was under control, I hoped his services wouldn't be needed again for a long, long time.

Amory had been promoted from sewers to candy canes and couldn't have been happier with the change. Therese was spending her first Christmas at a spa in Arizona. And my friend Juniper, heartsore but relieved at her near miss, was joining me for a post-Christmas tavern visit tomorrow.

After a while, Nick and I bundled up and strolled outside. All around the castle grounds the ice sculptures were lit like fountains at night. Decorated trees dotted the landscape most of the way down the mountain into Christmastown, which was ablaze with holiday spirit once again. I treasured every twinkle.

Overhead, the northern lights put on their own show, trailing wisps and swirls of green, yellow, and orange across the sky. During the past week and a half, I'd almost forgotten what a magical place this really was.

"Look," Nick said, nudging me.

Down the hill, a ribbon of torches came toward us, slowly. I could just make out the sounds of elves singing "The Holly and the Ivy."

"Finally," I said, "a musical event I didn't have to arrange."

He laughed. "They do this every year—going through town and then coming up here to serenade us. It marks the beginning of the post-Christmas season."

"One Christmas down," I said. "I survived."

He put an arm around me. "Next Christmas will be a little less hectic."

"Less homicidal, I hope."

"That, too." He drew me closer. "And now we can begin planning our summer in Cloudberry Bay."

I turned to him, thrilled. "You still want to go? Really?"

"Did you think I was leading you on?" He shook his head. "I intend to lounge on the beach for four months and decompress."

"But there's so much to do," I said. "Wait till you see our Fourth of July celebrations. It makes Christmas look tame. We have all sorts of displays, and parades, and music shows, cloudberry recipe competitions, and watermelon-eating contests—"

"How will I survive so much excitement?"

I gave him a gentle poke in the stomach. "Just don't think you'll be napping on the beach the whole time. Summer at the inn is like December here. We're busy."

The caroling grew louder as the elves neared. They'd switched to "I Saw Three Ships," but they were drowned out periodically by a loud *pop-pop-pop*, like a Harley-Davidson. I smiled.

Nick, on the other hand, wasn't amused. "What's that racket?"

"Jingles," I said. "I got him a souped-up muffler for his Snow Devil."

Just then, Jingles roared by on his sleek machine and let out a whoop of happiness. "Merry Christmas, Santa!"

"Merry Christmas!" Nick bellowed back, with such feeling, such authenticity, that it gave me shivers.

He looked down at me, concerned. "Cold again?"

"Nope." I nestled closer into that warm red coat of his. "Just right."

# Acknowledgments

For this book I owe a huge debt of gratitude to my wonderful editor, John Scognamiglio, who, not too long ago, asked me if I'd ever thought of writing a holiday mystery.

Special thanks to my agent, Annelise Robey, for her advice and also her steady calm during my panic attacks.

And to Joe Newman, my fellow misfit, thank you for proofreading, making all the dinners, and listening to me drone on about reindeer.